THE
REMAKING

THE
REMAKING

A NOVEL

CLAY McLEOD CHAPMAN

QUIRK BOOKS
PHILADELPHIA

Copyright © 2019 by Clay McLeod Chapman

Library of Congress Cataloging in Publication Number: 2019936668

ISBN: 978-1-68369-153-2

Typeset in ChaletComprime and Bembo
Cover and interior designed by Aurora Parlagreco
Cover illustration by Armando Veve
Production management by John J. McGurk

Quirk Books
215 Church Street
Philadelphia, PA 19106
quirkbooks.com

10 9 8 7 6 5 4 3 2 1

to the campers and counselors of 4-H Junior Camp
and the ghost stories we told
summer of '89
4-eva

PART ONE

THE WITCH GIRL'S GRAVE AT PILOT'S CREEK
1951

THESE WOODS WHISPER.

The pines at your back? You can practically feel the needles bristling in the wind. Lean in and listen closely and you'll hear their stories. Everything that's ever happened underneath that vast canopy of conifers. Every last romantic tryst. The suicides. The lynchings. You name it. These trees will testify to them.

These woods have witnessed it all.

Whenever somebody from town wants to do something in secret, they come out here. Where they think they're alone. Where nobody's watching. They hide in the shadows, performing their little rituals beneath these branches, as if they believe these trees will keep their secrets for them. Their lovers' liaisons, their midnight masses. They think nobody is listening in . . . but that's simply not true. That's not true at all. The trees are listening.

Always listening.

The woods know what the people of Pilot's Creek have done.

What we've all done.

I've lived in this godforsaken town my whole goddamn life. I know just about everything there is to know about the people here. Every last dark secret.

Know how?

I listen. I listen to what the trees have to say.

I listen to the woods.

So. What story do you want to hear? You want to know what drove Halley Tompkins to hang herself back in '46? Or which men it was who strung Russell Parr up? Or how about that baby they found half-buried back in '38?

No. You're not here for any of those stories.

You want to hear about Jessica, don't you?

Course you do. That's why you're here, isn't it? Tonight of all nights . . .

Twenty years ago on this very evening.

October 16, 1931.

We don't have much time. Here it is, almost midnight, and I haven't even begun telling you the tale of the Little Witch Girl of Pilot's Creek.

Poor, poor Jessica.

You brought me a bottle? Don't be stingy on me, now. That's my price of admission. You want to hear a story, you better goddamn well have brought me an offering.

Alms for the minstrel. Something to wet my whistle so that I'll sing.

And Jessica's story takes time.

Takes the life right out of me.

Her story takes its toll on the teller, you hear? The price is too high . . . unless you got something for me to drink. My throat's so parched, I don't think I can tell it without a drop of that Lightning Bolt. I'll sound like a bullfrog before I'm finished.

Did you? Did you bring me a little something? Just to take the edge off? Warm my insides? It gets so cold out here at night.

Thank you. Thank you kindly. That's much better. Feel that fire working its way down my throat. Settling into my belly, like a bonfire.

Now. Where was I?

Let's start with Jessica's mother.

Ella Louise Ford was born right here in Pilot's Creek. She'd come from good stock. Her family owned their fair share of acreage, growing tobacco. But there was always something off about that girl. Her mother sensed it from the get-go. None of that sugar and spice and everything nice for Ella Louise. No—that girl was touched. Little Ella Louise talked to the possums. She made charms out of dried tobacco leaves. She kept bees in mason jars and hid them underneath her bed. She couldn't be bothered with frilly dresses or dolls like all the other girls. Not the porcelain kind, with pigtails and rose-painted cheeks. She made her own dolls. If you could even call them dolls. Looked more like totems. Like effigies. Twined together from twigs and wheat. Moss and leaves. Insects in their chests. Beetle hearts.

Try as they might, Mr. and Mrs. Ford could never break little Ella Louise of her strangeness streak. She never mingled with other children her age. None of them trusted her. All the other boys and girls sensed something was off about her and kept their distance. Mother Ford took it all too personally, as if their rejection of Ella Louise were an affront to the family name.

You got to understand, a town as small as Pilot's Creek was crippled with superstitions. Rumors spread like cancer. Words hold power around here—and once word got around about Ella Louise's peculiar habits, it wasn't long before business for the Fords took a turn. It only got worse as Ella Louise grew up and became a young woman. Nobody wanted to be associated with her family. Be seen fraternizing with the Fords in the streets or paying them a visit at their home. Anyone who did suffered just as much of a cold shoulder as they did.

Understand now—all anyone ever had 'round here was their reputation. Simply to be seen in the midst of the Fords was enough to bankrupt businesses. Ruin entire legacies. You couldn't wash the stink of that family off once it clung to your skin. That family was cursed.

Mother Ford took to punishing her only daughter. Bending Ella Louise over her knee and trying to spank that darkness right out of her. Taking a switch to her thigh, until the insides of her legs bled. Anything that might exorcise this witchery brewing within her.

There it was. That word, at long last.

Witch.

It was whispered among the other mothers. Their children. All through town. In church, even. It wasn't long before all that gossip had grown into a downright din, the rumors spreading like wildfire, until everybody was talking about it. Until it was unavoidable.

Ella Louise Ford was a witch.

Her debutante ball was an absolute disaster. Her mother moved heaven and earth to make it a night to remember. And in a way it was. It truly was . . . just not how Mrs. Ford had hoped for.

Ella Louise had always been a sight to behold. She looked as if she had stepped right out of an oil painting. Something you might see in a museum. Her skin was pale, always pale, with the slightest hint of pink illuminating her cheeks. A grin always played across her face, but you'd never say she was smiling. Her lips just curled heavenward all on their own. Her eyes, if they ever locked onto yours, were a deep green, as green as the deep sea, I reckon, to the depths of which no man has ever ventured. Or ever will.

What mysteries lie behind those murky eyes, only the Devil knows.

Coming out to polite society had always been a part of the way of life for Pilot Creek's upper crust. Mrs. Ford had done it, her mother had done it, her mother before had done it, and on and on—so you damn well better believe Ella Louise was going to have her turn, no matter how much she protested. Mother Ford simply wouldn't hear it. She refused to let the ritual go. For a girl to become a woman, she needed to be presented. To be unveiled. That was their God-given rite of passage.

Ella Louise was meant to wear a beautiful ballroom gown, made just for her. Pink silk. Mother Ford could barely hide her high hopes for her daughter when she handed over that dress. Even then, she held on to the fantasy that her own Ella Louise had a fighting chance of being welcomed into polite society . . . But at the very moment of her coming out, when every debutante is presented to the upper echelon of Pilot's Creek, Ella Louise entered the dance room covered in mud from head to toe. Her gown was in tatters, all that pink torn to shreds. Dried leaves in her hair.

You could see her body moving beneath the ripped fabric, her pale flesh exposed to everyone. Practically the whole town, staring at her.

Nobody moved. Nobody breathed.

Ella Louise simply stood before them, smiling in that devilish way of hers, as if nothing were off about this at all. She asked her father for her first dance as a woman. Just as she had been instructed by her mother to do.

Mrs. Ford nearly fainted.

Ella Louise was cut off from that night forward. She was excommunicated from her own family. Disinherited. Her mother never uttered her daughter's name again. Her own flesh and blood. It was as if Ella Louise had never existed. Never lived another day in their house.

So Ella Louise moved into the woods.

She made this forest her home. It's unclear if she built her house herself or if someone had a hand in helping her, but a cabin manifested itself, seemingly out of nowhere. These woods are primarily composed of Eastern white pines that can reach up to a hundred feet, easily. They were originally used for building ship masts, centuries back, cut down and sent off to the naval yards in Norfolk. So much lush coverage, perfect for building a simple, one-story cottage with a fireplace cobbled together from stone and mortar. You could see the glow of a fire through its windows at night if you happened to be out here. But nothing and no one else actually lived out here. Not another soul.

Just Ella Louise.

And Jessica.

If I were better at my own arithmetic, I might surmise that it was the night of Ella Louise's coming out that served as the moment of her daughter's conception. Whatever had happened to Ella out there in those woods to bring her back in such a muddied state, well, nine months later . . .

But then again, I'm no mathematician.

And I sure as hell ain't no baby doctor.

Nobody knows who Jessica's father was. Or, more to the point, nobody owned up to it. Would you? Back then, in a town as small as this, you might as well have laid down with a leper. Ella Louise had become a burden for our town to bear. Pilot Creek's very own pariah. Weeks, months, would go by and nobody would see her rummaging about town. Hear her voice begging for pocket change. Even think about her out here, living alone, for all those years.

But then the sound of a baby crying lifted out from the woods. Jessica's wailing filled this forest. It echoed all the way into town. Into the ears and dreams of every last townsperson.

Ella Louise had a daughter now.

Other theories of paternity abounded. Such as Jessica had no father. She was immaculately conceived by the Devil himself. Ella Louise had made her pact with the Lord of Flies and he begot him an only daughter. Her very existence was a morbid reminder of her mother's unholy union with Beelzebub. Ella Louise and Jessica would come into town for their groceries, just like everybody else. Can't live off root vegetables alone, now. But when folks laid eyes on that little girl in Ella Louise's arms, all they ever saw was the princess of darkness.

We'd only see Jessica whenever she'd come into town. Watched her grow in these fits and spurts. Months would go by and there she'd be, traipsing down the road with her mama. Always holding her hand. Always keeping her eyes down low, on the ground. She didn't attend school with the rest of us. Didn't learn about life like the rest of us. Whatever lessons she got came from her mother back at their cabin. I can only imagine what she was taught out there in those woods. The Devil's arithmetic.

When Jessica turned nine, she started coming into town on her own. Always had a list of goods to fetch from the store for her mother. She didn't have Ella Louise at her side, holding her hand and braving the lane anymore, so some of us boys felt a bit more emboldened to share our inherited distaste for Jessica. Children took to throwing stones at the girl. Calling her all kinds of names. I'm not proud to admit that I myself fetched a pebble or two in my boyhood, tossing it at little Jessica's back.

Once, I struck her right in the shoulder.

My aim was true.

She turned right to me. Even though I was among a dozen other kids, all of them holding their own rock, she knew I'd been the one to throw it. Knew the rock had come from my very hand. She pinched her eyes—and without ever saying a single word to me, I heard Jessica's voice in my head, as if my own thoughts were boiling over in my skull. She whispered to me.

Cursed me.

What'd she say? I'll never tell. Not unless you've got another bottle on you.

Suffice to say, her curse worked. I can't stop thinking about her. Not back then, not even now. She left an imprint of herself, a shadow, on my mind.

Little Jessica has never left.

Nobody ever mentions how beautiful she was. Her mother may have been a picture of perfection, such a lovely face, but Jessica . . .

Jessica took my breath away.

She was an angel.

But for the life of me, I can't remember what the color of her eyes was. I can't remember the color of her hair. Or the features of her face. I can't remember any of her.

I can't describe her.

Words escape me.

She returns to me, night after night, for over twenty years now—and yet, the moment I wake, the vision of her dissipates. Gone. Just like that. I can only see her in my dreams.

As a boy, I was frightened of her. What she might do to me. But I couldn't stop myself from welcoming her into my head. Into my sleep. Now I wait for her. Yearning for her to return.

Why won't she let me go?

If Ella Louise had been touched with magic, then her daughter was downright blessed. Jessica had twice the talent her mother had.

Talent. What the hell else would you call it?

Ella Louise nurtured her daughter's *talents*. Taught her all she knew. If Mother Ford had done her damnedest to stamp out the fire brewing within her child, then Ella Louise went ahead and fanned those flames within Jessica. Out here, in these woods, nobody was going to stop them.

It was said that Jessica could commune with wildlife. She could mend a bird's broken wing with just the touch of her hands. Weeds would wilt from under her touch. Just a simple tap from her finger against the soil and out sprouted a toadstool. A dozen mushrooms.

This was what people believed, at least. What folks whispered among themselves in town. Nobody ever saw these things with their own eyes. Not that we needed to.

We believed.

Any boys brave enough—or dumb enough—to set foot into the forest and sneak a peek through the windows of their cottage would get pinkeye for their troubles. Anyone who came close to their home would break out in a rash, their skin scorched with poison ivy. Anyone who spoke ill of Ella Louise or Jessica within their earshot would suddenly discover an eruption of blisters covering their tongue.

None of this was simply a coincidence. None of this was chance. We all knew what Jessica was. What her mother was. What those two were up to out here in the woods.

But even a witch has got to make a living, right? Everybody struggles. The demands to make ends meet forced Ella Louise to set up her own apothecary shop in her house. For those folks in town who preferred to forgo the traditional medicine route, Ella Louise offered something a little more . . .

Herbal? *Of the earth*, shall we say?

It's all a bit hypocritical, I know, but sometimes modern medicine doesn't offer the solution. And it doesn't provide us with the destiny we believe we so richly deserve.

You want that fella to fall in love with you?

Ella Louise had something for that.

You want to get back at your boss for firing you?

Ella Louise had a little something for that, too.

You feeling sick in your soul?

Restless in the head?

Unhappy at your core?

Ella Louise had so many miracle cures. Medicines that had no names. Roots and leaves and fungi of all kinds. Flora and fauna, sealed within their own jars. The walls of her cottage were lined in glass. Hundreds if not thousands of mason jars, each one holding their own medicinal specimen. Herbs and insects and liquids of various viscosities. Each had a specific purpose, a particular healing property. Her medicines could do what the doctors in town couldn't. You just had to be brave enough to come out here and knock on her door.

You had to ask.

Please, Ella Louise, please help me.

Save me.

Please.

Nobody would come out and admit they had ever paid Ella Louise a visit. No one would profess to taking one of her cure-alls. You might as well confess to consorting with the Devil.

But we did.

We all did.

Men and women, mothers and fathers, boys and girls alike.

How couldn't we?

Ella Louise never judged. Never turned anyone away. She opened her doors to any soul in need who was willing to come knocking.

Shawna Reynolds had been suffering from severe cramps for the last few months of her pregnancy. She had only a few weeks before her due date, but the pain had become unbearable. Her family physician had failed her. Whatever prescriptions he provided did nothing. Shawna even crossed two county lines just to visit a prenatal specialist in the biggest hospital she could find, and even they couldn't get to the bottom of what was wrong with her.

Shawna and her husband had been trying—and trying—to get pregnant for years. *Years.* They prayed and prayed, but nothing ever took root. Just when they were about to finally give up, just when there wasn't any hope left of these two ever having their own child . . . It happened.

A miracle.

But the pregnancy took its toll on Shawna. Everyone could tell just by looking at her. That child was leeching the life right out of her. Rather than plumping up as most mothers do, she was only getting thinner. Skeletal. Shawna always had to rest after a few steps, sit down and catch her breath, but she never caught it. Always exhausted, and yet unable to sleep for more than a few minutes. The more her stomach bulged, the more the rest of her wizened away. You could see her rib cage rise up from her skin with every breath. Her cheekbones practically cut through her face. Her eyes sank into the depths of their sockets, all hollowed out.

Those cramps just kept getting worse.

Crippling her.

Killing her.

If you had no other choice, if modern medicine had failed you, I'd imagine you'd go visit Ella Louise, too. Shawna walked into these woods, alone, and knocked on her door.

And asked.

Please, Ella Louise, please help me.

Save me.

Please.

Ella Louise took a mortar and pestle and ground a few leaves and dried root into a powder. She scooped a spoonful and mixed it with water and told Shawna to drink.

Drink it all.

Whatever it was, it worked. Shawna's cramps stopped. All the pain, washed away.

A miracle.

Shawna was walking again. Color returned to her cheeks. Her ribs drifted beneath a layer of flesh. Her smile, her happiness, returned, and nobody was the wiser. No one, not even her husband, knew how. Nobody cared. All that mattered was Shawna had turned a corner.

A miracle.

It wasn't until Shawna was finally nine months pregnant that she woke to discover that her bedsheets were spotted. There was blood all over the bed.

Blood on her thighs.

Shawna's husband—Wayne Reynolds—rushed her straight to the

doctor's house in the middle of the night. Carried her the whole way, until they were both covered in blood.

The baby didn't make it.

Their doctor believed the miscarriage had been induced by some sort of chemical agent. The physician didn't want to alarm Wayne, but they'd found traces of toxins that nobody in their right mind would ever ingest. Especially while they were pregnant.

Had Shawna been exposed to any kind of rare plant lately, he asked? Like Jerusalem cherry? Water hemlock? Rosary pea? Had she eaten anything from the woods recently?

Shawna broke down and confessed she had been taking a spoonful of Ella Louise's special remedy for weeks. Perhaps a little bit more than a spoonful, she sobbed. Wayne was beside himself with grief. Son or daughter, he was prepared to love the child with his whole heart.

They buried a boy.

It doesn't take long before grief curdles into rage, now, does it? Wayne had always been a proud man. A pillar of society. A man of God. Every Sunday, he'd be first in line to receive the sacrament. So imagine how crestfallen, how crushed he was when he found out his own wife had been sneaking off into the woods, behind his back, for a remedy that balked at God's own divine providence. A potion that killed his unborn child before he was able to take in his first breath. That consigned their unbaptized lamb, as Wayne himself fervently believed, to eternal hellfire.

What would you have done if you were in Wayne's shoes?

What would any of us have done?

He wanted retribution. He wanted Ella Louise to pay for what she'd done. To his wife. To his child. To his family that would never be.

Who among us wouldn't have demanded the exact same thing? Who could have blamed him? Certainly not anyone from our town.

Certainly not the people of Pilot's Creek.

No—they understood. They saw his pain, his grief, his rage . . . and they knew what had to be done.

This had been a long time coming. Imagine a bonfire just waiting for the match.

Yearning to burn.

Now it was lit.

It didn't take much convincing on Wayne's part to get his friends all fired up. There were five men, all told. All members of the church. All law-abiding citizens.

Harold Smith. My own mailman.

Jeremy Hawthorne. Owner of Hawthorne Hardware.

Tom Watkins. Dentist.

Bill Pendleton. Accountant.

On this night, twenty years ago to the day, those five men went beyond the law. On this night, Wayne demanded justice no court could ever offer him and his family.

Tonight, they were going to burn a witch.

They circled around Ella Louise's cottage in the dark. Lord only knows how long they stood out there. Waiting. Staring through the windows. Watching Ella Louise and Jessica go about their business, none the wiser. Jessica reading to herself while Ella Louise sewed together a new dress for her daughter. Something pretty, no doubt. Humming the whole time.

Their plan was to smoke them out. Wayne tossed a bottle filled with diesel through the window. Then Harold Smith tossed in another. The flames spread over the pine floor. All those mason jars, all that glass lining the walls of the cottage—it all started to sparkle. The reflection of the conflagration lit up within each jar, hundreds of gleaming stars coming together in some unholy constellation.

The men waited.

And waited.

How long did those two hide inside? Longer than you might imagine. They must've known what was waiting for them. But the air grew thick. Dense with smoke. You could hear them coughing, gasping for air as glass started to shatter all around. All those jars, all their remedies, their life's work, was melting. Bursting. Going up in flames.

Ella Louise eventually burst through the door with nine-year-old Jessica clutched in her arms, hoisting her as best she could. That poor little girl was pressed tight against her mother's chest, coughing uncontrollably.

Jeremy Hawthorne and Bill Pendleton each grabbed Ella Louise by her arms. She struggled against their grip, trying desperately to pull herself free.

Jessica fell to the ground. Her mother yelled for her to run, *run*, so Jessica scrambled to her feet and raced for the trees.

She didn't get far.

Wayne Reynolds grabbed Jessica by her hair and yanked, sending her back to the ground. Ella Louise let out a howl as the man scooped her daughter up into his arms. Jessica's feet kicked through the air. But it was pointless. Hopeless. She couldn't wrestle herself free.

Tom Watkins was good with an axe, so in a matter of a few swings to a sapling, they had themselves a ready-made stake to tie Ella Louise to. They heaped kindling made of the branches of that sapling at her feet. Wet wood burns slowly. Very slowly.

The men circled around Ella Louise as she begged for her daughter's life. Pleaded with them to spare her. Do what they must to her, but let Jessica live.

The little girl yelled and screamed for her mama. Wayne Reynolds merely passed her off to Bill Pendleton. He fished out a box of wooden matches from his pocket and shook them next to Ella Louise's ear, those matches rattling.

Our town will not suffer a witch to live, Wayne said.

Then he struck a match.

Lighting her feet most certainly assured a slow burn. Took those flames a while to level with her head. Every mounting inch, every licking flicker was an invitation for her to shriek.

To plead for mercy.

To beg.

They made Jessica watch. Watch the fire rise. Watch the flames engulf her mother. Watch her body disappear beneath a sheet of orange and yellow. Jessica's screams had subsided into a keening. Just wet sounds. No shape or contours to it at all. Nothing but grief.

Suddenly little Jessica pulled herself free from Bill Pendleton's grip and ran right to her mother. Embraced her in flames. Wayne rushed to grab her and drag her back, but the girl wouldn't let go. The two ended up burning together.

Imagine, if you can, what it must have been like. Think about the flames at your feet.

Think about them climbing up your legs.

Your knees.

Your thighs.

Think about the smoke filling your lungs.

Think about the smell of your hair. That incendiary hiss filling the air, reeking of flame. Your hair, now burning, punctuated with an intermittent sizzle and pop. The smell of it is unavoidable now. Sulfur, scorched and organic. The odor of calcinated tissue wafting along. The smoke rising up from the smoldering web on your scalp, roasting for just a moment before combusting all together. Those chestnut tresses go up so quickly, as fragile as a bird's nest on fire.

Ever smell flesh on fire?

I have.

We all did. Everyone living within ten miles of Pilot's Creek smelled it that night.

I heard their screams. From miles away, in the safety of my own bedroom, under the roof of my parents' house, I swear I heard Ella Louise and Jessica Ford screaming together.

Mother and daughter.

October 16, 1931. Four minutes past midnight.

At dawn, the sun rose up to ash. All that was left were their blackened bones. The ribs of one skeleton were much smaller than the other, both charred chest cavities gripping onto each other in one last attempt to hold on. Stay together.

Those men buried Ella Louise in these woods. No gravestone. No marker of any kind. Wherever her body lies out here, those five men took that location to their own graves.

Nobody knows now.

Jessica was different. These men knew she was more powerful than her mother. They were afraid of her. She might rise from the grave and avenge her mother for what they'd done.

So what did they do?

You know this part of the story. Everyone in town knows. Those foolish men protected themselves the only way they knew how. With God. With consecrated ground.

Wayne and his co-conspirators buried poor little Jessica in a steel-reinforced coffin. They laid her body to rest right there, in our very own Pilot's Creek Cemetery, along with the rest of the dead from our town. After they lowered her coffin into the ground, they filled it with concrete. Three whole bags' worth. And they poured gravel over the top of her hardened sepulcher.

But those boys didn't stop there, did they? No—they went ahead and erected a metal fence out of interconnected crosses. Over a hundred crucifixes, arm-in-arm with one another, surrounding her resting place.

To keep Jessica in the ground.

To contain the ghost of the Little Witch Girl of Pilot's Creek.

Her grave is all that's left of this story. Their cottage is gone.

Nobody knows for sure where it stood.

See this patch of soil where we're sitting? The grass won't grow. Trees won't grow. Nothing will grow here now. Not in this tainted soil. I reckon this is where Jessica and Ella Louise last held on to each other. Where their bodies burned. Nothing but scorched earth.

You ever hear of that fungus that killed upwards of sixteen thousand trees back in 1935? Whole forest was nothing but gnarled skeletons in every direction. Dead chestnut trees as far as the eyes could see. The wood wasn't even good enough for lumber. Rotten all the way through.

What do you think did that?

Wasn't some fungus.

That was Ella Louise. Her body's buried in these woods still, somewhere. Out here. Her blood soured the earth. Made the trees sick. What was left of her body broke down, seeping into the soil, until those roots sucked her up and choked. Took ten whole years to replenish these woods. Another five for anything to grow. The chestnuts and Eastern pines have finally come back—but still nothing grows on this very spot where we're sitting now.

If you ask me, those two aren't done.

Not with this town.

You can chalk it up to fate, if you feel like it, but everybody knows about Harold Smith's car wreck. How Jeremy Hawthorne died in a freak accident while restocking his shop late one night. How Tom Watkins asphyxiated after inhaling too much of his own laughing gas, his pants puddled around his ankles. How Bill Pendleton's body was riddled with all kinds of cancer, every last cell blackened to a crisp.

And Wayne? Well, everybody knows Wayne Reynolds took his own life not long after what he and his friends had done. Brought a double-barreled shotgun up to his mouth, wrapping his lips around the muzzle. There's no way of saying for sure, but folks believe the last word he uttered before pulling the trigger wasn't a word at all, but a name . . .

Jessica.

I hear her in my dreams. Hear her calling for me. Pleading with me. Begging for us all to save them, spare her mother, make it stop, make the flames stop.

But none of us did. None of us did a damn thing. We let them burn out there that night.

We all let it happen.

The whole town.

I visited Jessica's grave. Once. Years back, when I was just a kid. Dumbest goddamn thing I'd ever done in my whole life. But you got to understand—you've got to believe me when I tell you—all that time, sixteen years up to that point, Jessica had been calling for me.

Whispering to me. *Come to me*, she'd say. *Come to me.*

I had to see her.

Just once. Just to know if I was really hearing her voice or if I was going out of my mind.

I snuck out of my parents' house in the middle of the night and slipped off to the cemetery. I hadn't considered the time, but when it reached four minutes after midnight . . .

I saw her.

Jessica. Waltzing along her grave in circles. She wandered as far as her crucifix-fence would allow. Never stepped outside it. The hem of her handstitched dress was still scorched in a ring of ash, while the rest of her dress was blinding white. Fresh cotton.

When she saw me—and she most certainly did see me—she smiled. That grin filled my chest with cold. My lungs locked up. I felt like I was drowning.

She reached out to me. Held out her hand.

Help me, she said.

I took a step closer. Lifted my arm.

Help me . . .

I stopped. There couldn't be more than a few inches between our fingers.

Help . . .

I couldn't move. Couldn't take another step, no matter how loud her voice grew in my skull.

Help . . .

I stepped back. Away from her Her smile withered. That was when I saw Jessica for what she really was. What she'd become, out there, under the ground, after all that time.

Her blackened bones.

Her charred lips.

Those mossy teeth.

They say little Jessica is still searching for her mother. Until they're reunited, her soul won't be at peace. She wanders about her grave, just waiting for someone to take her hand.

To let her out.

There it is. Four minutes past midnight. You can set your watch to it. Jessica and Ella Louise Ford breathed their last at this very moment, twenty years ago to the day.

Can you hear them? The trees? All those pines at your back, bristling in the breeze. You can nearly feel the pine needles against your neck, can't you? Piercing your skin. The branches will reach out. Grab you. Pull you away from the campfire and drag you back into the shadows.

You'll become a story, too. We all become ghost stories one day.

A good ghost story gets told . . . and retold. It's in the telling where the tale takes on a life of its own. A ghost story grows. It exists on the breath of those who tell it.

This one will live beyond me.

And you.

It'll live beyond all of us. This whole town. As long as there's someone around to tell it.

And tell it.

You hear that, Jessica? I did my part. Just like I was supposed to. Like I've always done.

I told your story. Again.

And again.

I'm so old now, Jessica. So tired. I can't keep doing this. Year after year. Let me go. Please. I'm begging you.

Let me go, you goddamn bitch. I'm sorry. I'm sorry. Please. Forgive me. Forgive me.

Free me.

Please.

Please.

Jessica, can you hear me? I know you're listening, damn it. Please. Please forgive me. Forgive our town. Forgive the people of Pilot's Creek.

We were wrong. We were wrong to do what we did to you and your mother.

Please. Please forgive us. Forgive us all.

Lift this curse. Release us.

Release me.

PART TWO

DON'T TREAD ON JESSICA'S GRAVE
1971

EXT. GRAVEYARD—LATER THAT NIGHT

The full moon casts an eerie blue glow over the headstones. An owl hoots.

CASSANDRA, HOPPER, GEMINI, DAMASCUS, and MOON-CHILD sit in a circle around Jessica Ford's grave, holding one another's hands. Candles are lit.

CLOSE ON Cassandra as she closes her eyes, ready to begin the séance.

CASSANDRA

We are speaking now to the spirit of Jessica Ford . . . We sense that you are with us, Jessica. We sense your presence. We sense that you cannot rest . . .

HOPPER

Yeah, lighten up, Jessica . . . Relax already.

MOONCHILD

Cut it out, Hopper. Be real.

CASSANDRA

Will you speak to us? Is there someone here you wish to communicate with? We are here to help. Will you tell us why you're not at rest, Jessica? Why don't you feel at peace? Why does your spirit remain here in this place?

DAMASCUS

I'm asking my spirit the same damn thing . . .

MOONCHILD

Knock it off!

BACK ON Cassandra, head weaving back and forth. Something strange is happening. Her eyes roll up into her skull, revealing nothing but pure white.

CASSANDRA

What happened? Tell us, dear spirit. Tell us and you will be free. Tell us. Tell us . . .

MOONCHILD

Cassandra!

HOPPER

What the hell—

Cassandra GROANS in a voice no longer her own. It's a child's voice . . . JESSICA.

CASSANDRA

(Possessed:)
Why have you woken me?

ONE

They looked just like her. All of them. Their faces, a harvest of apple cheeks. They had the same freckles as hers. Same soft lips framing milk-white teeth, each girl nibbling the tender flesh of her bottom lip. They were after a feeling. The sting without the blood.

How could there be so many of her? Amber counted two dozen at least. And that was just tallying the girls in the room right now. Who knew how many had auditioned already. There was no telling how many would occupy this very same seat after she abandoned it.

Just who exactly was Amber supposed to be today? She had already forgotten. The cattle calls were beginning to blur together in her mind. It was impossible to keep track.

A dead girl, that's right.

No, a ghost.

Wait. *A witch*. That was what she was reading for. It was a witch.

A little witch girl.

Today's auditions were taking place in some nondescript office building along the outskirts of Santa Monica. Whatever operation had used this space before had apparently gone under, leaving its gutted boardroom and empty cubicles behind. The waiting area was really nothing more than a hall lined with folding chairs on either side, swarming with girls. Yearning girls. All those searching eyes.

Hazel. Cerulean. Slate. Moss.

Brimming with hope.

Every time the casting director's assistant poked her head out from the boardroom, the coven of would-be witches all snapped their necks up at attention, the same look of desperation on their faces. Hoping to hear their name called next.

None of the girls made eye contact. Not with one another. That would be a big no-no. No one wants to see herself in the girl sitting next to her. Or sitting across from her. It feels like looking into a mirror at a reflection that's ready to hiss back, *I hate you.*

These girls were in competition with one another, weren't they? A fight to the death?

They are not your friends, her mother insisted in the parking lot, her breath smelling like peat far too early in the morning. A single-malt bog. *You're not on a playdate. This isn't a slumber party. You go in there and you show those sniveling little bitches what you're made of.*

The two never talked about it, not at all, but one time, when Amber was five or so, she found a stack of yellowing headshots in her mother's closet. She knew she wasn't supposed to be rummaging through her mother's stuff, but she couldn't help herself. The fresh face smiling up at Amber looked so familiar. It looked like hers. But it wasn't. It couldn't be. This young woman had to be in her teens. Much older than Amber. When she showed her mother what she'd found, asking if she knew who the pretty woman in the picture was, Mom only snatched the headshots from Amber's hand and promptly tossed them into the trash. Every last photograph.

Amber had done plenty of cattle calls, but she always lost herself within the throng of girls in the waiting area, no matter where her mother dragged her. She couldn't help it. Her eyes would roam over the dozens of girls who looked exactly like her, wondering who they were.

Today's audition was no different.

She was no different.

She could feel it happening again. That swell of anxiety. The mounting panic. Nothing set her apart. There was nothing of hers, not her face or smile or hair, that she could call her own. There was no distinctive physical difference between her and the rest of them. She felt herself begin to fade, to blend in with the multitude of girls. It was hopeless. There was no possible way she'd get picked.

Amber could practically hear the collective din of every yearning girl's thoughts. That silent prayer whispered under their breaths: *Pick me pick me pick me pick me pick me*—

She knew they were all whispering it because she was whispering it, too. Their thoughts were her thoughts.

That one and only wish.

Let me be The One . . .

What would it take to be chosen?

To be The One?

Mom had dressed her in her lime-green Jackie O pencil skirt, along with a matching plaid lime-green top with a high neck. Green tights. She had spotted five other Jackie Os in the waiting area already. Sorry, make that six. There were a couple Bardots. A few Mary Quants. Baby doll dresses. Turtlenecks and stockings. Even a few miniskirts. Miniskirts! She couldn't believe her eyes! How could their mothers let them expose so much leg like that? They weren't even ten!

Amber accidentally made eye contact with the girl sitting across from her. She was much prettier than Amber. Flaxen-blond hair, feathered just right. An eight-year-old Cheryl Tiegs.

Amber couldn't help but stare at her. Get lost in her beauty. When Little Cheryl Tiegs realized she was being ogled by this inferior doppelgänger, she glared at Amber until the air between them curdled. Amber only sank deeper into her seat, drifting below the surface of this sea of look-alikes and drowning herself.

An elbow prodded her in the ribs. "Sit up straight," Amber's mother muttered. The casting director might be watching her at that very moment. Spying on her. Assessing Amber, here and now, as if sitting in the holding area were the real audition. The true test.

Amber clutched the mimeographed copy of her sides. She had trouble reading the bigger words by herself—and yet she knew the lines, as if they were an incantation. A magic spell to be whispered, repeated over and over again, that would summon up the very character of this little witch girl from the ether—back from the dead—and possess Amber's body.

She was ready to be inhabited by the role. A ripe vessel.

Take me, Amber offered in solemn submission. *Take my body over the rest of these other girls. I am ready for you . . . I am The One.*

Looking over the lines was unnecessary now. Amber knew them by heart.

By heart.

What a weird thing to say. Was this dialogue in her blood now? Circulating through her veins? It certainly felt like it. Amber had spent the entire night drilling lines with her mother. She knew the dialogue inside and out. Upside and down. Backward, forward. She dreamed the lines. Recited them in her sleep. Mom had seen to it. A part of their prep was for Mom to read a line at random, then Amber would respond, no matter where they were in the script.

The words of this little witch girl were now in her heart.

Flowing through her.

Whispers of dialogue had followed her into her dreams. She could've sworn that witch girl spoke to her. Communed with her from beyond the grave. What was it that she had said?

Come to me . . .

Where was that line in the script?

Come to me . . .

Amber hadn't gotten nearly enough sleep last night. Her nerves were so stretched, but it wasn't because of the audition. She wanted the part, of course. Who didn't? They all did. Every last girl. But who wanted it the most? What were they willing to give up?

To sacrifice?

No, Amber was nervous because of her mother. What she might do if Amber didn't get the part. She had spotted a few envelopes on the nightstand that her mom had left unopened.

Each envelope had words stamped in angry red ink over the front. Words like *FINAL NOTICE*.

Mom was already on her second cigarette since they sat down in the waiting area, which Amber knew was a bad sign. Here it was, ten minutes after their scheduled call time. They had been running late. Always late. Their stucco bungalow was on the wrong side of the valley, far, far away from where all the auditions took place. The rush to get Amber dressed, get her fed, get her hair brushed, get her out of the house on time, the maneuvering through traffic, pinpointing the office building, finding parking, running to make it on time, always running, *running, running*.

Had her name already been called and they hadn't been there to hear it?

Had they skipped over her?

Amber glanced down and saw her mother's left leg juddering like a jackhammer. She had absolutely panicked at the sight of those alligator bags under Amber's eyes. She broke out her own bottle of liquid concealer and, with her pinkie, dabbed at those gray shadows until they disappeared. *There*, Mom said. *Those storm clouds are gone. Like they were never there.*

All the mothers sat next to their daughters. There was more variation here, more distinction among the older women. Their daughters may have looked as if they had all come off the same assembly line, but the mothers had their own looks. Brow-skimming bangs. Feathered locks. Shimmery eyelids. Pearlescent cheeks. Bronzed skin. Glossy lips. Tanned and athletic, effortless and au naturel, utterly done up.

She was always curious about what united these stage mothers. They must have shared the same competitive edge. That same cut-throat ambition. These women hired acting coaches for their children. Sent them to audition classes in lieu of soccer practice or swimming lessons or anything fun. Who had the best vocal instructor here, Amber wondered? Who had worked with the director before? Who knew the casting director or one of the producers on the film?

There were just so many Ambers.

Like dolls, she couldn't stop herself from thinking. *That's all I am. All any of us are.*

A Little Miss Amber doll.

Batteries sold separately! Comes with three prerecorded messages. Just pull Amber's string and she can repeat the dialogue from her sides, over and over again . . .

Hundreds, perhaps thousands of girls would read these exact same lines. That girl over there. And that girl over there. Her, over and over again. Her and her and her and her and . . .

Her.

They were all the same. She was the same.

A headshot.

A mimeograph, copied over and over and over again. Until the image itself began to degrade. Break down to hundreds of dots.

Amber couldn't stop herself from seeing their faces, all their faces, deteriorate. They were distorting all around her. Dissolving.

Decomposing.

Amber glanced down at her own headshot and realized it was nothing but a skull now. Black-and-white bones. Her lips had peeled away, her flesh gone, leaving behind that toothy smile that took hours to perfect. Her body had been buried long ago. Decades in the ground by now. Nothing but a charred skeleton. And yet they still poured cement over her grave to ensure that her corpse never clawed through the earth. To keep her in the ground forever.

Amber blinked back. Back to the hallway.

Back to all the other girls.

Waiting. And waiting.

Nothing but a purgatory of yearning girls, whispering the same lines under their breath.

When were they going to call her name?

How long did she have to wait here?

Couldn't they just put her out of her misery?

Nine years old.

Amber was only nine years old. Her mother was always telling casting directors that "Amber is very mature for her age," and that they should consider her for older parts. *What presence! What equipoise!* But this wasn't her choice. This was never her dream. It had always been what her mother wanted. The cattle calls and acting classes. All she wanted was soccer and ice cream and scribbling in her coloring books. She wanted to watch *The Partridge Family* and stay up late and not have to worry about saying the right thing or looking the right way or smiling. Always smiling. She couldn't hold her lips together much longer. She wanted to rip them off.

Just call me already, she thought. *Just call my name so I can say my lines and go home . . .*

Just call me . . .

Call me . . .

Kill me . . .

Call me . . .

Kill me . . .

Amber had done three commercials. One was a national spot for a dish detergent. *("Wow! Where did all that dirt go? Thanks, Suds!")*

Another was for an embarrassing off-brand Yoo-hoo drink that tasted like chalk. *("Mmm-mmm! Scrumptulicious! Nutritious and delicious! Go ahead and drink . . . Chocolicious!")* Amber threw up all over the set after twelve takes of sipping too much of the awful stuff.

Then there was a local spot for a used-car dealership. (*"Beep! Beep! Bring the whole family on down and take a ride!"*) She liked that commercial the best because she got to dress up like a cowgirl, her sleeves adorned in pink fringe, and ride a pony all day, even if it wasn't national.

But she'd never been in a movie before.

Never a feature.

You need to land this one, hon, Mom had said in the car, talking over her shoulder while Amber sat in the backseat, veering through traffic along the 405. They were already ten minutes late. Again. *Get this part. You hear me? This one's going to be your breakout, I can feel it. After the reviews roll in and the critics single you out, you can leave this god-awful schlock behind and play whatever part you want. You'll have the pick of the litter, hon. Trust me. Are you listening, Amber? Amber? You go in there and nail this audition. Kill it for me, honey. Kill it.*

Her tooth was loose. One of her upper central incisors. This was a problem. A major problem. Amber hadn't told her mother because she knew she'd get angry. If she lost a tooth before shooting began, they could fire her. *We didn't hire a gap-toothed girl*, the producers would say. But Amber couldn't help but run her tongue along the loose tooth. She couldn't stop herself from forcing the tip within the crevice of her gums, where it was most tender. She knew she was only making it worse, making the tooth looser. But she couldn't control herself. The root was raw, pain radiating out from her jaw. Worrying the nerve was the only feeling worth feeling right now. If she pushed at the tooth with her tongue, harder, just a little harder, Amber could feel the flesh flex and tear, the nerve ending separating, the very root ready to snap in—

"Amber Pendleton?"

Amber blinked back to the waiting area.

And smiled.

The casting director's assistant held the door open for her. Amber's mother was asked to wait outside, with all the other mothers, but she insisted on coming along. To observe. Her mother always made her more nervous. More anxious. Mom knew this, but she barged in anyway. Why was she being so pushy? Bickering with the assistant? Amber could feel her cheeks getting hotter. Was she blushing? Her mother's voice was rising. Getting shriller. Saying something about this being a horror movie. The things that would be asked of Amber, demanded of her daughter. Somebody had to make sure she was safe. That Amber was protected. But the only protection Amber felt like she needed right now was from her mother.

Not that she'd ever say that.

Not out loud.

The room felt empty. Emptier than she had expected. Hollow. There wasn't much furniture in here, even for such a wide-open space. Just a fold-out card table. The blinds were drawn, so no sunlight shone through. The dull thrum of fluorescents filled the room. Filled her skull. She felt the low-wattage throb in her jaw. In her loose tooth. The nerve ending picked up the electricity pulsing in the bulbs above, transmitting signals throughout the rest of her head.

Something in her lungs caught. A hitch in her chest. It felt like sandpaper in her windpipe. Was she choking? Was her throat constricting? She couldn't breathe. The air wasn't reaching her lungs anymore. Where had the oxygen gone? Was her face turning blue? Was she dying? Why wasn't anybody noticing her asphyxiating? Why wasn't anyone trying to save her?

The casting director hadn't made eye contact with her yet. Hadn't seen Amber. Hadn't acknowledged her presence. She was scribbling something down on her yellow notepad. Making a note about the girl that had just auditioned before her. What if that girl already got the part? What if it was too late for Amber? Why was she even doing this? Why was she here?

The casting director still wouldn't look up.

Was Amber supposed to wait?

Should she just start?

Get it over with?

Amber noticed the Pall Mall dangling between the casting director's fingers. The cinder had sunk through the cigarette, unsmoked, a slender tail of ash threatening to break at any moment, like a gray salamander escaping its attacker by snapping off its own appendage.

There was no color in the casting director's hair, as if it had been sapped of all its pigment, reduced to ash. She seemed tired. Her shoulders drooped. How many girls had she seen already? How many times had she heard the exact same lines, repeated the exact same way? The tone? The inflection? The singsongy lilt of hundreds of girls would haunt her dreams forever. Amber had been haunted by these words, too, the dialogue drifting into her own dreams. But when she heard it, she only heard one voice. *The* voice. The very voice of the ghost girl herself, as if this witch had tutored her on how to deliver the lines. The recitation.

Amber now knew how to cast the spell.

The casting director finally glanced up. Her eyes settled on Amber for the first time.

Actually saw her.

She hesitated.

Halted, even.

Amber wasn't positive, but she swore she saw the casting director's eyes widen. Did her pupils just dilate, like black holes widening within the cosmos, swallowing Amber whole?

The casting director took her in.

Savored her.

She leaned forward, holding the rest of herself up with her elbows. "What's your name, young lady?" There was warmth in her voice.

Amber cleared her throat as quietly as possible. "Amber Pendleton."

"And what part will you be reading for us today, Amber?"

Amber straightened her spine, trying hard not to glance over at her hovering mother. She exhaled, letting the room settle before responding, just as she had practiced with Mom a million times before. "I'll be reading the part of Jessica Ford."

Just then, the ash detached itself from the casting director's cigarette, as if the mere mention of Jessica's name were enough to send it toppling. When it hit the table, flakes of gray scattered everywhere, all over the casting director's notepad. Freckles on a ghost.

"Whenever you're ready, Jessica." The casting director abruptly caught herself. Laughed at her own folly, coughing wetly. "Sorry. I meant Amber. Whenever you're ready, Amber."

TWO

They were bleeding him out. Slowly. *Methodically.* They really wanted this to hurt. Sadistic sons of bitches. They wanted him to feel every last drip, until there was nothing left. Not a single drop of his life's work left in him.

A million and one paper cuts. That's how these financiers kill you. All the script notes. All the budget cuts and penny pinching. All the compromises he had to make, just to tell his story.

So many sacrifices. Lee Ketchum had to kill his darling just to get her onto the big screen.

His darling Jessica.

The financiers wanted to take his movie away from him. It no longer resembled his story. The story he'd been born to tell. The story he'd been dying to tell for years now. *Years.* Ever since he was a boy. Ever since he'd first heard the legend of the Little Witch Girl.

To this day, Ketchum could still recall what it felt like to sit around that campfire as a kid. The flames lapping at his face, warming his cheeks, while the back of his neck felt so cold. He sensed the presence of the pine trees at his back. Some old coot from town fancied himself the unofficial historian of Pilot's Creek. If you got him soused up enough, he'd mouth off over just about anything. All the seedy secrets the people from his hometown wished to keep cloistered.

But there was one story the kids from Pilot's Creek were always dying to hear . . .

The Little Witch Girl.

There's nothing like the feeling of a ghost story taking over your imagination. Seizing your dreams. The goose bumps rose up along Ketchum's arm as he let the story seep into his subconscious.

Jessica Ford had haunted him for years The number of bedsheets he'd yellowed throughout his childhood, all thanks to the nightmares she conjured up in his sleep. Jessica had made him a bedwetter. Not even Godzilla or Christopher Lee or Bloody Mary could've done that. Even when he was no older than ten, Ketchum knew her story would make a great movie.

A great *horror* movie. And he was going to be The One to make it. To tell her story.

He wanted kids all across this country to piss in their PJs, just as he had when he first heard her story.

Jessica Ford was his muse. If he didn't make this movie, somebody else surely would. Only a matter of time until some other filmmaker found out about her. Beat him to it.

Her story was dying to be told. Legends like hers don't stay local forever. They spread. They cross county lines. They pop up around campfires all across the country. They seep into the subconscious of other kids just like him. Ripe storytellers, all of them. One kid tells their friends and then those friends tell their friends and then they tell theirs and on and on, until there isn't anyone left who hasn't heard it. Heard about her.

Her.

Ketchum coveted the tale. He was like a possessive lover, all through his teens. He had to hide her. Protect her. Save her for himself. He wanted her story to be his and only his. He wanted desperately to keep her story a secret, like a butterfly sealed up inside a mason jar, until he had the opportunity to tell it the way he wanted to.

Jessica belonged to him.

Nobody else.

No one escapes Pilot's Creek, Virginia. His hometown was a black hole that sucked its citizens in and never spat them out. It was common for kids to graduate from high school, move down the block from their childhood home, and merely repeat whatever it was their parents did. They worked and married and had babies and died, not necessarily in that exact order.

Nobody made it out of this town.

Nobody escaped.

Ketchum was one of the lucky ones. He left right after graduation, and he never looked back. He was free. Finally free of Pilot's Creek. Its pull. But his thoughts often returned to Jessica. Always Jessica. There was a persistent whisper in his ear.

Come to me . . .

Come to me . . .

Come . . .

His time would come. Soon it would be his turn to tell her story. The fortieth anniversary of her death was just around the corner, coincidentally dovetailing with his final year in film school. He could hammer out a draft and raise the money and he could be shooting in less than a month.

But his version needed to have depth. To turn the screw, as it were. Really explore the darker themes that resonated for him. Focus on the mother–daughter relationship.

Focus on Jessica and Ella Louise. The tragedy of their story.

The true story.

Nobody would finance his film. Nobody wanted a melodrama with ghosts. His script collected dust. Ketchum was ready to give the screenplay a pauper's funeral, burying it in his desk among all his other unproduced films. A mass grave of hackwork. Nobody would mourn these unmade movies. Nobody would even know the ghost of Jessica Ford ever existed.

Until he met the Teraino Brothers.

Paulie and Butch Teraino swore they were in the plumbing business. They had some extra cash they needed to launder through a new business venture, and wouldn't you know it, everybody was making movies on the cheap these days. Porno or horror, take your pick. As long as something made its way onto the screen, the whole endeavor would be a perfect write-off.

Every filmmaker must make sacrifices.

Collaboration, it's called. The question for the director becomes, *How much of my own story am I willing to compromise in order to get this movie made?*

The concessions started off simple. They always do. Small tweaks. Swapping genders for a particular character. Perhaps raising the age for someone older to play?

And what about a little more skin? You know, for the drive-in crowd?

We want people to see this movie, right?

To sell tickets, we need a hook. For the kids. Something that's gonna rope them in. And what sells tickets better than a little T&A? Perhaps a bit more gore? Drench that screen in red, all right?

Before Ketchum knew what happened, he had sold the soul of his film. He sacrificed Jessica on the altar of a blank check. He had tried so hard to sell the Teraino Brothers on his personal vision and hadn't they agreed to bankroll his movie?

"So," Paulie had said, "what's with this story here?"

Neither of these men had necks. Their throats were swaddled in a stack of sweaty inner tubes. Chins upon chins. Their fingers looked more like raw, gray sausages. They had called Ketchum into their office, which was really nothing more than a faux-wood-paneled mobile home situated on a construction site that never seemed to have any construction going on.

Ketchum had painted the portrait as best as he could. Time to tell the story he'd been dying to tell all his life. "Imagine a woman disowned by her own family," he said. "A pariah among her peers. The local kids toss rocks at her whenever she passes. Calling her names. Spitting on her."

"Okay." Paulie had shrugged at his brother, more focused on his cuticles. "With you so far."

"Now"—Ketchum had kept at it—"imagine that woman having a child. Out of wedlock."

"Had a few of those," Butch had muttered.

"Nobody knows who the father is. Her daughter's birth is a riddle wrapped in a mystery, inside an enigma. An immaculate conception of the darkest kind."

"Did I miss something?" Butch had interrupted again. "Where's the blood?"

"The ending," Ketchum had cut in. "I was just getting to the ending. A group of superstitious men make their way to Ella Louise and Jessica Ford's house in the middle of the night. They drag them out into the woods. They tie them up and burn them at the stake."

"So . . . it's a witch movie?"

"Yes. Yes, a movie about what happens when we let our prejudices get out of hand. Consider *The Crucible*. The tragedy is in the fact that no one actually knows—"

"*The Crucible*?" Butch clearly had been annoyed by this reference.

"Arthur Miller? About the Salem witch trials? But it's really about McCarthyism?"

"So you're saying they're *not* witches?"

"No. No, they will be witches. Both of them. But . . . misunderstood witches. And therein lies the tragedy. Imagine the horror, the heartbreak, when Jessica gets her revenge on the townspeople of Pilot's Creek. She makes them pay for what they did to her and her mother."

Fine, his financiers had said, relenting. But need they remind Ketchum, this was supposed to be a horror movie. There better be some blood on the screen. They were more worried about the poster.

"Show a skeleton's hand reaching out from the ground or something," Paulie had suggested.

Don't Tread on Jessica's Grave.

The original title had been much, much worse. Paulie fancied himself a screenwriter. He wanted *Easy Rider* directed by Herschell Gordon Lewis. Hippies were in, big-time, thanks to Dennis Hopper. As long as Billy and Wyatt were still revving their choppers all the way to the box office, the Love Generation could easily be injected into just about every genre.

Hippie mystery. Hippie sci-fi. Hippie porno. Only a matter of time before there was hippie horror.

The storyline evolved—devolved?—into a quintet of cardboard counterculture stoners roaming the southern states in their Winnebago, scaring the local squares with their shaggy hair and talk of free love. One night, the group gets a flat in the middle of nowhere and decides to set up camp just outside quaint Pilot's Creek. One hippie chick realizes their RV is next to a cemetery, so she and her peacenik pals hop the fence and start toking up on a tombstone.

The grave of none other than Jessica Ford.

The Little Witch Girl of Pilot's Creek.

A mound of dirt encircled by interconnected crosses, as if to keep evil forces out.

. . . Or perhaps it's to keep them in?

The ground is choked with weeds. Nobody has cut through the swath of underbrush for years. The tombstone is overwhelmed with ivy. That hippie chick—Cassandra in the script—reaches over the fence and yanks the ivy away. Etched on the headstone, they read:

HERE LIES JESSICA FORD.
MAY SHE ALWAYS BURN.

What a bizarro thing to have etched onto a tombstone. Especially for some kid.

All seventeen years of her.

Cassandra gets the bright idea to hold some sort of séance, to commune with Jessica's spirit and all that. See if she died at peace. *Groovy.* The hippie quintet sit in a circle along the circumference of Jessica's grave and take hold of one another's hands, calling out to her. They pass around a spliff as Cassandra performs her special brand of hoodoo-spiritualist mumbo jumbo that doesn't even come close to sounding like an actual séance. The scene devolves into an orgy. All that free love happening on top of Jessica's resting place only ticks her off.

She rises. Rises from her grave. She's pretty sexy. Totally naked as she emerges from the earth. Not a single burn mark on her. The guys think this is all pretty far out. They've just conjured up some hot ghost chick and now she's beckoning, beckoning the boys to come closer.

Come closer . . .

Come closer . . .

Come . . .

The witch girl exacts her revenge against these pitiful hippies for the rest of the script, all sixteen remaining pages of it. Breasts and blood are spilled in grim, titillating fashion.

So what was the original title?

Jessica Drinks Hippy Blood.

They were killing him.

His story.

Couldn't they see that? The financiers were murdering his movie and they hadn't even started production yet. His story had been hijacked by hippies. A page one rewrite.

What about the truth, Ketchum kept insisting. *I want to tell the true story.*

Whatever that meant. The Teraino Brothers could care less.

It always went back to that night for Ketchum. That night around the campfire. Listening to the crazy old codger spin his yarns while slipping sips of whiskey. How many times had the old fogey told that exact same story to kids just like Ketchum? How many boys sat around that same campfire, listening to him yammer on about their hometown, just waiting to hear the story of the Little Witch Girl and her mother? How many dreams had she infected? How many short stories had she inspired? How many manuscripts for unfinished novels were collecting dust in desks or under beds at this very moment? How many notebooks had the mad ramblings of her tale?

How many movies?

No, she had chosen him. Ketchum knew it. Out of all the poets and novelists and troubadours, he was The One.

Jessica chose him.

It felt particularly galling to Ketchum that the investors insisted they change Jessica's age. For what? Just to get a little more T&A on the screen? He could just imagine her rolling over in her grave right now. No, Jessica had to go back to her real age. She had to be a child.

What if she was angry at him?

What would she do?

It was a silly thought, a childish thought, but Ketchum couldn't stop himself from dwelling on it. What would Jessica do if he didn't tell her story the right way?

The way she wanted it told?

What if he failed her?

He was the director. He was the writer. He was an *auteur*. But there was an unseen presence, a silent investor if you will, that Ketchum couldn't help but be aware of.

To hell with the producers. Fuck the financiers. Ketchum was working for one investor and one investor only. Jessica was the executive producer, as far as he was concerned.

She called the shots.

Ketchum was no Orson Welles. All the investors wanted was a drive-in cash-in delivered on time and on budget. All Ketchum wanted was to translate his nightmares onto the big screen. Production meetings became custody battles. Long, drawn-out hissy fits between filmmaker and financiers, with the producers serving as intermediaries.

There was no money. Two hundred thousand dollars, if that. Technically, the budget was more like $180,000—but the producers didn't tell the director that. That meant shooting on location. No sets. No building anything. Day-for-night. No night shoots, for the love of God.

Twenty days for production. Not a single day more.

The real tug-of-war was fought over Ella Louise. The financiers wanted a rising starlet cut from the same cloth as Fonda. Bardot.

They wanted blond.

Buxom.

Nora Lambert was the daughter of Russian Jewish immigrants. Nobody was going to ever mistake Nora as some cornfed beauty queen. Her olive complexion deepened on-screen, a Mediterranean siren. Not some fallen southern belle.

She's not right for the role, the Teraino Brothers insisted. *She doesn't look the part.*

What Ketchum hadn't told the financiers was Nora was his girlfriend. He had written the part just for her. He embedded the text with her cadences. Her inflections were Ella Louise's inflections. The voice that lifted off the page had always been Nora. When he started to assemble the movie in his mind, constructing the shots, he saw her. Always her.

This was the hill Ketchum was willing to die on. The role required intensity, he argued, a level of ferocity not seen on-screen. He needed somebody with chops. Someone unafraid to plumb the depths of feminine psychosis. Someone unapologetic. Willing to go the distance—and further. *Deeper.* All the way to the very depths of hell . . . and then crawl her way back.

The role, as written, would surely win the actress an Oscar. A first for any horror film. Hadn't any of them seen *Rosemary's Baby*? Ruth Gordon may have gotten Best Supporting Actress, sure, but this year—this would be the year Nora Lambert took home the top prize.

"If you don't let me cast her," he said, "then you don't have yourself a director and that means you don't have your movie anymore and you're up shit's creek with the IRS, aren't you?"

Ketchum got his leading lady. That was all that mattered.

Nora Lambert would light the silver screen on fire.

Let it burn.

So who would play Jessica?

THREE

The flames had chewed through her lips. What was left of her flesh now petaled outward, her cheeks peeling back until she saw her own teeth lined crookedly along her jaw.

An eternal grin.

The cartilage of her nose was gone, leaving behind a cindered cavity. The flesh along her forehead had flaked away. Swatches of exposed bone rose up from what little jagged scraps of skin were still webbed together across her temples. Whatever remaining hair that hadn't been scorched from the fire now clung to her scalp in matted clumps, seared to the sides of her skull.

It looked so real. So . . . lifelike.

Amber didn't mind the makeup chair. The endless hours of sitting. Staring off into nothing. Losing herself in her own reflection. Becoming someone—something—else.

It was quieter here in the special effects trailer. Much quieter than anywhere else on set. She wasn't supposed to talk when she sat here, in her very own swiveling dentist's chair. All the FX team wanted was for her to relax the muscles of her face. Simply sit still and let them apply layer upon layer of foundation over her skin, white now gray now black, shadows mounted upon shadows, until Amber vanished altogether beneath her makeup.

Her new skin.

All charred.

Not to mention she got to sip her soda from a straw while one of the production assistants held the can up for her, which she thought was just the funniest thing ever. The techs always fretted over her smearing her greasepaint. *Can't risk a dribble, now, can we? Can't get your new face wet* . . . That meant a poor PA was tasked with holding her can of RC and guiding the straw to her mouth. She'd sip, swallow, sip, then glance up and smile with her cindered lips.

Wasn't this how Cleopatra was treated?

She felt like royalty here.

If Amber was completely honest, the reason she liked the makeup trailer the most was that her mother was asked to mind her own business. Nobody engaged with her mom here. The makeup techs never seemed to listen to her, choosing not to answer her questions.

Do you know how long the shoot's supposed to go tonight?

What's taking them so long?

Weren't they supposed to start filming an hour ago?

Does anybody know anything here?

Am I just talking to myself?

She'd eventually get flustered or bored or hungry and leave Amber behind. Mom always promised she'd come back with a cheese sandwich from craft services, but rarely did.

That was okay, though. Amber just loved the silence.

The stillness.

The peace.

She'd get lost in her thoughts. In her own reflection. In her transition into this new person. This Little Witch Girl.

Amber ran her tongue along her lower teeth. She found the loose tooth and started to push. There, she felt that familiar flexing sensation of flesh tearing ever so slightly. She couldn't help herself. Couldn't stop herself. Something about it brought her great comfort. And pain.

So she pushed harder.

How far could her tongue push the tooth before it tore? Before the nerve snapped?

There was the slightest taste of rust in her mouth now.

Of blood.

Pictures of fresh flesh burns were taped all along the wall. Real burns. Real scorched flesh. Intense close-ups of waxen skin. Amber couldn't help but stare. She made a game out of trying to determine which part of the body had been burned in the photos, whether it was an arm or a cheek or a chest. The camera had gotten so close to the flesh, it was impossible to make out what part of the body it was. Amber stared at those pictures the longest. The rippled skin, losing its smoothness, looked like crunchy peanut butter spread over bread. Like cake frosting.

Her stomach would grow queasy if she looked too long at them. The deep burns. Cindered tissue. Rippled meat. Her attention would drift over the surrounding bottles. So many different elixirs. Gelatin and Gafquat and liquid latex. Spirit gums and KY jelly. A vast palette of cream-based makeups. Every pigment had its own container. Their own skin. Paintbrushes with various tips. Some were fine-tipped, others bulky. Plus sponges. Spatulas. Tongue depressors.

As much as she loved sitting in the makeup chair, the one thing Amber hadn't liked at all, that she prayed she never had to do ever again, was the lifecasting.

The lifecasting was the worst. It happened months ago, thankfully, but even thinking about it now made her shiver. Just remembering how dark it was under the plaster.

It didn't make sense to her that they needed a mold of her entire body. Still, they rubbed her skin down with petroleum jelly. It tickled. All those hands on her. Greasing her up. Like suntan lotion. She could almost imagine herself at the beach.

One makeup tech teased her that she would slip out of their hands if they tried to lift her. She was wearing a bathing suit, but still. All those hands. Her skin glistened under the lights. She'd never shimmered so much. They squeezed her scalp into a swim cap, stuffing all her hair inside so she wouldn't get any plaster in it. She felt like she was about to go swimming. She wanted to go swimming. She loved going to the pool, but her mother never let her. *All that chlorine saps the moisture right out of your skin,* she'd said. *Dries you all up into a scarecrow.*

The special effects people inserted a pair of straws into Amber's nose and told her to keep her lips sealed, her eyes squeezed shut, as they poured the plaster all over her body.

Thick, cold oatmeal-like fluid. Her skin broke out in goose bumps, it felt so strange. She felt the pressure of it against her, the plaster contracting against her skin as it started to harden, taking on the shape of her body. Her limbs. The slope of her torso.

All she wanted to do was open her eyes.

To breathe through her mouth.

She could feel her heart pounding against the inside of her chest as the plaster pressed down. It was squeezing her. This darkness. This cement.

She couldn't move. Couldn't move her lips. Couldn't scream.

She was buried.

Buried alive.

Amber was no longer in the special effects studio in downtown Santa Monica.

She was in the ground.

In the cemetery.

If she tried moving her arm, she was met with clammy resistance. The earth all around her was cold and compact. She could feel her eyes racing back and forth, like REMs in the thick of a nightmare, but no matter how hard she tried, she couldn't pry her greased eyelids open.

They were sealed shut.

The air. The air was all gone.

She couldn't breathe.

They had buried her. They had dropped her in a hole in the middle of the night and then they filled the earth back in all around her and then they poured all that cement over her, weighing her body down with concrete so that she could never dig herself out again.

Those men had left her below to asphyxiate.

To drown.

To die. She was going to die. Amber was going to die down here in the cold, cold ground and no one, no one would save her.

Let me out let me out please let me out . . .

Was she really screaming or was it all in her head? Her thoughts were racing far too quickly through her skull. Her throat burned. Her chest was on fire. Her whole body burned.

This must be how Jessica felt. Down there. In the ground.

Under the cement.

Waiting. Waiting for someone to save her.

To free her.

Let me out let me out let meoutletmeoutletmeeeeeeoooooout—

Someone squeezed her hand.

There was intense pressure around her skull. The earth shifted, tugging on her head, pulling her chest upward from her seat.

The plaster gave way.

An intense, blinding light seared her vision. The cylindrical lineation of fluorescent bulbs took shape over her head.

Amber slowly blinked back to the makeup studio.

When she asked how long she had been underground—wait, sorry, under the plaster cast, the tech grinned and said, "About fifteen minutes."

Only fifteen? *Minutes?* But it felt like . . .

Like years. Like she had been buried in the ground for years. Decades, even.

"This stuff hardens pretty quick," the special effects tech said. "Sure feels like an eternity, though, don't it?"

It certainly did.

Thankfully, the lifecasting was over. No more being buried alive. No more molds. The special effects crew took the cast and fashioned a series of burn appliances that would cover her body.

Now came the fun part.

They washed her face. Cleaned her skin. They prepared her hair, parting it where the burn would extend into her scalp. They applied the Gafquat to keep her hair upright, smoothing it down with a spatula and holding a hair dryer to it until it held its sculpted shape. They cut strips of nylon fiber, about a centimeter wide. Each was glued onto Amber's face, then dried. Spirit glue was applied through the nylon, seeping onto to her cheek. When the nylon was peeled away, her skin held its distorted rictus. They did the same with her eyelids. Her lips. They applied gelatin where the burns were meant to look their deepest.

The techs created smooth and rough areas, ragged and jagged edges of flesh. Hard ridges. Open chasms. Once the gelatin dried, they began to paint. Brushed flesh-toned makeup across the rippling skin. Shadows of red to create a raw sirloin complexion. Pink and vermillion to show where the flames had crept up along her neck. Across the jaw. They beefed up the purple in spots. Specks of blue to reinforce the burn and hint at the bone underneath. They swept charcoal-colored powder across the planes of her ravaged face. The ash and soot.

They had her sip some mouthwash laced with blue food coloring to give her tongue and teeth a darker hue. She rinsed and spit and smiled, exposing her newly decayed grin.

The latex made her skin itch, but she didn't care. She had conditioned herself to sit very, very still. She thought of herself as a statue. She was made of stone.

There was a solitude in this stillness that Amber quite liked. She found a calm tranquility rooted deep within her that she didn't even know she had, a haven at the very center of herself where she could go whenever she sat in the makeup chair. This was where she went for all those hours. The darkest depths of her being. When it was time to finally resurface, to rise up and start filming, she would no longer be Amber. She would be someone else.

Someone new.

Amber would be Jessica.

Jessica Ford.

The Little Witch Girl of Pilot's Creek.

She still couldn't believe she'd gotten the part. *Actually* gotten it. How many other girls had been hoping, *dreaming*, of sitting right here, right where she sat at that very moment?

She was chosen. She was The One.

There had been something special about Amber that made her perfect for the part, she'd overheard the casting director say. *A shimmer*, she called it. *A glow.*

You have no idea how many girls we saw, the casting director muttered to her mother. *Thought it'd never end . . . I started to go cross-eyed from all the kids coming through.*

Amber wasn't supposed to be listening to this conversation, but she'd eavesdropped on them anyway. *A glow*, she had said. Amber heard it. She had a glow. Something special. Something buried deep within her, burning bright. This woman, this professional, had seen it.

Unearthed it.

I never doubted she'd get the part, her mother beamed, lying through her smile. *She was born to play Jessica.*

Her math homework was piling up since shooting started weeks ago. A part of being on set was that her mother doubled as her tutor. Amber had been homeschooled for a year now, abandoning the public schools once Mom got it in her head that they could really make a go at this acting thing. The child labor laws were in her mother's favor. The film had to hire somebody to look after Amber.

Who better than her mother?

Her own flesh and blood?

Laws were laws, no matter how small the budget. Amber needed a guardian. A protector on this set. Someone who would have her better interests in mind. Who knew when to tell the director— wherever he was—that Amber had worked enough, thank you. That it was time for a break. A young girl can't work these long hours. She needs to study. She needs a rest.

But Amber hadn't cracked open her math textbook ever since they had arrived on set. That was almost three weeks ago now. Her mother kept promising they'd get to it. *Soon, hon,* she'd say. *Soon. Now let's go over your lines one more time. Tomorrow's a big day. They saved the best for last . . . Your big climactic scene! We wanna make sure we get the dialogue down, okay? We don't wanna make a fool out of ourselves in front of everybody, now, do we? Definitely not the director. Not if you want to work with him again. You never know. He might be going places. You can never tell with young filmmakers these days. They could stay stuck in the horror rut for the rest of their lives or . . .*

But Amber wasn't paying attention anymore. She was thinking about the girl.

About Jessica.

Who was she? She'd been told she was a real person. Or based on someone real, at least. *Inspired by . . .* That was what Mr. Ketchum had said. *This story is inspired by true events.*

Real events.

Just the thought of this all being real sent the slightest shiver down Amber's spine.

Jessica Ford had been a real girl. A living, breathing human being.

Flesh and blood.

Who was she? Who had she been? What had she been like?

Would they have been friends? Amber was the same age as her. Maybe they would've gotten along. Maybe they would've liked each other.

Amber found herself wanting to find out more about Jessica. Research for her role. Isn't that what actors were supposed to do? Learn as much about the characters they play?

She wanted to be Jessica.

In the flesh.

Amber would sit in this swivel chair while they burned her face away. First, the epidermis. Then the connective tissue and hair follicles. And finally the subcutaneous tissue, all the fat and muscle. All that was left was the blackened bone, her skull burned to a grinning crisp.

"All done," the FX tech said, squeezing Amber's hand. "What do you think?"

Amber stared at her reflection.

The scorched girl glared back.

Amber couldn't see herself anymore. She had been replaced, her body swapped with the charred skeleton of this little witch girl.

Jessica was here at last.

FOUR

The production team couldn't afford trailers to house the actors, so they improvised by corralling them in the graveyard chapel—the only roofed structure for miles.

The church had been built in 1888 from the pine scaffolding originally used for the erection of a granite column to commemorate Pilot Creek's very own dead Confederate general Alasdair C. Franklin, or so the pewter plaque at the front of the church read. The planks were occasionally replaced throughout the years until the proud people of Pilot's Creek were capable of mustering up the funds for a proper restoration.

It was so quiet here.

Even though the church served as a holding pen for the actors and crew, everyone in the production treated it as if it were a hallowed place. All conversations were in hushed tones, out of respect.

Craft services set up their station at the front. Soggy cheese sandwiches and hummus surrounded the pulpit. Amber watched each member of the crew come up to grab a bite. They would hesitate for a brief moment as if receiving benediction, the cold cuts their Eucharist.

Amber had never had much religion in her life. She could count on one hand the number of times her mother had dragged her into a church. But she liked sitting in these wooden pews, waiting for her call. Her attention drifted over the stained-glass windows lining the church walls.

Saints suffering from leprosy.

Angels tangled in serpents.

Jesus on the cross. Amber stared at him the longest. A sliver of colored glass was missing from his palm. The night's cool breeze blew into the chink, whistling through his stigmata.

Amber had to be guided to her pew by a production assistant. The PA held her hand and led her to her seat, insisting that she sit still. As still as possible. *Don't crease your costume.*

The latex kept itching. Especially around her nose.

Now it had reached her temples.

Her cheeks.

Amber had to stop thinking about it. Get her mind off the itch, no matter how much she wanted to scratch. *What time is it?* she wondered. *It's gotta be late . . .*

Amber shifted in her seat. The wood warped underneath her, echoing throughout the church. It was well past her bedtime. But she wasn't tired. Quite the opposite. Every bit of her body was wide awake, alive, brimming with electricity. Her first movie! Her first speaking role in a real movie! She felt naughty staying up so late. But she loved it. Absolutely loved it. These night shoots felt like a slumber party, only the other kids were much older than she was. Way cooler. She had been invited to hang out with the big kids, play their strange big-kid games. Like smoking cigarettes. Telling ghost stories in the cemetery. Playing Ghosts in the Graveyard. All Amber had to do was keep cool. Keep her giddiness to a minimum.

The other actors milled about the craft table. They must have been cold. They were hardly wearing any clothes. Their costumes exposed so much skin. She couldn't help but stare. All those shoulders. Those bare arms. And the lumps up front. Amber could feel her cheeks flush, even under all that latex. She had shot a few scenes with her adult co-stars already. They seemed much different then. Now that they were in the last week of production, everybody seemed tired. Less accessible. The actors treated her differently. They didn't talk to her at all.

Was it her costume? The makeup?

Did they think she was really the Little Witch Girl?

Were they scared of her?

Her tongue found her loose tooth once more. She jabbed at it this time, forcing the tooth further than she ever had before, like a tree toppling over in the woods.

Timmmberrrrrr!

The rusty tang of blood mingled with her saliva. It was pooling in her mouth now. It tasted gross. Like pennies on her tongue. She wanted to spit, but where? You can't spit in a church! She was supposed to sit still. But the flood of bloodied saliva was only rising, overwhelming her mouth. She had to get rid of it somehow. Get rid of it before her lips split—

Amber swallowed.

The warmth of it snaked down her gullet until it swelled up into her stomach.

She felt like she was about to barf.

Barf blood.

Amber shifted in her seat again, the warped wood creaking and echoing through the church. She instantly regretted moving. She didn't want to sit here by herself anymore.

Where was her mother?

Not her actual mother. The actress who played her mom in the movie.

Ella Louise.

Amber had spotted her on set earlier in the evening, before the sun had lowered over the surrounding tree line. She wasn't technically filming tonight, but now that they were shooting on location, here in this small, small town, there wasn't much else to do but hang around the set and help out however you could.

The production had squeezed in three consecutive night shoots just for the end. Mr. Ketchum wanted to get it right. He had demanded they film the final scene at night. He refused to shoot day-for-night, absolutely refused. You couldn't have the terrifying grand finale filtered through blue lenses! The audience would know it was shot in the middle of the day. Underexposing the shot in-camera might suggest the cool blue hue of moonlight, but the actors' skin would look like they were in an aquarium! He wanted to create a bonfire effect that had to be captured at night. There was absolutely no way those flames would contrast against the afternoon sky.

Amber wore a paper towel around her neck to keep her makeup from smearing. It felt like a bib. It was embarrassing. If she wanted to eat something, she had to ask a PA. So she didn't. She didn't want to seem like a baby in front of all the other actors, getting fed by somebody else, even if her stomach was churning, grumbling so loudly it echoed throughout the church.

Did anyone hear that? Her tummy? It must have sounded like a monster to everyone else, like a zombie clawing its way out from the ground.

Amber hadn't seen the director all night. Or during the day. He was always elsewhere. Always exhausted. He looked tired no matter what time of day it was. Amber could tell that Mr. Ketchum had been losing sleep ever since they started shooting here in Pilot's Creek. Always a disheveled mess. Unshaven. Purple bags under his eyes. He looked depleted to her. Drained.

Amber had learned that the director was originally from here. This was his hometown. How strange it must be for him. To come home. To make this movie here. Mr. Ketchum had even managed to secure three nights in the same cemetery where the real Jessica Ford was buried. Amber had asked her mother if she could see the grave, see the fence of crosses, but Mom kept sidestepping the question. Pretending she hadn't heard Amber, no matter how many times she asked. The grave had to be around here, somewhere. Maybe Amber could slip out and find it on her own. Nobody would notice, right? She could just sneak through the—

The church doors squealed open behind her.

There she was.

Her mother.

Not her real mother. Her cinematic one.

Miss Lambert.

Nora.

Even out of costume, without any makeup on, she looked other-worldly to Amber. Bewitching. She certainly didn't look like a lot of the women her flesh-and-blood mother hung around with. Her skin had a deeper hue to it. Not suntanned, but sun-kissed. She was stunning.

It made Amber feel warm inside, imagining this preternatural actress as her mother. Even if it was just a movie. Even if it was just pretend.

"Miss Lambert?"

The woman turned. Looked down. When her eyes settled onto Amber, it felt as if she had been looking for her, only her, searching for Amber this whole time—and here she was.

"Amber!" Miss Lambert smiled. Beamed. "Hello . . . You know, you can call me Nora now. Enough with this Miss Lambert stuff . . . You make me feel like my mother!"

Amber giggled at this. "Okay. Nora."

"How are you? Not too tired?"

Amber bashfully shook her head.

"I'm exhausted." Miss Lambert leaned in and whispered, mock-conspiratorially, as if the two of them were about to get up to something no good. "Ready for your spooky scene?"

Amber liked the feeling of keeping a secret. Something just for the two of them. She grinned and the latex along her lips tugged. Was her skin cracking? Were her wounds ripping?

"I wanted to come, just for you," Miss Lambert said. "Would you mind if I watched?"

Was she actually asking for Amber's permission? *Really?* She didn't know what to say. She was stunned. Honored. Amber shook her head: *No, of course not. Of course. Please stay!*

"Great," Miss Lambert said. "You'll be great. Knock 'em dead."

Someone cleared their throat behind Amber.

Nora noticed them first. Whatever mirth had played across her face washed away. She stood back up to her regular adult height and nodded.

Amber turned and found her mother.

The real one.

"There you are." Mom didn't look happy. Acting as if she'd been racing around town, desperately searching for her daughter. But where else would Amber have been? She had been sitting in the church for hours, ever since the makeup techs were done with her, waiting—and waiting—for her call, just like she was supposed to. Amber's mother knew she would be here, was sent here. Why was she acting like she'd lost her?

"Hi," Nora said, and nodded to Amber's mother.

Mom smiled back at Nora, even if it didn't quite feel like a smile. She quickly zeroed in on Amber. "Come on, hon," she said, taking her arm and pulling. "Time to go over your lines."

Amber didn't move. She wanted to stay in the church. Close to Miss Lambert. "Do we have to?"

This took Mom by surprise. Instead of looking to Amber, her eyes settled on Nora. A silent exchange passed between the women just over her head, some mysterious form of telepathic communication she herself had yet to master. The message was apparently received by Miss Lambert, loud and clear.

Mom gave a tug on Amber's arm. "Come," she said. "We need to run through your lines."

"But I already know my lines . . ."

Mom turned. Her eyes narrowed, taking Amber in. Her head turned ever so slightly to one shoulder, as if to assess this new willful streak. Where had this resistance come from?

"Excuse me?"

"But I want to stay."

She lowered herself to Amber's height. Staring her right in the eye, she said, "Listen, Amber. *Listen.* You're embarrassing yourself. You're embarrassing me. In front of everybody here. You want to make a fool out of yourself? Fine. But not here. Not on set. Act like a professional, 'kay?"

"I *am* a professional!"

Her words came out much louder than she intended. Poor Miss Lambert stepped back, away from Amber and her mother, silently excusing herself from the mounting tête-à-tête.

Amber's mother halted. "What did you just say?"

"*I am a professional.*" Amber had a flash to all the auditions. Racing from one cattle call to another in Mom's avocado-green Chevrolet Nova, speeding down the interstate. Mom would slam her palm onto the horn, cursing the traffic, swearing the entire way. As soon as they parked, they'd rush into whatever industrial building was holding the auditions, and then Mom would suddenly be all smiles again. Bright and beaming. Like nothing had happened.

The second they were back in the Chevy, it was nothing but panic. Outright chaos. Speeding down the streets. Running red lights. Just to get to the next audition.

Always the next audition.

Mom had been pulled over once. She had chewed the officer out as he wrote a ticket. *Don't you see we're running late here*, she'd berated the policeman from behind the wheel. *My daughter's got a callback across town and I have to get on the 405. And here you are, making her miss her chance. Happy now? Are you, officer? I bet you are. Asshole. Thanks, thanks so much.*

Amber had sunk into her seat, her cheeks flushed, praying she would disappear. She slid so far down that every inch of her made full contact with the leatherette. When she shifted, her skin had peeled away with a sticky sound.

Amber always prayed from the back of their Chevy that one day her mom might lose control of the wheel, simply glance away from the road for a moment, and ease into incoming traffic. Meet the fender of another car. An eighteen-wheeler careening toward them.

No more auditions. No more cattle calls.

Amber would be free.

Finally free.

But here, now, in the small church nestled deep within Pilot's Creek Cemetery, Amber realized that she would never be free. Free of family. This was her life. This was her mother.

"You done now?" Mom asked. "You done with your little hissy fit?"

"Mommy, please . . ."

"Enough. You listen to me, okay? We're going over your lines."

Even at nine, Amber knew this had nothing to do with going over her lines. Nothing at all. This had everything to do with the fact that she had been talking to Miss Lambert.

"I don't want to . . ."

"Amber."

"No."

"Amber!"

"NO!"

Their voices reverberated through the church, bouncing off the wooden rafters.

"You do as I say," Mom seethed. She'd had enough. She clutched Amber's arm and began to drag her away. Amber leaned the other way, pulling back.

"Let me go."

Amber felt the strain in her wrist. Her shoulder was about to pop out of its socket.

"Let go!"

Amber yanked her arm back. Hard. As hard as she could. Amber's mother let go, releasing her, both of them stumbling backward. She fell onto her back. Picking herself up as quickly as she could, she ran down the aisle. Away from her mother.

"Amber!"

Her shoulder struck the church doors and pushed them open, racing out into the darkness.

Into the cemetery.

FIVE

The sun. The sun was waiting for her outside. She ran right into it, straight out from the church and into the blindingly bright white light of a supernova. She brought her arms up to her face, shielding her eyes. It felt so close, so hot against her cheeks, she couldn't help but wonder if the intense glare was enough to peel her skin right off. Burn straight through.

Wait, she thought. Wasn't it midnight? Where had the sun come from?

Her eyes slowly adjusted. Back to the night.

To the dark.

There were several suns now. Not just one. An entire constellation of hot white spots hung throughout the cemetery, suspended over the graves on their own telescopic stands.

For the last few hours, the gaffer and his crew had busied themselves by setting up a handful of ground-mounted lighting fixtures all around the outer perimeter of the cemetery, illuminating the graves. Each headstone cast its own severe shadow. In the film, in the very celluloid itself, it would look like moonlight. But here, on set, they burned with an intensity that caused Amber to wince.

The cemetery wasn't so big. A town as small as this one, there weren't that many bodies to bury. Pilot's Creek hadn't expanded beyond its few stoplights. There were no plans to extend the city limits and there were certainly no plans to cut through the surrounding woods to make way for more graves. There was more than enough room to bury this town's own without ever setting foot into the neighboring pines, which was just the way the locals liked it. Preferred it. Nobody set foot in those woods. That much was clear.

But at night, in the dark, the graveyard lost its shape. The contours of it loosened within the shadows, bleeding into the surrounding trees. As far as Amber was concerned, it felt as if the cemetery went on for miles and miles. There could have been hundreds of graves, a thousand graves, lingering beyond these lighting fixtures. The crew had only set up their kit in the northern corner of the cemetery, isolating a row of graves directly in front of the church. Whoever was buried beyond the light's reach was anybody's guess. Amber didn't know.

"Finally," a man's voice beckoned from beyond the grave. "There you are."

Amber froze.

Mr. Ketchum marched straight for her. His breath fogged up before him, puffs of steam dissipating into the night air at a quick clip, as if he were breathing fire. She simply stood there, intensely aware of the fact that Mr. Ketchum didn't seem happy with her. Happy at all. With anything. The arc lamps cast a stark silhouette over his face. Amber had a hard time seeing his eyes. They had sunk back farther into his sockets, lost in shadows. He kept chewing. From where Amber was standing, staring up, it looked like he was gnawing on his own tongue.

"Let's get going, shall we?"

There were so few men in Amber's life. She'd never met her father. Any opinions of him were filtered through her mother's point of view. Mom occasionally dated, bringing home the odd boyfriend now and then. But none of them lasted. None of the men ever lasted.

Their names, their faces—some with mustaches, some not—all blurred together.

Mr. Ketchum had been around longer than any other man in Amber's life. She couldn't help but feel he just might be the closest thing to a father figure she had.

Telling her what to do.

Where to stand.

How to talk.

Demanding the most out of her.

Only the best.

And right now Mr. Ketchum was very, *very* disappointed in her.

"We're burning moonlight here, people," he announced, clapping his hands. "Let's get this shot before the sun comes, okay? We've got to bang out five pages before dawn . . ."

The setup was simple.

All Amber had to do was walk through a row of headstones.

Simple. A monkey could do it.

Cassandra and her hippie boyfriend were sitting on her grave, toking up after a little postcoital séancing. Their backs pressed against Jessica Ford's headstone. The boyfriend would stand up and mumble something about needing to relieve himself, leaving Cassandra alone.

The spirit of Jessica Ford would rise from the earth, out from her grave. Cassandra wouldn't be the wiser, wouldn't know Jessica was closing in on her, until it was too late.

It all seemed simple enough. They blocked the whole scene. Mr. Ketchum pointed to Amber's marks, where she had to walk. Where to stop and stand and look so the camera could see her. Where to say her line.

Easy-peasy, lemon-squeezy.

But as soon as Mr. Ketchum was standing behind the camera, muttering to the cinematographer about how to frame the shot, as soon as he pressed his eyes against the viewfinder to see how it all looked, as soon as the boom operator lifted the mic over Amber's head, as soon as Amber was standing alone, waiting alone, as soon as the intense glare of the lamp spread over her face, the heat from the bulbs causing her to sweat, her makeup starting to slicken, the perspiration chilling against her skin . . . she felt her skin prickle.

How could she be hot and cold at the same time? It made no sense to her.

"Sound," the sound tech called out.

"Camera."

"Rolling."

A young man stepped up with a clapboard in hand. He lifted it directly in front of Amber's face. The glare of the lights was suddenly off her eyes. Amber's attention drifted, her eyes wandering over the row of graves. So many bodies buried here. The light kits. The camera. The crew waltzing over their coffins. This didn't seem right. Didn't seem appropriate. Being here, like this. Making a movie, like this. Wouldn't the dead think they were making fun of them? Teasing them? Dancing over their graves? Amber couldn't help but feel guilty. Culpable.

"*Don't Tread on Jessica's Grave*," he announced. "Scene forty-three. Take one."

CLACK.

The arm on the clapboard came down so hard, so fast, it snapped Amber out of her daydream. She gave a start, wincing from the harsh smack of the wooden wand slicing down. Like a guillotine. Like a mousetrap. She needed a moment to settle her nerves. Settle down.

"And . . . *action*."

All eyes were suddenly on Amber. She felt them staring at her. The cast. The crew. The director. Mom. Nora. All of them. Watching her. Waiting for her to say her line. Her one line.

It should've been so simple.

All she had to do was waltz down the graves. Lift her arm and reach out to Cassandra. Point an accusing finger at the young woman and her frizzy-haired boyfriend and say . . .

And say . . .

What was her line again?

Her mind had gone blank. The words weren't there anymore. They all evaporated. They had just been there, only a moment ago. And now . . .

Now . . .

Now her tongue felt dry. It had shriveled in her mouth. Her throat constricted. She felt like a raisin. Like a mummy. A shriveled corpse on two feet.

Amber lost her mark. Her eyes darted away from her sightline. To the camera.

(Don't look directly in the camera!)

To the crew.

(Don't look at the crew!)

To her mother.

(Don't look at me! Whatever you do, don't ever look at me!)

Her mother had been standing off to the side, deeper in the cemetery, where the FX techs had been waiting for their cue to move in and prep for the next scene.

Amber lost herself in her mom's eyes. The telepathic missives she kept sending to her daughter. She was having a hard time deciphering her mother's expression. She looked frightened. Her own mother. Her eyes so wide. Her mouth hanging open, without breathing.

What was there for her to be so scared of? Why would she be afraid?

"Cut."

The call felt like a cut all right. Slicing through the air at Amber's back. She hadn't seen who said it, but she knew right away it had been Mr. Ketchum. The intonation. The anger.

"Set it up quickly, please. Back to starting positions. Let's do it again." And then, from whatever shadow he was hiding in, his voice bellowed out: "Do you need your line, Amber?"

She shook her head *no*. No—she knew the lines. They were in her, she swore it. They always had been. She just lost them for a second. Just a second. But they were back now.

She promised.

Her lines.

Her voice.

Her breath.

She had them all back. Back where they belonged.

Please don't be mad at me, she wanted to say. But she knew this would only make Mr. Ketchum madder. Adults always get angrier when you ask them not to be mad at you, because it makes them see that they're angry in the first place. You've made them aware of the fact that they're angry, angry at you, and you've called them out on it. You've shined a light on their rage, and nothing makes an adult feel more awful than knowing they've done something awful.

"Sound."

"Camera."

"Rolling."

"*Don't Tread on Jessica's Grave,*" he announced. "Scene forty-three. Take two."

CLACK.

Even though Amber knew the harsh sound was coming, it still startled her again. She took a moment to mentally check if all of her fingers were still attached to her hands.

"Action!"

Amber shuffled down the row of graves, just as she was told to.

Amber lifted up her arm, haltingly so, just how Mr. Ketchum had told her to. *Like it's really heavy,* he'd said to her, *like it weighs a hundred pounds.*

She pointed her finger off camera, toward the spot where

Cassandra was supposed to be, unaware that the spirit of Jessica Ford was approaching.

Amber's lips parted. She took a breath and . . .

Nothing.

The line was gone again. It had just been there, right there at the tip of her—

"*Cut*. Cut!"

Amber noticed that the moment Mr. Ketchum shouted *cut*, everybody else went limp. The crew clenched during filming, holding their breath. But as soon as the camera shut off, their limbs loosened again, all that pent-up breath spilling out in one big collective exhale.

Before Amber knew what was happening, she saw Mr. Ketchum approaching. Saw him storming down the row of graves. Heading straight for her. There was spite in his eyes. He was trying to hide it. Masked in a thin layer of impatience. But she knew, Amber knew it was all a façade.

Mr. Ketchum kneeled before her. He took a moment to breathe in through his nose. Take the little girl in. "Amber. You okay, hon?"

Treacle. His voice sounded phony. There was anger buried beneath that sugary tone.

Amber nodded her head. It's always better to agree with adults, she knew. Let them believe they're right so that they won't get angrier with you.

"Having a hard time remembering your line?"

Amber nodded again. "Yeah."

Her mother suddenly appeared. Breathless. She had raced through the graves and was now standing next to Mr. Ketchum. He was quick to notice, tightening his smile.

"That's okay," he continued. "It happens. Everybody forgets now and then. But it's really, *really* important that we get this shot finished so we can move on to the next, 'kay?"

Amber nodded. She glanced at her mother, who did nothing. Said nothing. She merely hung back, eyes wide, imploring with Amber: *Don't mess this up don't you dare mess this up . . .*

"So." Ketchum cleared his throat, drawing Amber's attention back. "The line in the script is: *Do you want to play with me?* Pretty simple, right? Now why don't you go ahead and try it?"

Amber nodded her head, up and down, as she intonated the line back to Mr. Ketchum, word for lifeless word. "Do you want to play with me."

Ketchum smiled. "See? That wasn't so hard, now, was it?"

Amber shook her head *no.*

"Try it again for me."

"Do you want to play with me."

"Once more."

"Do you want to play with me."

"Again for good luck?"

"Do you want to play with me."

"Ask it. It's a question."

"Do you want to play with me?"

"Perfect! Perfect! Once more?"

"Do you want to play with me?"

"Again!"

"Do you want to play with me?"

"Good. Great. Perfect. Think you can do that when the cameras start rolling?"

Amber nodded *yes.*

do you want to play with me
do you want to play with me
do you want to play with me
do you want
do you
me

But even then, from some bottomless depth within her chest, she could hear another voice inside her, a turf-ridden lisp, hissing out an altogether different response. Rejecting him.

Noooooooo

"Good," Mr. Ketchum responded. "Real good. Now, we won't start rolling until you say you're ready this time, okay? I'm not gonna call action until you're ready. We want to get this right, so you let me know when you're ready. Okay, Amber? Does that sound good to you?"

Noooooooo

Mr. Ketchum stood up and faced Amber's mother. The silent exchange between them seemed less than sympathetic.

do you want to play with me

do you want to play with me

do you want to play with me

do you want to play

All their eyes. Everyone was watching her. Waiting for her. Hanging on her every word.

These words seemed so silly.

So . . . *wrong.*

That was when it struck Amber. She suddenly realized what the problem was.

These weren't the right words.

Of all the things to say, this is the silly stuff they had written?

"Do you want to play with me?"

Who writes tripe like that? She could write better lines than that. She'd been hearing them in her dreams for days now. Weeks.

Amber had a story to tell. An important story. She was a vessel, a conduit for her character, for Jessica Ford, the Little Witch Girl, and this was what she was supposed to say?

Do you want to play with me?

It was wrong.

All wrong.

do you want to play with me

"Sound."

do you want to play with me do you want to play with me

"Camera."

do you want to play with me do you want to play with me do you want to play with me

CLACK.

do you want to play with me do you want to play with me do you want to play with me do you want to play with me do you want to play with me do you want to play with me do you want to play with me do you want to play with me do you want to play with me do you want to play with me do you want to play with me do you want to play

And just like that, before the camera, its film unspooling, whirring and clicking from within its sealed chambers, before the rest of the crew and her own mother, Amber nodded at the director and Mr. Ketchum called *action*.

Amber suddenly knew exactly what needed to be said.

"Tell my story," Amber said. "Let everyone know who I am."

The words flowed right out of her. She didn't even realize she was saying them until she spoke out loud, filling the air and embedding them onto tape.

"Cut, cut, CUT!"

Amber heard Ketchum coming before she saw him. His strides swept through the crisp air. Mr. Ketchum swooped upon her before she could retreat. "What the hell's going on here? You want to rewrite the scene? You want to play a little game and say whatever the hell you want to? Is that what you want to do, Amber? Is that what's going on here?"

Her mom rushed up. "Let me talk to her. We can work this—"

Ketchum shot back up and released his complete wrath on Amber's mother. "You want to tell me what the fuck this is all about? You want to talk to your daughter and let her know what this is costing us? That I only have three days left on the schedule to shoot? That every time she misses her mark or forgets her line or makes some shit up, she's losing us thousands of dollars? Can you please do that for me?"

"She . . ." Mom started. "She's just a girl."

Just a girl.

Her mother was sticking up for her. Fighting for her. Defending her against this . . . this ogre of a director. This mean man. Nobody should talk that way to a child. Even Amber knew that. Everybody knew that. And here was her mother, her mom, ready to put her foot down.

"Do you know how many fucking girls there are out there that I could've cast? Do you know how many fucking kids auditioned for this role? Do you know how many bitches are ready and waiting to take her place? Right now? At this very minute? Do you?"

Amber waited. This was the moment. The moment where her mom would say a bad word, a really bad word. Really throw it at him. Spit it right in his face.

Nobody talks to my daughter like that, she would say. *Nobody.*

Ketchum took her silence to keep on going. "I can get on the phone right now. I can call up Sheila and get her to send down whoever was next on the list. Hell, I could just head down to Pilot's Creek Elementary or whatever the fuck it's called and drag some kid out of class and get them all suited up . . . I could give a shit who plays her, *as long as she says the fucking lines exactly the way they are written.* Hear me?"

Amber's mom bowed her head.

And nodded.

She kneeled before Amber. Before she met her daughter's eyes, she took in a quick breath. Really gulped it down, like someone who didn't savor it but just wanted to imbibe.

"Amber . . ."

She still hadn't looked at her. Why wasn't she looking at her? Why wasn't she protecting her? Why wasn't she stopping this mean, mean man from saying these awful, awful things?

Save me, Mommy . . .

Save me . . .

"Amber, you need to do what Mr. Ketchum says. You understand?"

Amber croaked. "But . . ."

Amber's mom gripped her by the shoulders. Squeezed. "Listen to me. *Listen.* Do you see what you're doing? Do you? Do you understand how much trouble you're causing right now?"

"Mommy . . ."

"Just say the lines, Amber."

"You're hurting—"

"Say the lines the way they're written."

Amber tore herself out of her mother's grip. It took all her strength. She toppled over, her back smacking the tombstone directly behind her, smashing into the soft sandstone.

She bit down and instantly felt her teeth crack together.

Her tooth.

Her tooth bent backward, almost at a ninety-degree angle. The nerve tore even farther away, until the tooth flailed against her tongue, barely holding on any longer, just by a thread of flesh.

The force of impact was enough to send the headstone tipping over. Once it hit the ground, the slab shattered, crumbling into smaller chunks that rolled across the ground.

Amber's mom didn't move. Didn't rush to catch her. She only froze. The rest of the crew was watching. The cinematographer was watching. The director was watching. The FX techs were watching. The makeup assistants were watching. The production assistants were watching. The rest of the cast was watching. The actress playing Cassandra was watching.

Nora . . .

Nora Lambert was watching, her fingers pressed to her mouth in stunned silence, standing in complete stillness among all the others.

"Oh, Amber . . ." Miss Lambert said it. Not her mother.

Her mother said nothing.

Amber ran. She picked herself up and raced through a row of tombstones. The farther she went, the deeper she slipped into the dark. Into the shadows waiting beyond the Fresnel lamps.

The cemetery opened up to her.

SIX

Amber could hear her name. So many different voices, adult voices, men and women, all calling out for her. The soft contours of her name echoed in the surrounding trees. Rippling.

Amber . . .

Amber . . .

Amber . . .

They had come looking for her. They would find her here. Eventually. She knew that. Hiding in the cemetery. Balled up inside herself among the graves. Like a baby. Like a little—

She had gone where the lights couldn't touch her. Where the reach of the arc lamps receded into shadows. But the cemetery wasn't big enough to hide forever. Not if she really wanted to be alone. Away from all of them.

Her back was pressed against a headstone. The very grit of it scraped off her shoulders. The headstones were so old in this corner of the cemetery. Much older than the rest. The names and dates had all faded from the endless weather. She glanced at the inscription written behind her, barely able to read it in the dark. She ran her fingers along the name, the date of their birth, their death, trying hard to read the inscription with her fingertips, as if she were blind.

Amber . . .

Amber . . .

Amber . . .

A breeze blew through the tombs, whisking off with her name. She couldn't make out the distinction between voices anymore. She couldn't tell if it was a production assistant or her mother or the director or the cast. Whoever was shouting now, or however many, their voices were fading. As if they were heading in the other direction. They were going the wrong way.

Amber . . .

Amber . . .

Amber . . .

She knew she shouldn't cry. She knew she was ruining her makeup. All those hours in the spinning dentist chair . . . all for nothing. She would have to sit and stare at her reflection for hours again, forced to start from scratch. Hours to take the ruined latex appliances off and hours to glue completely new prosthetics back on. The makeup techs would be polite and say it was no big deal, *shit happens*, but Amber knew, she knew they would all be mad at her. Fuming on the inside. Furious for all those wasted hours. She was old enough to understand that time is money in this business and there wasn't nearly enough money to begin with for this cursed production and now she had wasted everyone's time, hours and hours and Lord only knows how many hundreds of thousands of dollars, all because she was crying.

Because Amber was nothing but a big crybaby.

I didn't raise you to be a crybaby, she could hear her mother saying already, scolding her in front of the whole crew. *Stop making a fool out of yourself. Pull yourself together.*

Amber brought her knees up to her chest and buried her face in the chasm between her legs. Her skin crackled. Peeled. The latex puckered around her cheeks. She could feel the tears worming their way through the nylon, winnowing within the crevices along her face.

It itched. It itched so much.

All Amber wanted to do was tear it all away. Dig her fingers into the fake layer of flesh and rip the makeup off with her own bare hands. Rip it all away, every last layer. Rip away her real skin even. Until there was none left. Until it was all exposed. Her bones. Her own skull.

She looked down at her costume. The ashen dress. What she must have looked like. A crying ghost girl. A crybaby phantom hiding among the graves.

Her tooth fell out.

Amber hadn't even realized it had torn free, but there it was, resting in her hand. The slightest puddle of bloodied saliva settled into the crevices of her palm.

Her tooth. She closed her hand around it, squeezing her fingers into a fist, until she felt the roots of her tooth dig into her flesh.

If she waited here long enough, the sun would eventually come up. It would be a new day. Perhaps some mourning family member would visit the cemetery to pay their respects to a dearly departed granny and they would stumble upon Amber in costume, her burnt skin in tatters. She could just imagine their reaction. Their screams. They would run. Run from her.

Jessica is back, they'd shout. *Jessica Ford is freeeeeeeeeeee . . .*

That would show them, she thought. *I'll show them all.*

A sob escaped Amber's throat. That wasn't what she wanted. Not at all. She didn't want anything to do with Jessica.

Amber wasn't going back. Wasn't going to star in this stupid, awful movie. They couldn't make her. They just couldn't. No matter how much her mother insisted, demanded that she do it. She could spank Amber if she wanted. She could bend her daughter over her knee and give her a good hiding in front of the whole crew. Amber didn't care. She didn't care what the contract said or whether she got paid or sued or whatever adults do. She wouldn't do it.

She just couldn't. She couldn't be Jessica.

Amber . . .

Amber . . .

Amber . . .

The pinprick of insect legs scuttled across the back of her hand. She yanked her arm away. Whatever bug it was, it was gone now. A beetle or centipede, maybe. They had to be all over her now. She could feel them. All of them. Crawling over her skin. She couldn't see them, but she knew they were there. They had to be there. So many insects skittering over the earth.

And what about the bodies buried just below her?

This was a cemetery, after all.

A real cemetery.

Why couldn't they have just made a pretend one? Styrofoam tombstones in a soccer field somewhere back in Los Angeles? Why did they have to come all the way out here? Why this cemetery in particular? What was so special about this place, this graveyard, with all of its dead? All those bodies, their pruned flesh, withered and shriveled and peeling away. Their toothy grins and their dust-covered charnel suits. They must have been so angry at them, at Amber, mad at her for coming here, making light of death by waltzing over their graves.

Jessica . . .

Someone called out for her. The voice sounded different. Distinct. There was a softness to it. A tenderness. Certainly not her mother.

Jessica . . .

Whoever it was, their voice drifted along with the wind and winnowed through the tombs, brushing over Amber's cheek.

Jessica . . .

It was a woman. A woman, calling out for her.

Jessica . . .

That's weird, Amber thought. *Why would they call out for her character?*

Maybe she was just imagining it.

Jessica . . .

But no. There it was again. A woman's voice. The tender lilt to it drifted over the cemetery. For a moment, Amber couldn't shake the feeling that the voice had started within her own head. Whoever was calling for her had access to her thoughts.

Jessica . . .

Jessica . . .

Jessica . . .

But Amber *wasn't* Jessica. She was just dressed like her. Pretending to be her.

This wasn't real. This was all for show.

Didn't they know that?

Jessica . . .

Amber turned herself over until she was kneeling before the headstone. She brought her hands up and grabbed hold of the crumbling sandstone. Pulling herself up, she peered over the edge of the headstone to see if she could spot the person calling out for her.

No one was there.

The cemetery was completely empty. Nothing but headstones. The lamps were still on, casting their shadows farther off. Amber sat within the inky puddle, curled inside the black.

Where had everybody gone? The crew? Shouldn't they be looking for her now?

Where was her mother? Why wasn't she looking for Amber?

Why was she alone?

Amber hesitated. Just a few rows ahead, she spotted a grave that looked unlike any of the other surrounding tombs.

This one had a fence. A metal fence that rose about a foot off the soil, sequestering its hallowed ground to prevent anyone from stepping on it.

Amber squinted, unsure of what she was seeing. But yes, yes, the fence was made up of crosses. Dozens and dozens of crucifixes, welded together into a rusted web. The same kinds of crosses she'd seen in the chapel. The larger crosses formed a scaffolding that impaled the ground. Several smaller crosses had been soldered along the arms of the bigger ones. The whole thing was choked with cobwebs and weeds. The ground itself hadn't been tended to for a long, long time, from the looks of it. The crabgrass rose up from the grave and wove its way through the fence. Amber hadn't even noticed the headstone. All those weeds were in the way.

Before she knew what she was even doing, before she could stop herself, Amber leaned forward and pressed her tooth into the dirt. She forced it down into the soil as far as her fingers could poke it, as if the tooth itself were a seed that would one day grow to bear wondrous fruit.

Jessica . . .

The voice was louder now.

Jessica . . .

Closer.

Jessica . . .

No—not closer. Not louder. Just . . . *clearer.* In her head.

Jessica . . .

Amber wasn't ready to be found. Not yet. She couldn't face anyone. Not from the movie. And certainly not her mother. She didn't want Mom to see her like this. Crying like a little girl.

She could hide. Hide somewhere else. The woods, maybe?

There was still time to slip through the tree line. She turned to run. Quick. Before anyone spotted her. She could slip through the row of tombs if she hurried. They wouldn't find her in—

The fence.

She hadn't remembered the fence at her feet. All those crosses rising up from the ground. The tip of her toes caught a crucifix, snagging her foot and sending her tumbling forward.

She was falling. Falling onto this caged-in grave.

The crumbling headstone filled her vision, coming for her so quickly, until there was nothing else for her to see. The weatherworn slope of it. The brittle edge. The weeds strangling its façade.

Amber's temple met sandstone. Shards of white-hot stars pierced her field of vision, like light from a projector burning through a snagged filmstrip, bubbling and distorting and chewing through the quivering celluloid until a black hole burst open and swallowed her, leaving behind nothing but darkness.

SEVEN

She felt her heartbeat in her head. Her skull was throbbing. Amber's eyelids fluttered open, slowly taking in the graveyard.

It was still dark. Still night. How long had she been out? Patting at her temple, she found the source of her pain. Just tapping the gash along her forehead sent a fresh sting radiating through the rest of her skull.

Her fingers felt wet. Blood. She was bleeding. Or was that just her makeup?

Amber sat upright. Too fast. The tombstones spun, circling around her head. She pinched her eyes shut and patiently waited for the dizzy spell to fade. It was here, in the darkness behind her eyelids, that the pain felt even worse. In the dark it felt as if her skull had cracked wide open.

Maybe it had.

Placing one hand on the nearest headstone, she struggled to lift herself back onto her feet. Another dizzy spell swept over her. Her knees softened. She was going to fall, fall over again, if she didn't plant her hand on the grave and hold the rest of herself upright. Hold on for dear life.

Jessica . . .

There. In the woods.

Just a step or two back from the surrounding tree line, where the shadows still lingered.

Amber could just barely make out the hazy silhouette of a woman. She was wearing a long white gown. The bottom of her dress was smeared with dirt.

No, not dirt. The hem of it was burned black, while farther up it softened to a gray. Like ash.

Even in the dark, Amber sensed this woman was looking right at her. Staring at her. She stood very still, making no moves, remaining in the woods. As if she were waiting.

Waiting for Amber.

There you are, the voice whispered gently within her head. *There you are, my love . . .*

Her makeup looked far more lifelike up close. Even better than Amber's. Lifelike wasn't the word for it, she realized.

More . . . deathlike? she wondered. *Is that even a word?*

Amber lost herself within the prosthetic work. The attention to detail. The special effects guys had really outdone themselves on Ella Louise. Her arms were outstretched, reaching out for Amber, as if she wanted to scoop the girl up and embrace her.

Amber couldn't help but marvel at the mottled flesh, how the upper layer had blackened to a scabbed crisp, cracking and curling back until it exposed the seared pink tissue underneath. Even her bones were on display. Amber could see all the way through the gap between the radius and ulna on her right forearm, as if the years buried in the ground had gnawed completely through.

How had the FX techs done all that?

Her gown had torn open along her torso, exposing bits of her flame-ravaged body. What little was left of it. Ashen ribs were stacked on top of one another. They flexed and fanned, in and out, with every wheezing breath. A gray sac that must've been her lungs shimmered underneath her charred chest cavity. There was a wetness to her exposed organs. The cemetery was lit, but she held back, standing in the woods, just out of the lighting fixtures' complete reach. Their residual glow cast an unhealthy sheen over her innards. To Amber, it looked as if there were a gray serpent coiled up within her rib cage, slithering about Ella Louise's skeleton.

Amber did it again. Thinking this was Ella Louise.

It's Nora.

Nora.

When Miss Lambert exhaled, Amber could swear she heard her insides whistle. Oxygen hissed out from the thinnest fissures within her windpipe, like air escaping a waterlogged tire.

But it was the eyes that were the most unsettling, Amber believed. The rest of Nora's face had blackened to a cindered crisp. Her scalp was nothing more than a blistered ball of waxen flesh and ash. Her nose, gone, revealed a yawning cavity at the very center of her face.

But her eyes.

Her eyes were *alive*. Two pulsing pearls were perched in their hollowed sockets, glistening in the dark. When Nora cast her gaze upon Amber, speechless Amber, the little girl could have sworn they were filled with some elemental sense of longing.

A sense of love.

A pale fire.

They had lost their color, the irises boiled away from the intense heat, leaving behind a creamy, maggoty hue. But they saw Amber. Stared at her and only her.

They're beautiful, Amber thought. There was love in her eyes. Her milked-over eyes.

Nothing but love.

Amber forgot for a moment, just a brief moment, that this was all pretend.

Latex and makeup.

Movie magic.

It just looks so real . . . She looks real.

It had taken hours for the makeup crew to get Amber to look the way she did. *Hours.* How had they gotten all the burn prosthetics on Nora so fast? The face paint and airbrushed bruises? The wig and the contact lenses? The false teeth? Just how long exactly had Amber been passed out? She hadn't realized they were shooting their reunion scene tonight. Maybe the director changed his mind and decided to film it this evening, shuffling scenes around. Maybe he told her mother and she had forgotten to let Amber know. Perhaps Mom simply chose not to.

Whatever the reason, it didn't matter. Amber was completely entranced.

"Do you . . ." Amber's voice faded, suddenly unsure of herself. She glanced down.

Why hadn't Nora said anything to her?

Why was she acting so strange?

Her feet. Even Nora's feet were done up. She wasn't wearing any shoes. The toe bones sank into the soil. A flimsy strip of singed skin dangling from her shin flapped in the breeze.

Amber glanced back up and realized Miss Lambert was still holding her arms out.

Reaching out for her.

For her. For a hug. An embrace.

To hold Amber.

"Do you," Amber started again, searching for the right thing to say. What was she supposed to say? What did Miss Lambert want her to do? "Do you wanna go over our lines?"

Nora smiled. It was an unnerving effect, watching her cindered lips peel back, like singed rose petals blossoming. There was hardly enough flesh to them, the vermillion border long gone, no longer lips, more like blackened worms. When Nora grinned, her upper lip halved itself through the center flap, as if there were a tear along the philtrum. Calling it a smile might have been a stretch, without enough flesh left along her mouth to lift. But what else could she be doing? What else could Amber call it? It had to be a smile. She looked happy, even with her face burned away. Her gums had receded to the roots of her charred teeth. And yet . . .

And yet . . .

There was joy in her face. Why was she looking at Amber like that? She hadn't blinked once. Her eyelids had burned back, leaving those pearlescent orbs to float within their charred sockets. For a moment, Amber imagined those eyes as fireflies bobbing about in the darkness.

Will-o'-the-wisps! That was what they reminded Amber of. She remembered reading about foolish fire in one of her books about fairies, their phosphorescence flickering over the marsh at midnight. Amber could have sworn she was staring at a pair of the tiniest ghosts, watching them dance about the atmosphere before her, glowing in the darkest shadows of the woods.

The woods.

Miss Lambert still hadn't left the woods. Hadn't crossed beyond the tree line.

Why hadn't she joined Amber? Why wouldn't she step into the cemetery?

Amber didn't understand why she was still hiding in the shadows, refusing to move beyond the surrounding circumference of trees. It was as if she wouldn't, or couldn't, cross some invisible barrier that separated the woods from the graveyard.

Something in the script bubbled up into her brain just then. A line her mother read out loud to her one night. Something about the ghost of Ella Louise Ford being unable to enter the cemetery or some weird superstitious rule like that. It didn't make sense to Amber at the time, she recalled. Why couldn't she? Wasn't Ella Louise a ghost, too? Why couldn't her spirit step into a graveyard with all the other spirits? What was so wrong, so awful about her soul that kept her locked out? Didn't she deserve to rest, too? Eternal rest? Didn't she deserve peace?

Stop asking so many silly questions, Mom had said to her, continuing to flip through the script. *It's just a stupid movie. They probably make up the rules as they go along . . .*

Her mother had read over the dialogue so quickly, tossing it out under her breath and forging ahead to the next line, the thought of it was gone before it even had a chance to resonate within Amber's mind. Mom always read these scripts to herself first. Then the two would read it out aloud together. Mom would skip over the parts that didn't involve Amber's character, which ended up being most of this movie. When all was said and done, Jessica Ford, the Little Witch Girl of Pilot's Creek, only showed up around the midpoint—and even then it was done in the dark, her ghost drifting through the shadows, in silhouette, withholding the ultimate reveal of her character at the very, very end. Which completely pissed off her mom.

Aren't you supposed to be the bad guy? she muttered as she flipped back through the pages, rereading them, searching for a spare scrap of dialogue she might have missed the first time. *What kind of horror movie is this? Why are they hiding you for half the movie? Who in the hell is gonna be scared if they don't show you?*

Miss Lambert still held out her hand.

Beckoning to Amber.

Each finger looked like a candle melted down to the wick, the flesh ebbing away to bone. The distal phalanxes had sharpened themselves into claws. Clumps of dirt clung to her knuckles. Had she been digging? What was left of her dress was covered in mud.

She kept her hand held out for Amber to take.

How long had she been holding that pose?

Waiting for Amber.

Waiting.

Waiting . . .

Amber glanced over her shoulder. She scanned the cemetery, searching for someone. Anyone. A production assistant or producer or even her mother. She hadn't heard her name in quite a while. It was as if they had all forgotten her. Or given up. Where had everyone gone?

Why was she all alone out here?

No, not alone. Not anymore.

Someone had found her.

Miss Lambert.

But Miss Lambert wasn't . . . acting like Miss Lambert. She was acting like somebody else.

Method.

That's what this must be all about. Amber remembered her mother muttering on about the Method. Certain actors liked to lose themselves in a role. They plumbed the depths of their own personal experience in order to become their characters. Amber thought it all sounded pretty silly when she first heard about it. The lengths actors will go to for a role.

Couldn't they just, you know . . . pretend? Say their lines? That was what Amber always did.

Supposedly, some actors get so caught up in the Method, Mom told her, they won't even answer to their real name. While on set, they prefer to go by their character's name.

Perhaps Miss Lambert was one of these method actors.

Maybe Nora wasn't Nora anymore.

So this must be Ella Louise then.

Amber smiled. *Method.* She decided to play along. It would be fun! They could pretend together. Just the two of them. They were no longer Amber Pendleton and Nora Lambert.

They were Jessica and Ella Louise Ford.

Mother and daughter, reunited at last.

Just like in the script.

Amber couldn't help but giggle. She felt like the two of them now had a secret to share. This was their own private game and no one—not even Amber's real mother—could intervene.

They would lose themselves in their roles and never look back.

No more Amber.

No more Nora.

Just Ella Louise.

Just Jessica.

Amber—*no*, she chastised herself, *remember, you're not Amber anymore, it's Jessica now*—Jessica slowly lifted her hand from her side and slid her fingers into Ella Louise's grip.

Her mother's skin was cold. Wet. The crags of burnt flesh crackled against the palm of her own hand. She could feel the hard metacarpals shifting beneath the seared layer of skin.

Her skin felt so cold. So cold.

But Jessica held on.

Ella Louise took a step toward the woods, tugging on Jessica's arm. She wanted her to follow. She wanted her daughter to step away from the hallowed ground of the cemetery and enter the forest. Where they could finally be alone.

Alone together.

Forever.

EIGHT

Where was she taking her? The two had been trudging through the woods for what felt like forever to Amber.

You're not Amber, remember? she said to herself. *It's Jessica now. Play along!*

You're Jessica.

Jessica.

Jessica.

She kept tripping. She was losing the feeling in her feet, clumsily stumbling in the dark. Her fingers had grown so numb. The cold had seeped into her limbs and was now working its way into her bones, an insidious chill that permeated every inch of her body.

These costumes weren't made for the cold. They were nothing but rags, really. She was shivering. The *click-click-click* of her own teeth chattering against one another filled her skull. She could see her breath spreading out before her with every exhale, short bursts of steam.

Not Nora.

Amber couldn't make out Nora's breath at all. It wasn't fogging up before her, like her own breath was.

Nora hadn't let go of Amber since she had first stepped into the woods. The woman's grip only tightened, her bony fingers clamping around her wrist and pulling.

Amber had to pick up her pace, just to keep from losing her footing and falling on the ground. She was practically running now. Her shoulder felt like it was one tug away from popping out of its socket. She wanted to ask Nora why she was in such a hurry.

She wanted to ask, *Where are we going? Shouldn't we be heading the other way? Back to the church? Toward the crew? Toward Mom?*

Nora hadn't looked back. Hadn't glanced over her shoulder at Amber—*Jessica*—for a while now. She seemed determined to drag the little girl deeper into the woods, where no one would find them. She was limping. One heel raked over the ground, scraping up leaves and pine needles in their wake. Amber hadn't noticed it before. It seemed like Nora was unable to bend her right leg. Like her bones had locked. Or had lost their mobility. Now that they were rushing through the woods, the woman's unsteady gait was unavoidable. Had she always had a limp?

The farther away from the lamps they walked, the thicker the shadows grew. Now there was no light, artificial or otherwise. The moon was barricaded behind a latticework of branches. Its beams barely reached through the dense canopy of pines overhead. What little light was able to find them cast the faintest glow over their bodies, but not much else. There was nothing Amber could see, nothing beyond the sloping torsos of pines, their boughs warping in the dark. She could hear the chirping of crickets, every snapping branch at her heels.

And Nora's ragged breathing. Every inhale had a wet drag to it, like burlap ripping. Her exhales were only worse. The air would enter her chest with a sharp intake, *rrrrrip*, only to seep out through her lungs, her throat, her corroded flesh. It whistled out from her in far too many places.

But still . . . it wasn't fogging up. Wasn't clouding over in the air, like Amber's was.

Pins and needles prickled the soft underside of her arm. She was losing the feeling below her shoulder. The flow of blood was no longer reaching her hand.

"You're hurting me," Amber said, tugging back.

Nora's grip only tightened.

Pulling her forward.

Deeper into the woods.

Amber had never noticed it before, but as the wind blew through the surrounding pines, their needles rustled in a soft timbre. Not like the rustling of leaves. These needles bristled. It had a fainter resonance to it. Gentler. Amber closed her eyes, and for the briefest spell, she convinced herself she was actually at the beach, listening to the waves rushing over the shore.

Fingernails raked across Amber's cheek.

Her eyes jolted open.

A low-hanging branch had brushed over her face, its needles scraping her skin.

"I want to go back. *Please.*"

There. She'd said it. The tone of her voice held no strength, though. No persistence. It was a whimper, a sound her mother abhorred. Whenever Amber talked in that voice, her mom would immediately respond in the exact same tone, only exaggerated to annoying effect.

Eeeeh, I'm hungry. I'm tired. I wanna go home.

Like a crybaby.

A big, fat, silly crybaby.

But Amber couldn't help it. She was scared. Cold. And lost. She had no idea where they were anymore or how far they had gone. These woods felt endless. There were no contours, no dimension to this endless stretch of trees. It just kept going on and on. No hills, no clearings . . .

The pines suddenly opened.

Just like that. As if they had been listening to Amber's thoughts.

A clearing.

The moon hung overhead, wrapped in a crown of quivering treetops. Nora stepped into the glade and immediately halted. She released Amber's hand for the first time in an eternity. Amber brought her arm up and massaged her wrist. The feeling of her own cold skin sent shivers down her spine. She'd gone so numb, her own flesh didn't feel like it was hers.

Nora stood in the center of the clearing.

At the very heart of it.

Amber had yet to step into the opening, unsure of what she should do. Was she supposed to follow Nora? Her head kept spinning. She felt dizzy, released from Nora's grip.

That was when she noticed the upturned earth.

All the dirt. So much soil.

It looked as if someone had dug a hole in the ground.

No. Not dug in.

Dug out.

The ground had opened from below, the dirt forced up in jagged mounds at either side of this gaping chasm. Something had clawed its way out from the ground.

From the dirt.

Nora stared at Amber. Waiting. Almost as if she were expecting something from Amber. Wanting something of her. *Yearning.* So much yearning.

What was she supposed to say? What was going on here?

"I want . . ." Amber started, only for her breath to catch in her throat. "I want . . ."

What was she going to say? What did she want? What did she *really* want?

"I want to go home."

There. She'd said it.

Home. That's exactly what Amber wanted.

She wanted to go home.

Nora breathed in, dragging the air through her ragged lungs, and responded in a voice that sounded nothing like Nora Lambert at all.

"*Home.*"

NINE

A warm swell spread down the inside of Amber's leg and instantly chilled within the open air. It only dawned on her that she had wet herself when she felt that her knees were dripping. She hadn't even realized it was happening, what her own body was doing, how it had reacted to the sound of Nora's scraping voice, until it was too late. Far too late. The rest of her body had gone completely rigid, her spine now ramrod straight—but everything housed within her bones, all the organs and squishy stuff coiled inside Amber, seemed to unspool all at once.

That wasn't Nora Lambert. It had never been Nora Lambert.

This was someone else. *Something* else.

All this time.

The cemetery.

The walk through the woods.

Holding hands with it.

Talking to it.

Trusting it.

A low mewling sound escaped from Amber's throat. She couldn't stop herself from moaning. It was too much. All of this was too much. She was just a girl. Just a little girl.

A crybaby.

It was—

It—

Ella Louise Ford reached her hand out to Amber once more, repeating the word.

"*Home . . .*"

It sounded so wet. Much too wet. The word slipped over her shriveled tongue. The breath supporting its intonations was so sibilant.

Words shouldn't sound that way. They should never sound so sodden.

Certainly not the word *home*.

But there was a yearning in Ella Louise. She was imploring with Amber. Entreating with the little girl to understand something that such a young girl couldn't. Or wouldn't. Her own fragile fabric of reality refused to unravel and accept that the woman before her was dead. Long since dead. She had been in the ground for years now. Years. Rotting away. Waiting.

Ella Louise stepped forward, holding out her hand to Amber. "*Home.*"

There was love in that one word.

There was hope.

And dirt. So much dirt clogged in her windpipe.

Amber stepped back. She stepped away from the heap of scorched bones that belonged to Ella Louise Ford.

Ella's neck cricked to her shoulder, like a curious dog tilting its head to one side. She didn't understand this. Why would Jessica suddenly retreat like this? After they'd come so far . . .

"No," Amber croaked, and took another step back. She was shaking her head, *no, no, no, no*, unable to stop herself. Tears wormed their way through the latex, ungluing the prosthetic appliances along her cheeks. The burns were already peeling free from her face. "Please . . ."

Ella Louise lumbered toward her. Her unhinged limbs swung at her sides, as if whatever corporeal force had been holding her together was now slowly losing its grip. Her movements were awkward, clumsy, like a tattered rag doll struggling to pick itself up and hold itself upright, all on its own. Each new step took more effort than the one before, looking as if it hurt to move.

But she kept coming closer. *Closer.* She refused to stop, no matter how much it pained her.

"Home . . ."

Amber took another step back.

And another.

"Don't . . ." Amber's foot found an uplifted root, sending her toppling backward. She felt as if she were suspended in the air, her free fall going on for an eternity, like Alice tumbling down the rabbit hole. She might fall forever, she thought, and never hit the ground.

When she landed on her backside, the sudden jolt electrified her lungs. The air rushed into her chest, sharp and cold, like a hundred pine needles piercing her diaphragm.

Amber screamed.

Amber screamed so loud, so abruptly, it echoed into the woods and never came back.

The woods woke. All the pines bristled at the sound of her voice.

And shivered.

What was left of Ella Louise Ford's eyes only glared. There was hurt in them. Moments before, they had been full of love, of longing, but now—now they were cold, cracked porcelain.

Now they were dead.

Truly dead.

Amber turned herself over and clawed at the earth. Her fingernails dug into the dirt as she pulled herself back up, her legs thrusting her body off the ground and leaping into the air.

She was running. Running so fast.

Amber never looked back.

Couldn't look back.

Not at her.

Not at—

"Home." Amber heard the word once more just over her shoulder, as she raced into the dense canopy of pine trees. The word itself curled into her ear. She swore she felt the cold, decrepit breath that had sent the word along its merry way, through the air and into her mind.

She couldn't stop herself from repeating the word over and over again in her head.

Home.

Home.

Home.

The pines seemed thicker now. More packed together. Amber felt the branches scrape over her face. Those needles, all those pine needles, clawing at her skin. Scraping her makeup away. Until they dug into her own flesh. Her real flesh.

She wouldn't stop running. No matter what.

No matter what.

Just keep running. Run all the way home.

Home.

Home.

Home.

The word was in her head now, inescapable, echoing through her skull, an earworm curling through the lobe and burrowing into her brain and chewing within.

Leaves crackled behind her. There was a familiar dragging sound. Something heavy scraping over the ground. A foot. Ella Louise was following her, chasing her. Right behind her.

Amber picked up her pace. Her lungs were burning. The cold air had left her throat raw.

Run.

Run.

Run—

The very last thing Amber heard before running straight into the trunk of a conifer and smashing her face, shattering her nose and blacking out completely, was Ella Louise calling her—

Home.

TEN

It was nearing three in the morning. Production had halted over two hours ago. Two, going on three goddamn hours. The crew had all dropped what they were doing to look for—

"Amber?"

The gaffer should've been setting up the final shot for the night, but no, instead he was searching the cemetery along with the rest of his team. When no one could find her hiding behind any of the tombstones, the cast and crew all took to the woods, weaving through the trees with their flashlights like some motley search party. The master electrician. The grip. The wardrobe assistant. Makeup. His DP. Even Nora was out here, fucking saint that she was. She wasn't even on the call sheet for tonight's shoot, and yet here she was, on set to show her support to her succubus of a co-star. She'd grabbed a flashlight along with everybody else, calling out for—

"Amber?"

They'd never make their shot list now. Thrown right out the window. All the scenes he was supposed to shoot tonight, all those pages—up in smoke. Burned to a crisp. Sabotaged by—

"Amber?"

She was ruining everything. Ruining his movie. This girl was going to deep-six the whole fucking film before he could finish it.

Before he could show the world and tell Jessica's story.

Ketchum was close to finishing the film.

So close.

He could feel it. It was a similar sensation to swimming underwater and racing back up to the surface just when the oxygen in your lungs begins to burn. The surface is so close, so close you can see it, yet the rest of your body can't wait and is beginning to revolt. The back of your throat. Your chest. Your ribs.

All his body wanted was air . . .

To breathe.

He was just tired. So tired. He hadn't slept in days. Probably weeks by now. It certainly felt that way. He hadn't gotten a solid night's rest since shooting started. Not since coming back to Pilot's Creek. The pine needles always bristled in his ear, like static from a television set. He'd wake up in the middle of the night and wonder if he'd left the TV on. Whenever he made his way back to his hotel room after an endless day of shooting and he'd crash in bed and close his eyes, that rustling sound washed over his eardrums, like a wire brush stroking over a snare, keeping him awake.

Just a couple more days of production left. Just a few more rolls in the can and the film would be complete. Nothing else mattered. Not anymore.

He'd come so far. Just another day, two days, and he'd have all the footage he needed.

Now he just needed to find—

"Amber?"

Just needed—

"Aaaaammmmbeeerrrrrrrr?" He might as well have been howling at the moon—wherever it had gone. His dull inflection came back to him as others called the girl's name.

"Aaaam . . ."

". . . berrrr . . ."

"Aaaam . . ."

". . . berrrr . . ."

Her name didn't sound real anymore. The letters had already lost their elasticity. Their aural shape. How many times had he called out for her? His voice was so hoarse. There was no concern left. No tender intonation that would compel this bratty kid to come crawling out from whatever hidey-hole she was curled up in.

Hiding from *him*, he just knew it. The little witch.

"Amber?"

Perhaps he was some fairy-tale beast. An ogre prowling the forest for Little Red Child Actress. He couldn't keep the anger from rising in his throat. Taking over. But what else was left of him? Look at what she'd done. Production had halted. Shooting had halted. The crew had completely abandoned their posts. The cast's costumes were all covered in shit. They'd need to be retouched by hair and makeup, but by then the sun would be coming up. And for what? *Because some cunt couldn't remember her lines.*

The deeper into the woods he went, the more that grim, singular revelation took root.

It's already over. Done. It's all ruined.

His movie was ruined.

Most of the film was in the can. Could he shoot around her? Film the rest of Nora's scenes without her? He could slip a costume on a PA and shoot her from over the shoulder. Make it look like Jessica from behind. He could cobble some B-roll together and fill out the last few scenes.

What other choice did he have? What other options did she leave him?

"Amber!"

Of course he wanted to find her. Find her first. Find her before her vexing wench of a mother stumbled upon her. The two had been walking side by side for a while. As the director, the captain of this sinking ship, he had to console her, swearing up and down that they'd find her daughter. Ms. Pendleton had been blubbering on and on about something or other. The words simply weren't there for him. He wasn't listening to her, not anymore. Not since they'd entered the woods. He'd held her hand for a while in some half-assed conciliatory gesture. *There, there, Ms. Pendleton, we'll find your daughter, don't you worry, she has to be out here somewhere* . . . But she clenched his wrist, digging her lacquered fingernails into his skin. There was a pearly shine to her manicure, even out here in the moonless woods. Whenever his flashlight caught her nails, the beam illuminated them like teeth. A big white smile. Biting his hand.

Ketchum eventually broke away from her. Left her behind. She was slowing him down. Dragging him down. He picked up his pace until the sound of her steps faded into the trees.

Because let's be honest with ourselves here, Ketchum mused. Of course he wanted to find Amber—not because he wanted to be the one to rescue her. He wanted to strangle her. Squeeze the life right out of her. Nothing was going to get in the way of him telling his story.

Nothing.

Not the producers or the financiers. Most certainly not some kid. Some whining, crying, pleading little kid who couldn't remember her fucking lines.

Didn't she see how important this was? Couldn't Amber understand how special she was? How she'd been chosen for this immense task? This awe-inspiring mission? She had been picked! Hand-selected over all the others . . . So many others. It was *her* that Jessica had wanted. The casting director had narrowed it down to three choices for Ketchum to mull over. Three headshots. Three freckle-nosed, sandy-blond-haired girls smiling up at him from their glossies.

Ketchum glanced at the first girl.

Flipped to the second.

When he first laid eyes on Amber, holding her headshot between his fingers, the faintest breath spread over the back of his neck.

Her.

A whisper. Barely even a breath.

Her.

Ketchum knew. He knew he'd found her.

Found his Jessica.

Didn't that mean anything to her? Amber had been given the opportunity of a lifetime, the awesome responsibility to inhabit the role of Jessica. Bring her to life again. Tell her story.

Hadn't he made it easy for her? The lines were so simple. A child could recite them. That was the whole goddamn point! He had written the script in a fever dream. It had poured out of him—so why couldn't she just do her part and say the words the way they were meant to be said? The way they were intended to be heard?

"AMBER!"

Ketchum wasn't thinking clearly. The low drone of a migraine thrummed through his skull. Or maybe it was a hangover. His thoughts weren't his own anymore. Stumbling out here when he could be making his movie. The flashlights swept through the woods. Their beams reached in every direction, passing over the trees. Ketchum couldn't tell if he was imagining it or not, but in his eyes, he saw that the flashlights were swaying in a figure-eight motion, arcing overhead and then circling back and doing it all over again.

Like searchlights. Spotlights. As if this were all a movie premiere.

His premiere.

Ketchum could see it now. See it very clearly. The woods receded, as if the branches themselves were a curtain parting. Splitting just for him. Showing him opening night.

The waving beams of a carbon arc lamp streaked through the sky, slicing at the air overhead. Brighter than the moon.

His limo pulled up before the theater. The red carpet was waiting for him. The moment he stepped out, he spotted the marquee. His name in lights. Next to Jessica's.

The stars. The stars were all out tonight. For him. Him and his movie.

He had to find Amber. Find her and finish this.

Ketchum followed the spotlights. They kept sweeping through the air. It didn't even seem as if they were coming from his flashlight anymore. They burned, burned with an intensity that led him along, deeper into the woods.

Ketchum walked down the red carpet. A mile's worth of blood leading him into the picture house. His premiere was waiting for him. The show was about to start.

The applause. It was faint, at first. Soft, like waves. No, not waves—needles. Pine needles. They bristled all around him. Clapping just for him. *The director is here! Bravo! Bravo!*

When he stepped into the clearing, Ketchum expected to see every last seat in the theater filled. The tuxedos and gowns. The glitter. The house lights would dim and the film would begin.

But the clearing was empty.

Nothing but grass.

Where was he? The flashlight in his hand felt heavier than ever. He couldn't hold on to it anymore. It slipped, slipped right through his fingers. It fell to the ground and didn't make a sound.

The beam stretched across the clearing and found something pale. White petals. A flower wilting at the wrist.

A hand.

A *girl's* hand. Rising out from the ground. The surrounding dirt appeared to have been disturbed very recently. Whatever was buried below hadn't been there for long.

"Oh," someone said. "Oh God . . ." A woman pushed past Ketchum and rushed forward. He didn't see who it was, hadn't realized he had company.

Nora. She dropped to her knees and began clawing at the ground. Her jeans were now covered in mud as she unearthed this pale flower.

This limp body half buried in the ground.

"Is she dead?" Ketchum heard himself ask, even if he wasn't entirely convinced he was the one asking the question.

Nora brought Amber's body up to her chest. She swept the dirt from her face. Soil spilled out from her lips. One of the girl's arms flopped to the ground. She wasn't moving. Wasn't breathing. Her eyes remained shut, the dirt still pocketed within her sockets.

"Don't worry," Nora whispered. Not to Ketchum, but to Amber. "I've got you. I'm going to take you back home." The heartbreak in her voice was quite palpable. Award worthy.

Ketchum's chest locked. A clenched sensation took over his lungs, like a seizure, his own ribs gripping his heart.

Love. He loved Amber in that moment. Loved that fucking little witch girl with all his heart. For everything she had done to him, every little miserable torture she'd put him, his film, through—if she was dead, *actually dead*, it would have all been worth it. Completely and utterly worth it.

Amber Pendleton had just saved his movie. Everyone would want to see it now.

Everyone would know Jessica.

Bless you, Amber . . .

Bless you.

PART THREE

I KNOW WHAT YOU DID ON JESSICA'S GRAVE
1995

EXT. CEMETERY—LATER THAT NIGHT

CASS, TOMMY, DREW, JADA and *KEVIN wander along the graves, flashlights out.*

JADA

I don't think we should be here, guys . . . I got a real bad feeling about this.

Kevin gets straight into Jada's personal space, holding his flashlight up to his face.

KEVIN

(Perfect *Night of the Living Dead* impersonation:)
"They're coming to get you, Barbara . . ."

TOMMY

Dude. Cut that shit out. This isn't another one of your stupid horror movies . . .

KEVIN

Case in point: It's always the dumb macho jock waving around his johnson who ends up meeting a grisly fate first.

Mark my words, Tommy . . . You're toast.

                          TOMMY
Your mouth is gonna meet my fist if you don't can it, *comprende?*

Cass suddenly HALTS, her attention fixed on JESSICA FORD'S GRAVE. We know it's her grave because it's surrounded by a fence of rusted metal CRUCIFIXES.

                          DREW
Holy shit. It's really her . . . Jessica Ford! I thought she was just an urban legend.

                          CASS
She's real. The legend is real. And it's almost twelve . . . They say, at exactly four minutes after midnight, you can see the spirit of Jessica Ford wandering along her grave, yearning to be reunited with her long-lost mother. But whatever you do, no matter how much she begs . . . never, ever, take hold of her hand. If you do . . .

                          KEVIN
. . . What? What happens?

                          CASS
She'll drag you down into the ground. Into her grave. Forever.

                          TOMMY
As if. Come on, Cass . . . Nobody really believes that BS.

CASS

Oh yeah? Tell that to Jessica. In three minutes, you can meet her for your . . . Wait. Did you see that? Think I just saw someone. Behind the headstone. Oh. Oh God—

ONE

There are so many of them.

So many faces. Pale skinned. Larval-complexioned. They haven't seen the sun in days. Maybe months. Hiding in the shadows. Lurking in whatever subterranean space they call home.

Their mother's basements.

Their sex dungeons.

Their tombs.

They've seen me now. Oh God, their eyes. All those hollow eyes . . . Looking right at me. *Staring.* Not even blinking. Any of them. Gray eyes. So wide. Glassed over. Gummed up in something phlegmy, like oysters. Nothing but pearls of gray snot floating in each socket.

Now that they know I'm here—*She's here! She's here!*—they've all grown giddier. More agitated. I've stirred them up. Just my mere presence is enough to rouse them. The scent of me gets them excited. A charge of dead electricity ignites their dull eyes as they shuffle up closer.

Closer . . .

Closer . . .

There's no escaping them now. It's too late to run. To hide.

I'm trapped.

Just go away go away just please make them all go away—

They keep coming. Lumbering up to me, one right after another. Closer . . .

Closer.

A horde. A mindless, shambling horde. Mostly men. Always men.

Where do they all come from?

Why are they here?

What do they want from me? Ogling me with those dead stares. Those mucosal, oyster eyes. *Please I can't do this I can't do this don't make me do this I can't I can't I just can't—*

There have to be a hundred of them. Maybe more. I've lost count. I can't see the end of the line. Just when I think they're gone, that it's finally, *finally* over, I look up and see more.

And more.

More.

All of them reaching out for me. Trying to touch me. Grab me. Those hands. Their fingernails gnawed through. Raw pink cuticles.

Always bring antibacterial hand sanitizer, I've learned. Stock up. Never leave home without it. I always have a little bottle in my fanny pack, ready to pull out before I embark upon shaking these hands by the hundreds. Strangers' hands. Greasy little sausage fingers. All of them reaching out for me. Taking hold. *Squeezing.* Warm cold cuts slipping and sliding across my skin. Never take a whiff of your fingers after a con because it'll smell worse than a deli counter after the power's gone out during a heat wave. I'd swear one of these fans slipped me a bologna sandwich when I wasn't looking.

"It's, uh . . . It's an honor, Miss Pendleton."

I smile. Have to smile. But inside I'm screaming. One long, drawn out, internal yet eternal shriek.

"Could you make it out to John, please?"

I smile. Nod. Yes, of course.

To John. My #1 fan.

I can't keep my hand from shaking.

Don't fall apart on me. Not now. You can do this. It's almost over.

Only one more hour to go.

My contract said I'd only have to sign from noon until three, but that doesn't stop the line from stretching on and on and on. If you cut them off, if you send your fans home without signing their VHS box covers or their posters or their T-shirts or their own flesh, if you don't give them exactly what they want . . . they will haunt you. Come back to you. Accost you. Word gets out that you're difficult. That you're a *genre prima donna*. And then you have nothing. Nothing. And I'm already dangerously close to rock bottom. Most actresses bring their boyfriends to help set up their booths. Me, I had to park my Volvo thirty blocks away from the convention center just so I wouldn't have to pay eighty bucks in a lot, schlepping my headshots the whole way here. I'm thirty-three years old—fine, thirty-four—and nobody's carrying my swag for me. No significant other on hand to help arrange the booth, deal with the bank, keep the line moving smoothly. Nobody makes sure the fans don't slow things down with too much small talk. Just get their autograph and go. Next. It's just me, setting up and signing, signing, signing until the line finally goes away.

Until they all go away.

Sign and smile.

Smile . . .

The pen trembles. I can hardly read my own handwriting anymore. It doesn't even look like my name, so abstract to me now. Every letter has a serrated edge to it, like the jagged line on a heart-rate monitor from someone in the midst of a coronary, spiking and plummeting.

There, I say to myself. *You did it. You got through it. One more autograph down. Only . . .*

Fifty-seven more minutes to go.

Fifty-six.

Fifty-five.

Fifty-four.

Klonopin is a godsend. Those tranqs get me straight through the day. To all you up-and-coming scream queenies out there, a little word of advice: Get a prescription for that, *ASAP*, if you know what's good for yourself. My medications have evolved over the years, going back to you-know-when, thanks to Mom and her own half-assed stabs at salvaging my childhood. What little was left of it. Wasn't until I began foraging through the pharmaceutical sphere on my own, somewhere around, oh, say, twelve, that I came upon klonnies. Pop a couple K-pins and the line of fans loses its edge. I try to make sure I'm finished with my photo-opping for the day before taking one. No panels or any speaking engagements, because those benzies will knock you out. *K-ooh.* Makes your mouth all mushy. Your tongue's suddenly a hundred pounds heavier. At first, I figured I was speaking coherently. I could even hear the words coming in loud and clear in my own ear . . . But to the fans, the convention organizers, my fellow panelists, I was nothing but a mealymouthed mess. Just a faux-Gucci-clad cow chewing her tongue in front of everyone.

Now I only take half a Klonopin before beginning my signings. Otherwise I might not remember what I said and to whom I said it. Too many black holes to fall through. The second half I save, as a treat for myself, at the end of the day. When it's all over. Finally over. When I want to forget.

Not to mention the doxepin for depression. The diazepam for dozing off during all the sleepless nights. The Ritalin for cutting through the fog. And the ergotamine for migraines.

I'd be remiss if my travel nips were left off the list, along with a half gallon of coffee and Lord knows how many cigarettes to get me through the rest of the day. To keep me balanced.

Keep me sane.

Next in line is a family of three. They shuffle up, beaming, prodding their daughter up to my table. She's just a girl.

Just a child.

"Hi, Miss Pendleton," her father says. "It's such an honor to meet you . . ."

"Huge honor," her mother adds. Both parents have stuffed themselves into a T-shirt screen-printed with a different horror movie. Movies I've never heard of. That I'll never, ever subject myself to. *Children Shouldn't Play with Dead Things* and *Don't Torture a Duckling*.

But their daughter. Good God, they've dressed their daughter up to look like me.

Just like Jessica.

Scorched skin. Burnt cheeks. Hair in calcinated clumps, a sea urchin of cinders. Her dress has been spray-painted with black spots, masquerading as ash. It's a pale comparison to the actual costume I wore. The makeup is nowhere near as authentic. One close look and I can see where the prosthetics are glued onto her cheeks. The fake burn on her forehead is peeling off, revealing her real skin. That tender pink. She silently stares back at me, unsure what to say.

The girl can't be any older than nine, for Christ's sake.

She's just a child.

Just a child.

She didn't ask for this. Nobody that age ever asks for this type of abuse. It's obvious she doesn't want to be here, doesn't want to be dressed up in this crappy costume—but her parents, *Christ, her own flesh and blood*, thought it would be a gas to subject their kid to this fanatical act of public humiliation. To mortify her in front of everyone for their own perverted pleasure.

I can't stop staring at her.

Like looking in a mirror. A mirror of me as a—

girl

I'm losing the soft focus of my surroundings. That cozy cushion in my cranium. The Klonopin is ebbing. The edges of everything are starting to sharpen again. Knives in my temples.

I'm looking into a mirror, at my reflection, but I have to remind myself that the image of me staring back isn't me . . .

It's Jessica.

Her dad clears his throat. "We've watched *Don't Tread on Jessica's Grave* together, uh . . . I don't know how many times." He chuckles as he says it, too. He's so nervous, he can't help but bray. Nobody mistakes *Jessica* for a classic. It's niche at best. Niche within niche. On a scale of one to ten—one being *Shriek of the Mutilated* and ten being *The Exorcist*—the scrappy obscurity I have found myself imprisoned within lands somewhere in the three to four range.

But it has its followers. And they are legion. Devoted to the very end. Whenever I ask why, and believe me, I'm always asking why— *Why this movie? Why me?*—the answer from the fans is always some variation of the same refrain: *It just spoke to me, you know? It felt real.*

What I can't help but hear, in my head, whether these fans say it or not, is:

There's a ghost in there. Somewhere in the movie . . . You can just feel it. Can't you feel it? Feel her? Inside the movie?

Inside you?

This father is still talking to me. I have to snap back. Pay attention. Smile. "I've watched it probably, like a hundred times," he says, "by myself, but now we all watch it. The whole fam."

"Oh." What else can I say? I smile, feigning gratitude, but I'm already calculating the years in my head. These parents had to be in their early twenties. Maybe younger. They must have had their daughter when they were still in their teens. Seventeen? Sixteen? Jesus, fifteen?

Kids having kids.

"I first watched it when I was five," the mom adds. "So we figured it was about time to watch it with her."

Her.

This poor girl is trapped between her mom and dad, gripping her mother's hand. She won't let go. I'm stuck sitting behind my table, so I'm eye-to-eye with her, staring at this poor rendition of Jessica. She's in a costume she doesn't want to wear, pretending to be someone she doesn't want to be.

I know what that feels like.

I lean in until I'm only a few inches away from her. I want this just to be between her and me. "I hope you didn't get any nightmares watching it . . ."

The girl only shakes her head, *no, no*. Then, thinking twice about it, she slowly nods. *Yes.*

Yes, there were nightmares.

Of course there were nightmares.

So many nightmares.

I know those nightmares. Had plenty of them, myself.

Too many.

I glance around the convention center, pretending to check that no one else is listening. This is just between the two of us. Just between us girls.

Just us Jessicas.

When I deem the coast is clear, I ask her, "What's your name, honey?"

"Jessica."

"No, honey," I say. "I mean, what's your *real* name?"

She only stares blankly back at me, repeating herself, "Jessica."

Holy shit.

I want to call social services, right then and there. I have to struggle to suppress the rising tide of bile filling my throat. "Can I let you in on a little secret, Jessica?"

She nods. Slower. Unsure what else she should do. If this is okay. Is this okay? Can she keep a secret? With me? This older woman? This . . . stranger? The source of all her nightmares.

"I was your age when we made that movie," I said. "It was pretty scary to me, too. I had some bad dreams back then. Really bad dreams."

The girl takes this in, absorbs it.

"But it was all pretend," I lie. "Make believe, you know? It was—it's just a movie."

Just a movie.

Just a movie.

I don't know how any times I repeated that to myself. All through my childhood.

Well into adulthood.

A secret mantra to keep the ghosts at bay.

It's only a movie . . .

Only a movie . . .

Only a movie . . .

Only . . .

We take our photo. I can feel the lie eating away at me. My throat is still burning, the words wrapped in stomach acid. I can still taste them in my mouth.

Only a movie only a movie only a movie only a . . .

I wish I could protect her. Save her from this awful movie. From her own awful goddamn parents. I should've stood up and grabbed her and taken her away or called the police or just run out of here or—*or something.*

Anything.

She's just a child, for Christ's sake.

Just a girl.

No one that young should ever watch that movie. Jesus, no one that young should have been *in* that movie.

Why hadn't somebody tried to save me?

She turns her head back to look at me one last time before she's completely eclipsed by the next fan in line, beelining his way up to the card table, impatiently waiting his turn.

And Jessica is gone. Just like that.

Nothing but a ghost.

My attention drifts over the card table to my setup. All the head-shots. The production stills. It's been a while since I've subjected myself to a horror convention. I thought I could get through it. I thought I was strong enough again. I was keeping the panic attacks at bay. The benzies helped, yes. But glancing over all the pictures of myself in costume, as a child, nothing but a little girl, I feel that familiar tug, that gravitational pull back into the dark place.

Back to Pilot's Creek.

To the woods.

These last twenty-four years have felt like a dream. Like I never left that hole in the ground.

I'm stuck here.

In the ground.

I never left . . .

I never left . . .

I never left . . .

I never—

"It is such a pleasure to finally meet you, ma'am," this next fan says. "You have no idea how long I've waited for this. When I heard you were coming to TerrorCon, I took off from work. I had to switch shifts with Chet, but that's okay. I drove three hours just to get here. I made sure that there wasn't anything . . ."

I give him a faint smile, but I'm distracted.

I'm searching for the girl.

That poor girl.

For Jessica.

Maybe it's not too late. Maybe there's still time. Maybe I can still save her—

". . . thought you'd never do another convention. I read your last interview in *Rue Morgue* and it sounded like you had sworn them off for good. So thanks, thank you, for coming back."

Back from the dead.

He plops down a glossy headshot of me onto the table. Of course he's brought his own. I start signing it without looking at the picture. The motions of my wrist are so automatic now.

But when I glance down, my hand juts out, sending my Sharpie flying. The *P* in *Pendleton* stretches across the whole image. Over my face.

It's one of my childhood headshots. From my commercial days. Before *Don't Tread on Jessica's Grave*. I haven't seen one of these photographs in . . . Jesus, I don't even know how long. The edges of the image have yellowed. How did this guy get his hands on it?

"I found it on eBay," he says, as if he were listening to my thoughts, proud of his rare acquisition. "Only cost me five bucks . . . Totally worth it. *You* are worth it, Miss Pendleton."

I finish signing my name before sliding the picture toward him.

And smile.

"Oh, ah, actually, I was wondering . . ." he begins, only to stop himself.

Christ, this one wants to ask for something special. I can sense it. It's in his body language. He's being sheepish. Bashful. But he won't go away.

That's how these conventions work. They all want something. Need something. That's why they come here. They've all come because they want something from me. Anything. Everything. An autograph. A picture. A hug. An ear to whisper into. A shoulder to cry on. A wisp of my hair. A drop of my blood. A piece of my soul. They want to tell me how much my movie meant to them. How it changed their life. How I was their first. Their only. Their everything.

But this movie nearly killed me.

It took everything from me.

Everything.

Can't they see that?

Don't they know?

I have nothing left. There's nothing left of me to give. My bank account is nearly overdrawn. I've become well versed in the off-brand macaroni and cheese at my local deli. I have to put on a face that doesn't feel like my own. *It's not mine . . .* I have to relive this one moment from my life, over twenty years ago, over and over again, a broken record that keeps on skipping, just to get by. Just to survive. To live. But I don't even know what I'm living for anymore.

Even if I tried, the fans, all these fans, they won't let me forget. Won't let me move on. Run away. I have to reexperience it for them. Reenact it for them. The trauma of it. Like I'm trapped in an endless loop. Reliving that night over and over and over and over and over and—

"Could you, uh . . ." He takes a deep breath. "Do you mind signing it as Jessica?"

"Of course," I manage to say.

And smile.

His cheeks flush red, his skin splotching over in a patch of pulpy, mushy strawberries. "Thank you, Miss Pendleton . . . Thank you. I, uh . . . I'm such a big fan of yours. *Don't Tread on Jessica's Grave* is one of my all-time faves. Top five, easy."

"Don't let the other four films know that," I kid.

"Have you heard they're remaking it?"

Everything in my head goes quiet. A hush rushes through the entire convention hall. Every conversation diminishes. Every costumed fan continues to chat with the costumed fan beside them, but their voices are gone for me.

The din is gone.

All I hear is her breath. Raspy. Wet burlap ripping in her chest.

Ella Louise.

"I'm sorry," I say in a slow, measured tone. "Remaking . . . ?"

He can tell I don't understand. *"Don't Tread on Jessica's Grave,"* he beams. "They've been talking about it for years. Now that the film is about to celebrate its twenty-fifth anniversary, the producers nailed down the rights. Ketchum finally let them go, I guess. They're updating it for, like, you know . . . a *modern* audience."

The excitement on his face dissolves as soon as he realizes I'm hearing this news for the very first time. He is the messenger of this revelation.

To my awakening.

"You, uh . . ." He licks his lips. "You didn't know?"

"No," I manage to say, my voice barely registering. "I didn't."

"Pretty cool, huh?" He beams at me. "I wonder who they'll get to play Jessica?"

TWO

There's no air. No space. No privacy here. Nowhere for me to go to be alone. If I want to get back to the green room, I have to willfully immerse myself in the throng of costumes and cross the entire convention center.

I can't do it. I just can't. Not alone. Not by myself. But there's no other choice. Nowhere else I can go. I don't have a boyfriend bodyguarding me. I'm not one of the higher-end scream queens who can afford a handler. I'm all alone out here.

Contractually speaking, I'm supposed to sit and sign autographs for another forty-five minutes. The organizers will dock me, I'm positive, insisting I didn't fulfill my end of the agreement. I've been in breach of contract before. I started showing up to a few too many autograph signings smelling a *weeee* bit besotted, making an ass out of myself in front of all the other scream queens, so that earned me a scarlet letter in certain circles for a while.

Fine by me. I needed a break from these conventions anyhow.

Needed to breathe.

Just to be clear, I have never considered myself to actually be a "scream queen." That designation is for my bustier genre-compatriots. I get lumped in with the final girls all the fucking time, no matter how much I try to qualify my character to these programmers. After two decades of hitting up the circuit, I've had to resign myself to the label.

I'm not judging my sisters. We're all just trying to get by here. Make a living. If people want to pay ten bucks for a signed headshot, then who am I to complain? If they want to pose for a photo for five, let them.

But I never screamed on screen. All my screaming happened between takes.

Off camera. In the woods.

It's been over two decades since *Don't Tread on Jessica's Grave* came out. It was supposed to pop up on a few drive-in screens across the country and that was it. People would move on. Forget it.

Forget the film.

Forget me. I could move on with my life.

We all would.

But the story behind the movie took on a life of its own. *Did you hear what happened on set?* horror hounds whispered among themselves. *True story. Supposedly, the kid playing the ghost girl saw the real deal and nearly died . . . They found her buried in a shallow grave, like, a mile off from where they were shooting. I've heard, if you watch the movie real close, you can even see the ghost in the background . . .*

All lies. Just stories to tell. But it was enough. Enough for people to seek it out. Hunt it down in the video store. Plop down two bucks to see if they could spot her. Then rewatch it.

That's when Jessica gets her fangs into you.

No one was supposed to remember a piece of low-budget crap like *Jessica's Grave* five years from when it first came out. Ten years. It was supposed to be consigned to the trash heap of cinema, lost alongside all the other awful tripe that got cranked out. All the schlock that didn't deserve to be remembered, wrapped in webs of celluloid. Toss those prints into a landfill. Bury them forever.

But the next time you rent *Three Men and a Baby*, see if you can

spot a little boy in the background, hiding behind the window curtains, peeking out behind Tom Selleck's shoulder.

See him?

That boy was murdered in the house they filmed that scene in.

A ghost.

What you're looking at is the spirit of a boy trapped in celluloid
for all to see.

Everybody loves cursed movie productions.

The Exorcist was cursed.

Poltergeist was cursed.

Hell, even *The Wizard of Oz* was plagued with mishaps. Dead
munchkins and noosed monkeys. Whatever your opinions on the
movies themselves might be, people eat up the idea that a film is
doomed from the get-go because it tampered with the supernatural
balance of things. The novelty of a production getting too close to
its subject matter and paying the price sends the conspiracy theorists
salivating. *Don't Tread on Jessica's Grave* is yet another entry in the
canon of cursed movies.

And I'm the living embodiment of that curse.

For a few bucks, you can see for yourself.

The role seared itself onto me, like a brand. People didn't know
my name, my real name, but they remembered her. Jessica wouldn't
let go. I couldn't escape her.

Hey, aren't you that creepy kid?

Always calling me Jessica.

You're Jessica, aren't you?

Stopping me on the street.

Hey, Jessica!

I lost myself. I wasn't me anymore. Not to the rest of the world.

To them, I was Jessica. To nonfans, I was the child actress who
buried herself alive and blamed it on a ghost.

Either way, it was a legacy I couldn't escape. If I auditioned for another movie, all the casting directors would whisper to my mother that they just couldn't see me shaking off my previous part. It followed me. Haunted me. When I looked back at my career now—or what Mom passed off as a career—I couldn't help but laugh. What an idiot I was. Hopeless. I never stood a chance. I could see that now.

I wasn't made for this life. Not a life in the movies.

I wanted to be a kid.

Just a girl.

The only offers coming my way were for horror movies. It was always the same role. Always some diluted version of Jessica. Just another spooky ghost girl with her hair covering her face. Always seeking revenge from beyond the grave. But that wasn't me. That was never supposed to be me.

Mom had promised me, had sworn up and down during the casting call, that this movie was merely a diving board, a launching pad into the rest of my burgeoning, blossoming career.

Hello serious roles. Hello awards. Hello Hollywood Walk of Fame. Every serious actor does it. Demi Moore. Jennifer Aniston. Brooke Shields. I just had to follow in their footsteps . . .

It was a lie.

All a lie.

I was trapped. Trapped in a film I didn't want to be in. I never wanted to act again. Never wanted to set foot on set ever again. Not after what happened.

Not after—

When Mom tells the story of how I was discovered, she's always the one who finds me. When I was younger, her version sounded the best. Hers was the version that I wanted to be true. She found me and uprooted me and clung to me, pressing my limp body against her chest and squeezing so hard until I gasped back to life, ushering the air back into my lungs. Reviving me. She wouldn't let me go. Held on to me the whole way to the hospital, no matter how much the paramedics pleaded.

"Don't worry," she whispered. I can almost remember the warmth of her voice drifting into my ear. "I've got you. I'm going to take you back home."

But the older I got, the more I didn't trust her version. It didn't sound right anymore. Didn't sound real. It didn't help that Mom's telling of it changed whenever I overheard her whispering to others. Embellishing certain bits. Her role in my rescue.

When I was asked what happened, I told them the truth. I told them about Ella Louise Ford. Mom didn't believe me. Nobody believed me about what I saw. Nobody believed my story. Not the director or producers or the crew. There were only a couple days left to shoot. Too late to recast now. Too late to replace me. Ketchum took what little footage he had and creatively edited around me. Made the most of it. The most of me. I was his Jessica whether he wanted me to be or not. Whether I wanted to be or not.

I didn't ask for this life. I never asked for it.

That movie nearly killed me.

It still wants to. Even now. Now more than ever. It won't die. This goddamn film won't die! For a while, I was able to avoid my rabid fans, always begging for an autograph.

A picture with me.

A slice of me.

A drop of me.

They want my life.

All of it.

They want Jessica. That's what they're really after. They want to see her. See if she's lingering somewhere within me, hiding behind my eyes. These fans have heard all the stories. They've volleyed their own personal theories of what actually happened. They've convinced themselves it's all true. How strange is it that the only people who believe me, after all these years, are the fans? They live for this shit. They eat it up. Because if it's true, if Jessica is real, then maybe she's still here. In me. Maybe they can see her. Touch her.

I need her, too. Or just the money. That's the only reason why I agree to do these goddamn horror conventions in the first place. *Just one more*, I swore to myself. *One more weekend signing autographs and I can cash that check and it'll go straight back to the bank and I can move on.*

Run. Run far, far away.

They're remaking it.

Remaking *Jessica*.

There are three Smirnoff travel nips in my fanny pack. Now I wish I'd brought four. Maybe I did and I'm just forgetting it. Three mini vodkas will be enough to get me through the day, right? I haven't started yet, have I? *Drink responsibly*, as they say. All in moderation.

Someone steps in front of me. He's wearing a hockey mask. I let out a brief shout, so he pulls back the mask, propping it on top of his head to show me he's just a fan. Just a man.

I wish he'd left the mask on.

"Hey . . ." he starts. "Are you, uh . . . Are you the gal who played Jessica in—"

But I didn't let him finish, forging ahead.

Plowing through the crowd.

Run.

Run.

I can hear more and more fans start to pick up on my scent. Most times, if I just keep my head low and move in as straight a line as much as humanly possible, pushing past the people as fast as I can, most of these fans won't even notice me among all the slashers and demons and dead witch girls. I just have to move—

"Are you Jessica?"

I don't answer. I just keep forcing my way through. But once one person notices, more catch on. There's blood in the water now.

My blood.

"Hey! It's Jessica!"

"Holy shit! Hey, Jessica!"

"Jessica!"

I can feel the smile on my face start to crack. I can't hold much longer. I have to look like I'm touched by all the attention, that I'm appreciative, *thank you, thank you, hello, yes, hi*, but it's too hot in here. There's not enough air to breathe. It's so crowded in the aisle. Everyone ambles along, our bodies caught in the general flow, wandering along the convention center.

But now everyone's stopping. Everyone's staring.

Staring at me.

"Can I get a picture with you?"

"Can you sign my arm?"

"Can you tell me—"

I can't breathe.

Can't breathe.

Can't—

There's a back alley behind the snack bar. A pair of doors leads into a long concrete corridor. Convention center employees only. It's my best shot. My only shot. I push through the doors and wait for them to close, pressing my back against the cream-colored cinder blocks.

I try waiting for my breathing to balance. Let the inhales even themselves out.

But they don't.

I can't stop myself from shaking. I'm trembling all over. Practically convulsing. My wrists. My knees. My legs give out. I'm sliding down the wall, my back pressed against the cinder blocks.

I'm on the floor. In a heap. I can feel the tears running down my cheeks in hot streams. Drowning me.

The sounds of my sobs echo down the corridor as I lean against the concrete walls.

So much concrete. Those men poured concrete on top of her, so much concrete, just to keep her down. In the ground. The cold, cold ground. To stop her from digging her way out.

But she had found a way to come back. Through another.

Jessica rises.

THREE

I finally got the call from my agent a week later. At least I think it was a week. Maybe it was longer. There are a few black patches on my social calendar that I can't quite account for.

It's not like I've been waiting around the phone for it to ring all day. Just waiting for him to call me. Waiting for someone, anyone, to call. Break the news to me that this was real.

That Jessica was back.

I hadn't heard from my agent in months. Who am I kidding? It had been closer to a year. I'm surprised he still had my number. Maybe he didn't. Maybe he had to scrounge through the dumpster out back just to find his dusty Rolodex. Our last conversation hadn't been, ah, shall we say . . . cordial? Businesslike? I believe I called him a leech or tick or some kind of parasite. An easy dig, I know, but I was sick of these conventions. So sick of the signings. The video store visits. All the screenings of a film that should have been dead. I wanted to move on. Find work. New roles. But my agent, my blessed agent, kindly suggested that fresh roles probably wouldn't be on my horizon anytime soon. Not unless, of course, I would reconsider my staunch position on which type of roles I constantly turned down. That was when I declared he was draining me of ten percent.

"Honey," he purred from the other end of the line, "to be a leech, there's gotta be some blood in the bank worth sucking on . . . and you're just about bone dry."

Nobody wants a former child actress. Particularly one still haunted by her most popular role. It didn't matter how many years had gone by since *Don't Tread on Jessica's Grave*.

Remember Reagan? Of course you do. Everyone does. How many years did it take Linda Blair to claw her way out from *The Exorcist*'s shadow?

Beep. Wrong answer. It was a trick question. She never did. She's still trapped. She hasn't crawled out from beneath the eclipse of her most infamous character. That role has haunted her for decades. Even now. She's still billed on the poster as ". . . from *The Exorcist*."

Even as a grown-ass woman, her fans always see her as her twelve-year-old self.

As a child. As a little girl.

Not a woman.

She never grew up. Her fans wouldn't let her.

I know that feeling. It's demeaning, is what it is.

Infantilizing.

Suffocating.

But I bet Reagan never visited Linda in her dreams. I bet Pazuzu or whatever the hell that demon was called never sabotaged Linda's short-lived and ill-fated marriage with a TV stuntman.

Or racked up a healthy amount of therapy bills.

Or led her to freebase off-brand sleep medication.

Or put her on a first-name basis with the clerk at the liquor store down the block. I bet you there isn't an autographed headshot of her nine-year-old self tacked up to the wall behind the faux-wood-paneled counter of said liquor store (*"Boo! Drink responsibly. Love, Amber Pendleton."*) along with all the other alcoholic actors who patronize this particular spot.

You're goddamn right I had sworn off horror. I wasn't going to subject myself to that form of cinematic servitude. For years, I've put my foot down about taking parts that even came close to mimicking Jessica. I refused to do slasher films or killer shark films or haunted house films or zombie films and I most definitely would never, ever do another creepy kid flick.

I wasn't some creepy kid, for Christ's sake.

I wasn't a ghost girl.

I was a human being. A fucking flesh-and-blood, living-and-breathing human being.

An out-of-work human being.

The conventions were a necessity. I only booked a horror con if the bank account was looking particularly low. But I was getting pinned for being a tad problematic on the convention scene.

She's too demanding, I heard.

Or how about *high-strung*.

Neurotic.

God, how horror movies just *loooooove* their neurotic women. Nearly half the horror films getting cranked out there—written by men, might I add—had some emotionally unstable, fucking fragile, porcelain-skinned waif at the center of their narrative. Such a genre trope. Such a torture device. These movies were about making their female characters suffer. Sure, they could survive. They could be the final girl and live through the end credits . . . But at what cost?

Look at what it did to Marilyn Burns.

Or Catherine Deneuve.

Or Karen Black.

Or Mia Farrow.

Let's hear from Roman Polanski about how he treats his female protagonists, shall we?

And what would Alfie have to say about his dear Tippi?

Or how about Dario Argento? First he marries his leading ladies and then he daydreams up all the different and colorful ways he can kill them in supersaturated celluloid.

Why put us women through this?

Why torture us?

Whoever Slew Auntie Roo? Whatever Happened to Baby Jane? Trilogy of Terror? The Strange Vengeance of Rosalie? The Strange Possession of Mrs. Oliver? Sisters? Séance on a Wet Afternoon? Play Misty for Me? The Haunting? Burnt Offerings?

There just haven't been enough whispers about me, have there? Number one on my Top 5 Don't-Cast-Amber-Pendleton-in-Anything list: *She's unhireable now. The woman's damaged goods.*

Christ, if they knew. If they only knew the truth.

I've never asked for someone to pick out my green M&Ms for me or anything like that. I never demanded my own green room or security detail—even though it definitely would have come in handy. I come to each convention with my own stack of headshots and banner, ready to rock. I do everything myself. All of it. I never ask for anything more than space. For privacy.

It's just the fans. The fans are everywhere. Always staring. Always wanting more.

I have nothing left to give them.

I feel empty.

Drained.

But Jessica isn't done yet.

Not with me.

My agent was just as stunned as I was to be calling. "But here we are," he said. Water under the bridge, just like that. Bygones. You're never really truly out of this business. Not these days. Not when someone wants something from you. The producers will always find you.

The movie always finds you.

Your sin will find you.

"So I take it you heard the *neeewz*." He started right in, wasting no time getting down to business. Time is money. "Word on the street is Jessica is getting the reboot treatment."

"I heard."

"Not the best part, you haven't. Ever hear of this kid Sergio Gillespie?"

"Should I?"

"He's one of these young, new, hotshot directors. Made a short film right outta NYU that made a splash on the festival circuit. He's been getting a lot of heat. The studios have been circling him for months and, well, now this kid's got the keys to the castle. He can direct whatever the hell he wants and . . . guess what? He wants his first feature to be none other than our little darling *Jessica*. Back from the dead."

"Good for him." Home for the last three years had been a loft house in Echo Park. I had some cats around here, somewhere. Or maybe they had me. They only came around when there was something worth eating. Them and the junkies. I can hear them rummaging through the trash cans out back at night. Tiny claws scraping against the aluminum: *scritch scritch scritch*. I think it's the cats. Please, God, I hope so.

"This Gillespie wants to do some serious meta-casting," my agent said. "It's a complete gas. He actually wants to hire a bunch of former child actors. Like, right from the Mickey Mouse Club or whatever. The bright-eyed, bushy-tailed, totally wholesome types."

"Why?" I asked.

"You know how it is. These teen stars are all desperate to be taken seriously. They're looking to break out from their picture-perfect Disney mold. Horror's the way to go."

No, I thought. *No, it isn't. Not by a long shot.*

"Sounds amazing," I said in a monotone into the receiver. "Can't wait to see it on HBO."

"Amber? *Helloooo* . . . Are you even listening to me, hon? They want you. *You*, Amber!"

"For what?"

"For the movie! I figured you'd be jumping up and down. Dancing in the streets. This is big! Huge! The director demanded, insisted, that you be in *Don't Tread on Jessica* . . . or whatever they're going to call it now."

"Last time I checked, I wasn't in the Mickey Mouse Club."

The sun eased into the living room. A sliver of light passed through the half-polished-off bottle of Smirnoff on the table and refracted itself into several smaller shards of color. A distilled rainbow cast across my bare feet. I could feel its warmth in my toes. I hadn't realized how thirsty I was. *I should put some orange juice in this,* I thought, bringing the bottle up for a sip, *it's still morning. Is it still morning? What day is it?*

"I'm a little old to be playing Jessica, don't you think?" I asked as the vodka blossomed in my empty stomach. "Christ, I'm old enough to play Ella Louise now . . ."

It was true. Don't think I hadn't done the math in my head a hundred times already.

A thousand times.

I was around the same age as Nora Lambert now, maybe a bit older than her. That bitch. She never talked to me after the shoot. Never wanted to see me again. Not after what happened. The hell I put her through on set. With the police. Guess who got grilled the most after I proclaimed that the ghost of Ella Louise Ford had nearly buried me alive? The actress playing her in the movie, of course. Poor Nora . . . I know she blamed me for that whole fiasco. They all did. Ketchum. The cast. The crew. I nearly ruined their movie.

What was it that W. C. Fields always said? *Never work with animals or children . . .*

Yeah, well, guess we all learned that lesson the hard way.

Nobody believed me.

Nobody listened.

Nobody saw.

But here I was. Older now. Alive. The same age as Ella Louise

Ford. The real Ella Louise. I could have been Jessica's mother now. That witch could've been my daughter.

My little girl.

I hadn't realized how long the silence from the other end of the line had stretched. Who had spoken last? I'd drifted for a moment, losing myself in my thoughts.

What the hell is he waiting for?

"Amber. Darling. Sweetie."

Whatever warmth I'd leeched off the vodka went cold.

"No," I managed to say.

"It's perfect, Amber . . ." There was a sincerity to his tone. He really believed this BS.

"I won't do it."

"*Ella Louise Ford* . . . It's genius. Who knows the role better than you? Tell me! Who?"

"Nora Lambert," I said.

"She's dead, Amber."

"Oh."

"Two years ago. Cervical cancer."

"Oh. I—I didn't know." Of course I knew. There wasn't any mention in the trades. Nothing beyond an obit in her hometown newspaper. Lambert never escaped her role, either, but she got to walk away. She never reached out for the limelight again . . . by choice.

She was the lucky one, I thought. *At least she ran when she had the chance. I was trapped. That movie kidnapped me. Erased me.* I was like that terrorist heiress. What was her name? The one who lost herself and joined her captors' cause? Patty Hearst! For me, I'd been shanghaied by a horror movie. The world lost Amber Pendleton. The world was brainwashed into believing I was Jessica Ford.

"It's what Nora would've wanted," my agent said. "To honor her legacy."

I had no idea what he meant by that. Nora wouldn't have wanted me anywhere near that movie. I had been invited to her memorial service but I chose not to go. Not to see her.

In the open casket.

In the ground.

I felt so small. My body felt so small. My voice, where was my voice? I couldn't find it. I couldn't find the air to take into my lungs, to breathe back out and manifest the sounds that would take shape in my mouth to say the word I needed to say over and over and over and . . .

No . . .

No.

NO.

"Amber. Please. Take a moment. Think this through. It's perfect. You played Jessica in the original . . . And now you'll play Ella Louise in the remake. The fans will love it. Absolutely go rabid for it. Instant box office success. *Boom.* You're back on top. Hello, new roles. Hello, work!"

A very, very dark thought took root in my head just then. I couldn't shake it loose the longer it wrapped around my brain.

What If I wasn't actually talking to my agent?

What if this was all in my head?

This could have been just another one of my childhood episodes. *A mental lapse,* the doctor suggested to Mom, *a momentary rift from reality.* Sometimes, one's imagination breaks from the truth. A snap. That fissure quickly fills in with its own alternate reality. A story made up in one's mind to make sense of the trauma they've been subjected to. A fantasy.

A ghost story.

What if, after all these years, after all the conventions and autographs, I had finally cracked? What if I was holding my phone up to my ear and there was nobody there, no agent, nothing but a dial tone, and I was having this entire conversation with myself, with my own fragmented personality?

What if I was crazy?

God, I wanted that to be the case. So wanted it to be true. If I was nuts, if I really was just a loony tune here, my mind lost to the funnies, then it would have been me doing this to myself. It would be my mind's fault. Not some movie. Not some real ghost.

I could finally be free.

Free of her.

With the right medication, the proper prescription, some time to rest in the hospital—

"Amber," my agent said into the phone. "Still with me, hon? *Hellooooo*."

"I won't do it," I croaked.

"Can you tell me why? Why you're not taking this seriously? Why you're not even considering it? They're coming to us with this. You know that, right? This is not me banging down their door. The director wants *you*, Amber. *You*. He asked for you and nobody else."

"I—I can't. I just can't."

"The studio absolutely loves the idea. The director wants you to come in right away. Read some pages. Get in front of the camera again. It misses you, Amber. It's time. Time to come back . . ."

"Please." Was I crying? I couldn't tell, but it felt like it. "Please don't make me do this."

Why did my voice sound so little? Why did I sound like a child? Just a girl . . .

"They're offering low six figures," he said. "I think I can talk them up at bit. At least to lower-mid. You can't turn this down. I know you need this, Amber. It's good money. The best payday you've seen in years. Speaking frankly, hon, it's the best payday you're liable to get from here on out. So take it. Please. Just consider it."

I told my agent I would, just to get him off the phone. "Don't sit on it for too long," he warned. "The offer won't stay on the table forever."

My bare feet were still on the table. I was staring at them. My toes. I can remember the wet leaves clinging to them. How cold it felt running through those woods. All that mud. The cuts and scrapes. The blood. Little slices up and down my legs. The kudzu and thorns reaching for me, holding me back. Pulling me down into the ground. Into the soil.

Into Jessica's grave.

I don't know how long I sat there, in my living room. In the silence. I don't know how long I stared at my feet. When I snapped out of it, I picked up the phone and started dialing.

There was no answering machine to pick up the call, so it rang and rang and rang and—

She finally picked up.

She didn't say anything. Didn't say hello or ask who's calling. She didn't need to.

No one called her nowadays.

No one but me.

"Hey, Mom . . ." I waited for a beat, just a breath, to see if she might have something to say. But all I got was her breathing. Those wet, jagged inhales that sounded so familiar to me.

The doctor demanded she stop smoking, but of course she never did. Never would. What else did she have at this point? I hadn't visited her in months. Her own daughter.

"I thought you might get a kick out this, but . . ." But what? What was I going to tell her? Why had I called?

You know exactly why, a voice embedded deep within my chest answered.

Of course I knew.

"The movie. *Jessica's Grave.* They're—they're doing it all over again. Remaking it."

More breathing.

Only breathing.

"New cast. New story. Or, I guess, the same story. Just . . . told differently. Fresh start."

I imagined her. Still in bed. Slumped over. She probably had her breakfast tray in front of her. Diced pineapple in a plastic cup. She hated eating the pineapple cubes, leaving them behind to congeal. I could picture the pack of Pall Malls. One freshly lit, nestled between her fingers. Smoking in bed, even though the nurse on call would have a hissy fit.

I heard Mom take a long drag.

Exhale.

I could almost smell the smoke seeping through the receiver, into my living room. I knew that smell. I grew up with that smell. Never got rid of that smell. It was still in my clothes.

My hair. My skin.

My skull.

Just say it, Amber, the voice pushed. Prodded. *Tell her. Tell her the gooood neeeeewz.*

"They—they offered me a part. A big part, actually. You're not gonna believe who . . ."

Nothing. Still nothing from the other end.

"Ella Louise," I blurted. "Can you believe it? They want me, me of all people, to play Ella Louise Ford this time. After all these years. After everything, they want—"

"Don't."

At first, I didn't believe I'd actually heard it. I must have imagined it.

But Mom said it again. Louder this time.

More wet.

"Don't do it, Amber," Mom said. "Please."

That wasn't what I was expecting from her. At all.

She hung up before I could say anything more. The dial tone hummed through the receiver, like a cigarette stubbed out in my ear. I was back in the silence of my house.

Back in my own head.

This story of Jessica and Ella Louise Ford. It had become my story. I had intersected with it, stepped into it. Now there was no separating us. We were connected. Tethered together, I guess you could say.

Our story wasn't finished yet. There was still more to tell. This story, our story, would finally have a chance to come full circle. After this chapter, I could find my way out

I had to find my way out. I needed to be free. Finally free of the Fords.

It was time I took control of my own narrative.

FOUR

"The camera loves you."

He's so young. Younger than me. Just a kid, really. He can't be much older than twenty-two. Twenty-three, tops. Fresh out of film school. Christ, *daycare*. I look at his grin and the word *cocksure* comes to mind. His confidence exceeds his age. How can someone so young be so self-possessed? He's used to getting exactly what he wants. Nobody's ever said no to him before.

What studio in their right mind would give this kid fifteen million dollars to reignite their horror property?

I'm professional enough to take the compliment and smile. "It's been a while."

"It's missed you," Sergio insists. His tone drops an octave and I can't help but think of a teenager pretending to act older than he really is, trying to buy beer by lowering his voice—

Uh, I must've left my driver's license in the car.

"I've missed it, too," I said.

The backless baby doll dress was a bold choice, but I wanted to make an impression. I was aiming for Mia Farrow in *Rosemary's Baby* but I really just feel like a Spice Girl.

I've perfected the rearview mirror makeup routine, putting on my face in the parking lot just before every audition . . . but today, I went to the salon. I wanted to make an impression.

But has this kid even noticed me? I feel as if he's evading eye contact. He frames the shot, looking at me through the viewfinder, but not in person. Not face-to-face.

I'm crawling out of my skin. The Klonopin was a bad idea, but I needed to take the edge off the fluorescents. The studio had already given Sergio his own production office on the lot. Just another bland boardroom. Reminded me of the office space where I first audi tioned for Jessica, years ago. These rooms with their dull lighting blend together. The faint hum of electricity pulses through the tubular bulbs directly over my head and I can't help but feel the electricity sinking into my teeth. My skin soaks in the stray radiation coursing through the lights.

"I told the studio you were the only one for the role of Ella."

"Better not let Meryl know," I kid. "I heard she's been campaigning for the part."

Sergio pretends to laugh. *Who's Meryl?*

He won't come out from behind the camcorder, keeping the lens between us. It's one of those new Handycams. I can't stand looking at myself on these digital cameras. Their resolution is so low, I feel like my skin is all washed out. I look pale. Sapped of all my blood.

Don't Tread on Jessica's Grave had been shot on Super 16mm. The camera was so small, it felt like we were all making some homemade movie in our backyard. Not a real film. The film stock would be blown up to 35mm and get shipped around from one drive-in to another. They could only afford to make a handful of release prints. When one theater was done with its run, those reels would get stuffed into their steel canisters and shipped off to the next screen, hopping from one town to the next.

And the next.

And the next.

That was how our movie made its way across America. Infecting the country, one screen at a time. After a year on the road, the film reels were so fatigued, the celluloid barely held itself together anymore. You could see the spots where the strip had snapped, reattached with tape.

Like snake skin. Flimsy. Translucent. Scaly.

This was my big-screen debut. It was supposed to be my big break. But there would be no big premiere. No gala opening. No searchlights in front of the theater, sweeping through the night sky. No limo pulling up to the red carpet. No photographers rushing up to take a picture, setting their flashbulbs off in my face. Blinding me.

These starlet fantasies were reserved for real movies. Not horror films.

Not for me.

Not Jessica.

The movie had its "premiere" in Kansas. What a joke. Just some drive-in miles outside town. There was no fanfare. No newspaper reviewed it. Our film was paired with an anonymous slasher flick, just to fill out an evening's double-billed creature feature. I can't even remember what the second movie was called, if I'd ever known in the first place. That film was the lucky one. Long forgotten by now. Lost for all time.

I had to wait until the release print made its way out west to finally see it. It took over a year for the film to reach California. Even then, it was a two-hour drive to the nearest theater. It screened in some rundown movie palace all the way in Pismo Beach. Mom drove me; she wanted to make a big deal out of it. Celebrate the occasion. Treat it like it was a gala premiere, even if no one else cared.

"I'll be your limo driver, hon," she said, forcing a smile. "What do you say? Let's be movie stars for a day."

I didn't want to go. Didn't want to see it.

See Jessica.

But Mom was trying. Trying so hard to make me feel special. To make amends for everything that happened.

We went to a noon matinee. The first screening of the day was always a dollar cheaper. We bought our popcorn from the greasy-haired concession girl reading her dog-eared copy of Daphne du Maurier's *Don't Look Now and Other Stories*. She barely looked up as we paid.

The theater was completely empty, save for one gentleman sitting alone at the back. We gave the guy a wide berth. For the most part, it felt like we had the whole place to ourselves.

We sat in the front row. The screen loomed over us, a vast expanse of blank space. The seats were so old, so rusted, they squealed every time I shuffled around. The upholstery had torn, with tufts of foam padding spilling out. I remember that the floor was so tacky with coagulated cola. I could feel the soles of my shoes peel away from the ground, so I tucked my feet under my thighs.

What would I look like? All the way up there? How big would I be?

Would I even recognize myself?

What would my voice sound like?

The house lights slowly went down. Mom took my hand. Her grip tightened, her fingers squeezing mine. We looked at each other as the last bit of light in the theater faded. The expression on her face puzzled me. Before we were both lost to the dark, I could've sworn I saw a look of sadness pass over her. There wasn't enough time to focus on it, and I was nowhere near mature enough to understand.

Regret. Reflecting on it now, I think it had been regret.

Too late to dwell on it now. The screen lit up.

Blinding white.

I had to brace myself for this. To see myself. How many years had gone by since the shoot? I had moved on with my life, hadn't I? Wasn't I getting better? The production was already receding into the deeper chasms of my memory. My recollections of what happened on set were now fuzzy around the edges. Like it never happened.

Like it was all a dream.

Just a dream.

A nightmare.

For every second on-screen, twenty-four frames of film pass through the projector, causing a fluid movement of images. Implying motion. Implying a continuous thread of action. The celluloid slips through the light so fast, the human eye never realizes it's actually looking at a series of snapshots. The photographs are moving so fast, your mind never grasps the notion that it's being tricked. Your brain wants that motion. It needs things to remain smooth. Connected. Tethered together. *Persistence of vision.*

I saw myself on-screen. My face cast across a stream of guncotton and camphor.

In makeup.

In costume.

I looked so sandy. Gritty. The film stock had a granular aspect to it. A gauzy quality. Everything was so hazy. I wondered if a piece of cloth—my costume, maybe—had slipped into the projector and was now flossed across its lens, illuminating the movie in this silken mist.

I was there all over again. Back in Pilot's Creek. In the cemetery.

The woods.

This all had to be a dream. It wasn't real. It wasn't. I had to believe this. Had to convince myself none of this was real. None of this was actually happening. I was crazy. I had made it up.

That wasn't me up here. That towering phantom girl. It couldn't be me. It just couldn't.

It was only a movie, I repeated to myself, hoping it would go away. *Only a movie . . .*

Only a movie . . .

Only a . . .

Only . . .

But it wasn't until I glanced over at Mom and saw how transfixed she was by the screen, watching her watch me, that I felt the first inkling of something being so wrong, so foul, with this movie. It felt like the film was an entity in of itself—a phantom with my face.

It wanted to be watched. It was using my likeness, my smile, to lure people in.

It wanted me to see. See it.

See *her.*

I ran out of the theater, shrieking all the way up the aisle. Mom had stayed in her seat. She kept watching. Watching that wraith on the screen who had taken my identity from me.

Mesmerized by Jessica. Hypnotized by that witch.

I burst through the doors and collapsed in the lobby. The greasy-haired girl behind the concession counter put down her book and gathered me up from the floor, wrapping her arms around me. "Hey, hey," she consoled me as best as she could. "It's okay. It's only a movie . . ."

Only a movie . . .

Only a movie . . .

Only . . .

With my eyes closed, for a moment there, I thought I was back in the woods. I was getting scooped up by someone—my mother, a production assistant, whoever had stumbled upon me first.

Don't worry, they had said. *I've got you. I'm going to take you back home.*

home

home

home

But it was just some college kid running the concession booth. This popcorn girl had no idea what to do with me. Who I was. All she saw was a little girl.

Just a girl.

I was too young to be watching this type of movie. What kind of parent lets an eleven-year-old watch this piece-of-crap horror movie?

"Are you okay?" she asked, running her hand along my shoulder. "Didn't you come in here with your mother or . . . ?" Her voice faded. I could see her eyes widen.

That was when it struck her.

I watched it happen. That familiar epiphany that would soon haunt me for the rest of my life. The moment of recognition solidifying itself in her mind. She had been subjected to my burnt face projected onto the screen, three or four times a day, for the last week.

Of course she'd recognize me.

"Hold up. Are—are you Jessica? From the movie?"

The film should have died.

It should have gone to its grave and stayed there. Buried. Forever. We shouldn't be here, I shouldn't be here, all these years later, talking about it like this. Honoring it like this. As if it were some—some kind of fallen war hero of horror movies. As if Jessica were something to pay respects to. So many films slip into obscurity. They're released, they're ripped apart by the critics, and then they're supposed to slip off into oblivion, to be promptly forgotten about. There're too many movies. Too many to remember. Too many to live.

Thou shalt not suffer a witch to live.

Why this film?

Why did this particular movie survive while so many others slip into obscurity? Why did it outlive all the others? What was it about Jessica that inspired such a rabid fan base?

It was, without a doubt, a shitty movie.

There was no story.

No budget.

The acting was terrible. Community theater kids from the '70s in skimpy outfits gallivanting about in the graveyard.

It was awful.

I was awful.

It's true. Let's just be honest with ourselves, okay? I was terrible in it. I was a kid, just a clueless kid, scared out of my skull, pretending to be dead.

There's nothing to redeem *Don't Tread on Jessica's Grave*, nothing to salvage it from the landfill of cinematic history.

Why couldn't the film just go away? Why wouldn't it die?

What if it didn't want to?

What if it wanted to live?

"The execs think I'm crazy for remaking it," Sergio says, snapping me back to the present day. To the boardroom. To the camera between us.

To my screen test.

Oh. Oh God. I'm panicking. There's cement in my chest. *How long was I daydreaming? How long was I staring off into nothing? Did he notice? Does he think I'm a nutcase?*

"I could give a shit," he says. "Sorry."

"It's okay," I say.

And smile.

He's grinning back at me, a bit sheepish. His hair keeps falling into his face. I can't tell if he's being bashful with me or not. There's only ten years between us. Maybe a bit more, but I'm not budging on my birthday. But who's in control here? Who has the power? He's the director. My director. I feel that internal inclination to wait for his command. To mold me. Move me. But he won't look at me. He just peers at me through the lens. Taking me in, like I'm something to behold. To marvel at. To—

To—

Oh. Oh God, he's one of them.

A fan.

He's a fan. Just like the others. Just like the rest. I can tell by the way he's looking at me.

His eyes. He has that look.

That *gaze*.

"Did you know the studio didn't realize they held the rights to the film?" he asks. I perk up to feign interest. "They had completely forgotten they even owned it after all these years. It had just been collecting dust in their vaults. I had to remind them about it. Can you believe that? I had to tell them the story of one of their own movies. They'd never even heard about it. Didn't even know it existed. Most of these execs were still in their diapers when Jessica first came out. Some of them weren't even born. They don't get it. They'll never get it."

"I've got to say," I say, finally finding my voice. An echo of it, at least. "I don't know if I really get it, either, Mr. Gillespie."

"*Gillespie?* Nuh-uh. Don't even. It's Sergio from now on, got me?"

"Sergio."

He's a fan. A fucking fan. A fan *with those eyes a fan with that stare a fan licking his lips a fan with a basement a fan with his autographs a fan with his fantasies* . . .

I have to go. I have to get out of here. Out of this boardroom.

I have to run.

Run.

Run!

"So many people don't know this movie exists," he says. "The genre die-hards do, sure. But not the rest of the world . . . this story is dying to be retold. It'll reach a wider audience now."

"Why?" I ask—can't help but ask. He's still looking through the viewfinder so I'm not sure if I should speak to his forehead or look directly into the camera.

"Because I'm ready to tell it."

I'm not sure how to respond to this, so I just let him fill the silence.

"Ever since I saw *Jessica* as a kid, I worshipped that shit. I can't even tell you how many times I watched it. But I knew, I fucking knew everything Ketchum got wrong on that film. What he should've done. So I started hearing this little voice in my head say:

You can do better than that. You can tell that story right. And so . . . you know. I'm going to. I fucking will."

The confidence. Even without the lack of eloquence. The resolute, absolute certainty.

Like he was chosen. Like he was The One.

"Why am I here?" I say it straight into the lens, imploring with the camera, hoping my words pass through its digital innards until this young man, this fanboy, sees me. *Actually* sees me. Sees what he is doing to me. I'm begging for him to look.

Look at me.

Not gaze, not stare, but see the human being pinned down by the lens of his camera.

See Amber. Not Jessica.

Sergio stands up straight. "I want to make a film that burns into people's subconscious just as much as the original *Don't Tread on Jessica's Grave* did for me when I first watched it. Something they will talk about for years. Something terrifying. When I watched *Jessica* as a kid, I'm sorry, but it wasn't you who I saw on-screen. I saw *her.* I saw the ghost of the Little Witch Girl. She spoke to me. Right to me. I—I heard her. And now I can't stop hearing her. That's what your movie did to me. So now I want to do that. Just that. I want to create that experience for the next little pipsqueak who sneaks into the video store. But to do it right, the way I see it in my head—I need you. I need you so I can tell this story the right way, the way it's meant to be told . . . I can't do it without you."

I have to turn away from him. "Stop."

"It's true. You've always been horror royalty to me, Miss Pendleton."

"Just . . . just call me Amber."

Sergio steps out from behind the camera. There's nothing separating us now. Nothing between us. He's walking toward me. He kneels.

Takes my hand.

"You are a goddess, Amber," he says. "You are my scream queen."

This little boy will never see me for who I am. I'll never be Amber to him.

All he sees is who I was. On-screen.

All he sees is Jessica.

FIVE

Sergio's story is like any other fan's story. It's a story I've heard so many times before, from so many different film buffs exactly like him. It doesn't change the fact that he's very passionate about what he's talking about. Not one bit. It's just that his story is no different from the legion of fans who've shared similar tales of stumbling upon Jessica for the first time.

His story isn't his own.

It's hers.

I can't help but take pity on these kids, these boys, when they tell me their story. Always so heartfelt. So impassioned. They have this burning desire, this innate need to express how much this movie meant to them as kids. How it changed their lives. Haunted their dreams.

I haunted their dreams, they all say.

But it's not true.

Whenever I hear them say this, I always want to respond—*No, no, it wasn't me. It wasn't me at all. It was Jessica . . .*

Always Jessica.

She is the one on-screen. She's the one in the movie. I was just her conduit. A ripe vessel for possession. But instead of saying this, instead of saying a goddamn thing, I simply nod and smile and listen to them. *I'm all ears, boys* . . . Listen over and over again to the same story.

The name of the video store might change . . .

Video Kingdom.

Hollywood Video.

Video Emporium.

The town might be different . . .

Minneapolis.

Winnipeg.

Richmond.

It doesn't matter which state . . .

Arkansas.

North Carolina.

Nevada.

The song remains the same, as they say, no matter where I hear it. No matter who sings it. Like a cover version. A broken record.

I could tell Sergio's story for him, if I wanted. I could tell the story, all their stories, for these boys, if I chose. I know their story by heart now.

By heart.

Sergio was seven when he first saw the VHS cover for *Don't Tread on Jessica's Grave.* Every day after school, he would ride his bike to the local video store. Video World was tucked into a topiary-bordered alcove of the Stony Point Shopping Centre, just a swift five-minute Schwinn sojourn from his front door. No bigger than a boutique, this early-'80s video store was tiny in comparison to the cancerous sprawl of the Blockbuster Video chain that would begin to metastasize its way through suburban strip malls. It would eventually put all the mom-and-pop operations like Video World out of business, but not yet.

Sergio was one of the lucky boys. He pushed through his pre-adolescence just before the big blue-and-yellow Blockbuster awnings started cropping up across his quiet hometown.

He had found his home away from home.

Walking into Video World after locking up his bike, he lost himself in a Shangri-La of Betamax and VHS. Every inch of wall space was lined, floor-to-ceiling, with videocassettes. Each four-by-seven-and-a-half-inch VHS cassette contained a different story, just waiting to be told, and Sergio made it his mission to watch them all. Or as many as his allowance would bear.

Hidden at the very back of the store, buried behind comedy, family, and drama sections—but before he reached the "private room" of adult films at the very, *very* back—there was a single row of videos that were off-limits to children such as himself.

The horror section.

This—this was where fear resided. Every kind of horror Sergio could think of—or not think of—was on display. Boys and girls weren't allowed to rent videos from this shadowy edge of the forest. A kid like Sergio couldn't help but feel a shift in the atmosphere upon entering the aisle, suddenly surrounded by so many R-rated movies. The carpet seemed to darken, was stained somehow. Even the air had a miasma of decrepit breath to it, thicker than the air in the children's section. He knew he wasn't supposed to be here. But he had to go deeper. Take just another step in. See if he could make his way past the titles that begin with the letter *A*.

Past the *B*s.

The *C*s.

He was suddenly immersed, surrounded by images of sheer terror. These horrors were captured on magnetic tape and sealed inside their own cardboard boxes, like gift-wrapped packages. The horror section presented a series of portraits as if they were on display in a gallery. A monstrosity exhibition. *Evil Dead. Night of the Creeps. The Company of Wolves. The Deadly Spawn. Faces of Death. Def-Con 4. Xtro. The Stepfather. The Driller Killer. The Stuff. The Texas Chain Saw*

Massacre. I Spit on Your Grave. The Dead Pit. Black Roses. Headless Eyes. Magic. Black Christmas. He Knows You're Alone. Cellar Dweller. Mother's Day. The Prowler.

Too many to count.

Too many to see.

But Sergio knew he had to watch them.

Watch them all.

Video after video displayed its own package. A snapshot of a victim caught in that instant just before the axe crashes down or a zombie covered in the gory remains of its last meal.

Sergio could still describe them all.

Every last cover.

The corpse of a college coed sitting in a rocking chair, a clear plastic bag still wrapped around her head. A pair of living eyeballs slithering out from their sockets. The silhouette of a man wielding a butcher knife, inches away from his stepdaughter and her defenseless dog.

Come on, kid, each box seemed to whisper. *Go ahead. I dare you. Slip a video off the shelf. Go ahead and pick any horror film and take the cassette into your hand. Rub your finger over the cardboard cover. Feel its softened edges? Feel how fuzzy and worn the corners are?*

Now look at the cover . . . Pick one.

Take it.

See.

Sergio grabbed *Don't Tread on Jessica's Grave*.

It's me on the box.

Me as Jessica.

Just a little girl.

A scorched ghost, complete with an intense close-up of my bare skull. A pair of milky eyes, settled into my sockets, stared right back at him. Sans eyelids. Sans flesh. Sans any space between us. I'm reaching out for him, my hand outstretched as if the spirit of the Little Witch

Girl of Pilot's Creek were a breath away from lifting off the box and grabbing him by the throat.

The tagline at the bottom read: *Jessica wants to play . . . with you!*

There was nothing left of me but the bones. My skin had burned away in the picture.

But the eyes. A pulpy wetness remained. There was a shine to them. They shimmered. How they had survived the fire while the rest of me had completely flaked away is anybody's guess, but here they were, silently accosting this young boy. Pining for him and only him.

Yearning for him.

Sergio couldn't tell if this incinerated girl was in pain or in a fit of horrific ecstasy, but her eyes—my eyes—continued to stare straight at him, boring their way into his psyche. They followed him through the aisle. All they did was look—look at Sergio, watching him as he dropped the cassette cover to the floor and ran crying out of the store. He thought they were alive. That the cover had come to life, possessed by the ghost of Jessica. She had come for him.

The truth was much duller than that. Thanks to a particular 3D-printing effect the studio did for the VHS cover, the glossy eyes on every cover popped out from the rest of the box. They'd spent more money on that gimmick than on the movie itself.

And it worked.

That was all it took to separate Jessica from the rest of the films on the shelf.

Boys just like Sergio had the exact same experience, all across the country. They all thought I was staring at them. That I was haunting them.

Coming for them.

Most of these horror movies drifted off into a sea of beta-obscurity, lost forever in a back catalog of forgettable movies.

Not Jessica. Somehow, the cover art remained indelibly sketched on Sergio's subconscious. The image wrapped itself around the deeper recesses of his brain and refused to let go. For years, even to this day, the one VHS cover Sergio could never shake, could never free himself of . . . was mine.

Was me.

"It was like you were reaching out to me," he said. "Like you wanted to touch me."

Of course he wasn't the first person to tell me this. I'd heard it so many times before. But I acted as if he were the first.

My first.

That he was the only one who'd had this personal experience with the movie.

With me.

Sergio may have been too young to actually watch the movie at the time—but he didn't need to. The cover artwork was enough. This was the true horror: not the film, but his preadolescent mind taking that snippet of visual information from the front cover—an act of violence, a look of terror, a ghost girl—and letting his own narrative develop from there.

The cover was all it took. For him, the cover was the movie. He watched his own personalized version of *Don't Tread on Jessica's Grave* in his imagination that night, every night. He didn't need his parents' VHS player. He had his dreams. He couldn't escape the made-up movie manifesting itself in his sleep. He couldn't escape me.

So he came back.

To me.

He rode his bike back to Video World the very next day. He marched straight into the horror aisle and found me, back on the shelf, waiting for him. Staring at him. Hungering for him to play.

And then the next day.

And the next.

Always back to me. To that hungry look in my eyes.

That *yearning*.

He had to have me. He knew these cassettes had a plastic chip embedded within them that would set off an alarm at the front of the store. He knew he couldn't steal the cassette. That didn't matter.

All Sergio wanted was the cover.

All he wanted was me.

He slipped the cassette out and left it on the shelf, naked. He stuffed the softened cardboard box down his pants and waltzed right out of the store, acting perfectly normal.

He freed me. Now he had me all to himself.

Forever.

Sergio tells me all this during my screen test. He keeps talking over dinner afterward. Over drinks back at his apartment.

He tells me his story in between kisses. As he undresses me.

He tells me his story as his breath deepens, intensifies. He tells me when he finally climaxes and rolls over onto his bed.

He tells me his story as the sweat along my skin begins to cool and suddenly, I'm cold again. So cold. The story never changes. The only difference is the person who tells it.

"So," I ask in my best Greta Garbo voice, just next to him. "Did I get the part, Mr. Director?"

SIX

My flesh is on fire. The flames are everywhere, consuming me. I'm burning, burning . . . I can't shake the flames away. I'm screaming. Pleading. But I can't hear myself. The sound of my own voice isn't there. I'm not making any sound no matter how much I scream and scream and—

That's when I wake up.

When I always wake.

Sergio is still fast asleep next to me. He's curled into himself, like a puppy.

I'm still at his place. It takes me a spell to settle back into my surroundings. Realize where I am. Catch my breath. I see the posters framed on his wall. The thread count on his sheets is stupefying.

Never slept with a fan before.

He's taken a part of me.

A keepsake.

Something he can possess forever now. Frame it, bottle it, cherish it. But I took something back, too—didn't I? Didn't I get Jessica again?

Don't I get to return now?

To the woods?

Sergio had told me this would be my comeback. My triumphant return to the big screen. This remake would bring my acting career back from the dead.

But what if it should stay dead? I thought. *Dead and buried . . .*

In the ground.

I need to leave. Need to get out of here. Out of this bed.

My purse has to be around here somewhere. There's a travel nip still in there, I think. Should be half full, at least. I had taken a swig when I had excused myself to use his bathroom earlier that night. Now for the life of me I couldn't remember where I'd left it.

I've made some pretty bad judgment calls in my life, but bedding the director has never been one of them. PAs, perhaps, but never a director. Nothing like deep-sixing your job prospects before they even begin. I must really want to fuck this all up for myself.

I wander about his apartment as quietly as possible. The mission to find my purse slowly ebbs into a bit of recon. What would it hurt to look around?

I find his workspace. I know I shouldn't do this, that I'm jeopardizing my job before I'm actually even hired, but to hell with it. I've already slept with the director. What's the worst that could happen?

I can't help myself.

I need to see.

Sure enough, there I am. The VHS cover Sergio stole all those years ago as a boy. The box is framed and hung on the wall, just above his desk, like a butterfly pinned and dried inside a glass case.

Preserved.

The cardboard has been pulled apart and unfolded at the seams, laid flat and pressed down so the front and back of the cover are visible. The edges are worn down, nothing but white fuzz. The image itself has faded, washed of its color, now a muted blue.

Except for the eyes.

My embossed eyes still have a glossiness to them. I'm staring right at myself. No matter where I stand, my own eyes follow me through the room. I'm looking into that same mirror all over again, in the makeup trailer, after all these years. I never left.

Jessica wants to play . . . with you!

It's time to go back and play. Back to Pilot's Creek.
Back home.

This time I'll be ready for her.

SEVEN

There's cement in my chest. I can feel it filling up my lungs. I can't breathe anymore. Everything within me hardens. *Congeals.* Jesus, even my blood is suddenly thickening over.

Stupid. So stupid of me. I shouldn't be here. I shouldn't be in Pilot's Creek.

In the cemetery.

At her grave.

Sergio had asked me to come with him. Escort him. Like I'm some fucking tour guide. Practically begged. He wanted to walk around the cemetery, just the two of us, as if it were all some kind of romantic leisurely stroll. We could walk through my scene together, block it out, but he just wanted me there. With him. Like I'm some kind of token. His good-luck charm.

Always acting like a boy with stars in his eyes.

This time the star is me.

Too bad that when you see the light from a star in the sky, the star itself has already died. Didn't Sergio know that? It's simply taken that long for the light to travel across the cosmos to reach his eyes, across billions of miles of darkness. I'm already dead.

What he's actually laying eyes on is a ghost.

It's just like acting, I thought, *just like any other part. Come on, Amber, you can do this.*

I could get on the plane. I could fly all the way across the country. Back to Bumfuck, Virginia. I could land at the nearest airstrip and hop in the car that would drive me the remaining two hours to Pilot's Creek, the town that time had forgotten, the town that hadn't changed at all.

The flight was a blur. Thank God. I can't even remember where we landed. I had carefully scheduled my complete med intake for all eight weeks of principal photography.

Eight weeks. That was downright unheard of for the original film. When we did it the first time, we barely had three weeks for the whole production, pickups and reshoots included.

Ketchum had to scramble to film as much coverage as he could with those last couple days without his Jessica, praying he'd gotten enough footage, realizing he hadn't, forced to edit around the potholed plot holes in his own storyline and pray the critics didn't call him out on it. But of course they did. Every review hammered Ketchum on the lapses in logic. The glaring inconsistencies. The downright contradictions in narrative. His ghost story without a ghost.

And yet, against all odds, the film had something . . . *else*. An otherness that no one, not even Ketchum, had accounted for at the time.

There was ambience.

There was tone.

A celluloid fog hung over nearly every angle. All those ponderous shots of nature. The countryside at dawn. The sun sinking into the surrounding trees. The granulated glow of the moon, seeping through the saturated 16mm. The glacial pace cast a spell over the viewer, which in truth was the effect of obnoxiously long takes to pad the running time.

Gradually, over time, there would be a reappraisal of *Don't Tread on Jessica's Grave*. Critics slowly came around to it. Not overnight, and definitely not all of them.

But some.

Enough.

Even Ebert took back his original assassination and rebranded *Jessica* as "a tone poem more than a horror movie. A ghost story where the ghosts aren't in sheets and rattling chains but lingering within the very celluloid. The movie itself feels haunted."

That ghost was coming back to haunt audiences again, thanks to Sergio. Thanks to . . .

I Know What You Did on Jessica's Grave.

Imagine a ghost under a white sheet with holes cut out for its eyes, but instead of a blanket, it uses a movie screen.

I need to face that ghost. Head-on. Time to take back my story from Jessica before it's too late. Before some other poor child succumbs to her family. If I can just keep it together long enough to make it through the shoot. That meant pacing myself. Doling out the benzodiazepine at an even clip. Not too much, not too little. Like Goldilocks, my treatment had to be *just right*.

The studio wanted to set up camp in Vancouver. They'd save a million in production costs if Canada could double as Small Town, USA, like every other film did these days.

But Sergio wasn't having it. He demanded they shoot in Virginia. Right here in Pilot's Creek. The balls on this boy! He could care less about tax incentives. He wanted to film where the original had filmed. Where the real story took place. *For authenticity's sake*, he insisted.

Fifteen million. The budget for the original had been south of two hundred thousand dollars. Ketchum could have made almost a hundred movies with the budget for this remake.

Sergio convinced the studio they wouldn't need to build anything. Pilot's Creek was already here, just waiting for them. It was a production designer's wet dream. Everything had already been constructed. The shuttered storefronts. The ramshackle houses. The dilapidated cemetery. The grave of Jessica Ford was wrapped in its rusted fence of soldered crosses. The Pilot's Creek from the script had been reared into existence decades ago, impeccably weatherworn and aged to perfection, sinking into the soil with every passing day. Waiting.

The locals took in the crew with a resigned sense of complacency. Their most famous resident was buried below hundreds of pounds of cement. The only reason anyone ever talked about Pilot's Creek was because of Jessica. If it weren't for this town's actions, their sins, nobody would know this flyspeck on the map even existed.

I wondered if they would remember me. If anyone would ever remember me.

How could they forget?

Production overtook Pilot's Creek. The townspeople offered no resistance. Imagine a small army of electricians and C-list celebrities swooping in and ransacking this sleepy southern town. The rigs rolled up with their equipment like the circus had just arrived. To the people of Pilot's Creek, it might as well have been a circus. There hadn't been this much activity here since—

Not since—

I haven't left the motel yet. Can't.

Not just yet.

I need to pace my panic attacks. Baby steps. One hurdle at a time. Now that I've gotten over the flight, I have to settle in. A stint at the Henley Road Motel off Route 60 wasn't the worst lodgings I'd ever found myself in. If I'm not mistaken, this was where we stayed the first time we filmed this movie. Same room. At least, I think I'm staying in the same room. They've all blurred together by now. We were given two adjoining rooms back then. Mom was supposed to stay next door, but most nights we slept in the same bed. Especially after filming a scary scene. Mom had to hold me through most of the night, until I finally drifted off to sleep.

Nothing has changed here. The rooms look exactly the same. The sun-sapped curtains still look like muscle tissue. I think they'd been red before. Now they're a dull pulpy orange. Rotten meat hanging from the windows. Sheets of sinew.

Every so often, there comes a tapping, as of someone gently rapping, rapping at my hotel door. Most of the time I won't answer. But Sergio keeps knocking at night. He waits until it's late. When he thinks nobody is listening. He's even come up with a secret knock. Our own little code. *Knock-swipe, knock-swipe, knock-knock-knock.*

He stayed until dawn last night.

Talking about the movie.

His vision.

"Come with me to the cemetery tomorrow," he begged. God, his eyes. His boyish eyes. Cobalt blue. Who was he even looking at? He was staring right at me, pleading with those baby blues, but who does he see? Who was that woman?

"I don't think so . . ."

"Why not?"

"I've still got to go over my lines and . . ."

"Bullshit. I wrote the script. You can say whatever you want to say."

"I should probably rest while I still can . . ."

"Please. Please? I want to see Jessica's grave with you. Don't make me go there alone. I need you by my side. Jessica might get ticked if I show up alone, without you."

"Fine," I managed. "I'll come."

I should've said no. Should've resisted. Here it was, the next morning. I had less than an hour before his car would pull in and pick me up and take me to—

Take me—

I've kept the windows closed ever since I checked in, leaving the TV set on through the night to drown out whatever sounds might try seeping their way into my room.

I have been, how should I say this . . . *hearing things.* Things I don't particularly care to be hearing. Things I know shouldn't be there. I half imagined Mom was still in the room next to mine. If I had the same room, maybe she did, too. Maybe she was still there? Waiting for me?

A pair of internal doors connected our two rooms. When I opened mine, I knew I would be greeted by another door, locked from the other side, so I couldn't open it and barge in. I never quite understood the reason for these doors, such useless doors that nobody really uses. When it had been me and Mom, we left them open, expanding our private space.

I had no idea who was next door now.

Over there.

I went ahead and pressed my ear against it. Listened in. I couldn't be sure if I heard the sound of a TV from the other side or not. I thought I heard someone walking into the bathroom.

Turning on the faucet.

"Mom?" I called out. I don't know why. I don't know what I was thinking. It just came spilling out of me. My silly mouth. I immediately felt like an idiot, but the damage was done.

Just as I pulled my ear back, away from the paneling, and was about to close the—

There was a knock.

Someone knocked on the internal door.

From the *other* side.

I leapt back. Staring at the door, I waited to see if the knock would come again.

But nothing.

Nothing.

The door opened.

The young woman from next door realized she had startled me. She had one of those overly emotive faces, where every sensation plays out in a dizzying array of fireworks. Her tan seeped into her lips until it bled across the vermillion border.

"Sorry, sorry." She winced. "Didn't mean to scare you—"

The woman cut herself off. She gasped, holding the pose. Her eyes widened as she began to fan her face with one hand, her mouth still hanging open. A squeal giddily built itself up within her throat. "*Oh my God*," she screeched. "I am such a big fan! It is such a *huge* honor to be working with you, Miss Pendleton! *Don't Tread on Jessica's Grave* is one of my all-time faves . . ."

She took my hand in hers, both of hers, wrapping my fist into a protective cocoon of her own manicured fingers. She gave me a good tug into her hotel room before hugging me.

"We're practically roomies! How insane is that?!"

I had absolutely no idea who this woman was. I lost myself in the disarray of her room. All the clothes strewn about and gutted luggage. There had to be a dozen suitcases open along the floor, their sequined insides spilling everywhere. How long had she been staying here?

"I haven't been making too much noise, have I?" She asked, still hugging me. I hadn't reciprocated, I realized, my arms held out at my sides as this woman kept squeezing.

She wouldn't let go.

"No," I finally said.

"*Whew*. Good. What a relief." She released me and fell back onto her bed. "The producers rented some farmhouse for me, but as soon as I got there, I was all like, *creeeeepsville*. No, thanks. So . . . here I am." She smiles, her irradiated teeth beaming back at me. "Here we are, *roomie*."

I'm supposed to say something. I know I should say something.

But the words aren't there.

"Oops. Sorry. I'm Jenna." Her hand darts out, ready to take mine. "Jenna Handley."

Jesus Christ, I think. *She's the Mouseketeer.*

She's in the goddamn movie.

Our final girl.

"Of course." I manage a smile, taking her hand. "Of course. It's such a pleasure to meet you. I'm . . . Amber. Amber Pendleton."

"I know who you are, *obviously*. Everyone knows who you are. You're like . . . the guest of honor." She snorts ever so daintily with that cute button nose, reminding me of Elizabeth Montgomery. A teen Tabitha. "It must be so crazy. Being back here. Doing this all over again."

"You got that right."

What does this Mouseketeer want from me? Are we going to have a slumber party now? Are we going to braid each other's hair? Stay up all night talking about our crushes?

Are we going to watch horror movies together? Pop a video in the VCR and munch on popcorn in our pajamas and scare ourselves silly until we jump at the slightest sound outside?

Are we going to watch *Don't Tread on Jessica's Grave*?

What does she want from me?

"I was thinking of grabbing some breakfast. Takeout from the diner. But I, um, I haven't figured out how to call out on my motel phone. Do you know how to reach the front desk?"

This girl has had everything done for her. Cooked for her. Cleaned for her.

Prescribed for her.

Maybe there's a potential friendship blossoming here after all.

"Bet you're already getting up to no good here, aren't you?"

She looked genuinely concerned. "What do you mean?"

"No paparazzi in Pilot's Creek, now, is there? Seems like you can have some fun. Let your hair down. Get wild and crazy with the farm boys."

She avoids the insinuation. "It is such an honor to be working with you. You have no idea how many times I've watched and rewatched the original *Jessica*. Just to get into the right mind-set, you know? I feel like I really understand the story now."

"Come on," I press. "Don't be coy. I'm talking about after the day's done. Cutting loose. I bet you kids brought along a little something extra to help unwind . . . Right?"

She looks like a tangerine chihuahua to me. The slope of her broad forehead. Her saucer eyes seem just a little bit too big for the rest of her head, growing wider. "What d'you mean?"

"That squeaky-clean image isn't so spotless, is it?" I sit next to her at the edge of her bed. She has to have a little something buried at the bottom of one of these suitcases. "Your secret's safe. I won't tell a soul. Did you bring some party favors with you?"

I should've noticed the gold crucifix wrapped around her neck. My mind lapsed back to all the crosses wrapped around Jessica's grave as Jenna Handley, virgin megastar, Miss Purity Power, Miss Abstinence absent-mindedly touched her own with her fingers. Clutching it. To give her strength.

"It's such a pleasure to meet you, Miss Pendleton," she says.

Very evenly, I might add.

I heard the lock to her inner door click the second she closed it behind me, sealing me out.

The rest of the cast looked so young. So innocent, even though I bet they fucked like bunnies. Even their skin looked as fresh as newly fallen snow. A homogenized wholesomeness. So soft. They looked so familiar to me, even if I could never pin down where I would have seen them before. They came from *that show*. Or *that other thing*. You know the show I'm talking about. We've all seen it. They were born into show business, acting since they were babies. They felt unreal. Like they weren't actually real. Test tube stars. They had been genetically bred to optimize their performance abilities.

The plasticine efficiency of this new generation of child star unnerved me. I can't imagine what their mothers were like. Did they even have stage mothers anymore? Or were they all raised in some laboratory for actors?

Stepford children. All of them. And here I was, the Old Guard. My presence on set was as the torchbearer. *My good-luck charm*, Sergio called me, sounding an awful lot like he meant to say *keepsake*.

Let's be honest with ourselves here, shall we? My part is a trumped-up cameo. I know that. Jenna Handley knows that. The rest of the cast knows that. It's no big secret. My screen time would be relegated to the pre-credits teaser and then at the very end. I'm here to establish the backstory. I'd pop up at the film's terrifying climax, rising out from the grave.

My involvement in the project is supposed to put the fans at ease. Let them all know their film is in good hands. A fan's hands, just like them.

Their sweating, slithering hands.

Have no fear, dear fans, the studio wanted to say through me, *your movie is not some callous cash-in. We're taking this remake extremely seriously. Fear not, we're handling your Jessica with care. See who we've got? It's none other than the original Jessica Ford herself . . .*

The one, the only . . . Amber Pendleton! How's that for stunt casting?!

Just a joke. I was nothing but a joke.

I didn't deserve this part. It's not like I had gotten it because I was right for the role. I hadn't nailed the audition. I nailed the director, for fuck's sake.

But the story needed me. Or maybe I just needed this story.

I needed Jessica.

EIGHT

Horror is dead. The fans have been griping about it for years. Nothing but the same canned slasher narratives told over and over again. Sequels are all direct-to-video now. Even I knew these pale imitations had squeezed whatever last drops of blood their franchises had left. The killers all punned. The fans were fatigued. Critics didn't review these movies anymore. The studios never held press screenings anyhow, knowing they'd be eviscerated. How many times could these films bring the same supernatural serial killer back from the dead, just to slash through another batch of stock characters, only for the final girl to save the day and start the process over again?

Mix, repeat.

Mix, repeat.

Mix . . .

But Sergio worships these sequels. Even the god-awful ones. Particularly the god-awful ones! He studies them as if they're masterworks. He can quote them, line for line. He wrote his senior thesis paper on *Friday the 13th: A New Beginning*. He doesn't make a value judgment over high or low art. To him, these movies are everything. He's a fan.

A fan a fan Jesus Christ he was a fan . . .

Horror is dead? Long live horror!

Viva la Jessica!

The studio couldn't care less about *I Know What You Did on Jessica's Grave*. They let Sergio do whatever he wanted. As long as he came in on time, on budget, they wouldn't even bother watching the dailies. What was fifteen million to them? Just a drop in the bucket. That was barely the equivalent of the catering budget for one of their action flicks.

But Sergio is obsessed with his remake. His rendition of Jessica. His love letter to her. He needs it to be perfect. It's vital to him that the DNA of the original *Jessica* remain intact.

"The soul of *Jessica* is still there," Sergio says, sitting next to me in the back of his rental car, "because you'll be there. You are the lifeblood of this project, Amber. You are my movie."

This was wrong of me. Being with him. Sleeping with the director, *Christ*. Such a cliché.

I am his muse, he says.

His muse.

When was the last time I inspired anything out of anyone?

No more hippies. Cassandra and Moonbeam or whatever the hell her name was have been replaced by a group of erudite teens who were raised on a steady diet of horror films. These kids speak in a lingo steeped in *Fangoria*. A horror patois. They know all there is to know about serial killers and creepy ghost kids because they've seen every last slasher film there is to see. They're genre savants. They still do all the stupid-kid-stuff stupid kids did in horror movies, of course. The toking up. The premarital sex. But when these idiots do these very idiotic things, they comment on the fact that they're doing them, referencing them while doing them. These characters can somehow critique the very movie they're in.

Take page thirty-six in the script, when Tommy and Susan are fooling around:

TOMMY

This is totally the moment where some masked redneck is gonna step out and machete us.

SUSAN

Then we better hurry and do it before he slices and dices us . . .

I've never read anything like it before. I don't know what to think, to be honest. Is this a joke? Some elaborate prank? *Candid Camera for Scream Queens?* Is Sergio messing with me?

Take this snippet from page eighty-four:

WES

Don't you know the rules? Just because you think you've killed her, the creepy ghost girl always comes back for one last jump-scare.

CASS

Save it for the sequel, bitch.

These kids are breaking the fourth wall. They're so self-aware, meta-contextualizing everything that happens to them, as it happens to them. It doesn't feel real.

None of this feels real.

"Do teens even talk like this?" I asked Sergio when I first read the script, realizing how old that made me sound.

"I do," Sergio says. He has just finished another draft and he wants, *needs*, to share it with me. At this very moment in the car, as soon as he picks me up from the motel. I'm his first eyes on the script, a dubious distinction I don't think I truly deserve. I can't stand it.

"Yeah, but . . ." How can I say this? "You're not like other people, are you?"

He certainly isn't like Ketchum. Everybody loved to mythologize the man as some mad genius after the fact. There was one story floating around that Ketchum had used hypnosis on set. He held ritualistic rehearsals that tapped into some expressionistic mumbo jumbo bordering on human sacrifice. He wanted his actors to achieve the highest level of spiritual awareness, personally believing it would feed into our characters until we *became* our characters. So he pumped his cast full of LSD and we all performed shamanistic orgies and slit the throat of a goat on set and on and on and on.

It was all bullshit. Just another cinematic urban legend. A myth made up by pimple-faced movie hounds like Sergio. Ketchum was a hack. He'd always been a hack.

Jessica made that movie. She was the real storyteller here.

Not him.

But Sergio is a believer. He's read all the interviews with Ketchum in the horror magazines. He knows everything there is to know about the troubled production, what it took to bring Ketchum's vision of Jessica to the big screen. But it was a lie. All a lie. How can I break that to Sergio? It would crush him. He won't understand. He's just too much of a fan to see the film for what it truly is.

A reckoning.

"If all your characters speak in this meta, self-aware, horror talk," I say, "it'll sound like they're all the same. That they're just extensions of one person. Of the screenwriter . . . Of you."

He takes back the script, tugging it out of my hands. "You're missing the point . . ."

"Okay. Tell me. What's the point?"

"My babysitter let me watch my first horror movie," he says, staring out the window. "I started to sneak out of my bedroom in the middle of the night while my parents were asleep so I could watch whatever slasher was on HBO. These movies are everything to me. And I'm not alone. My whole generation watches horror movies. Now we're the ones remaking them."

"But real people don't talk like this . . ."

"Everyone talks like this." He's mad. Wounded. I must have really hurt him.

Of course I did. He's just a boy.

A little boy with a camera.

He's a fan. And when fans get hurt, when you don't give them what they want, they take it out on you. They make you suffer. Now Sergio is making me pay by giving me the silent treatment. Pouting like a child.

"Serg," I say, "nobody knows about us . . . right? Our relation-ship?" *Relationship*. Christ. Who had I turned into all of a sudden?

"No," he mutters out the window. "Still a secret, I swear."

I don't want anyone, anyone, to know. Not the producers. Defi-nitely not the studio execs. This is so idiotic of me. Completely idiotic. I'm feeling like a washed-up joke enough as it is. The last thing I need is to feel like I'm some sort of charity case for the director.

I need to feel like I belong here. On set. In this film.

That I deserve this.

Someone's holding my hand. I glance down and notice that Ser-gio's fingers have woven through mine, a knot of flesh. His hand squeezes mine. "Lot of memories here, huh?"

Too many.

The world outside the car drifts in and out of clarity. The town of Pilot's Creek is a ghost in and of itself. Not much has changed since the last time I was here. I'm surprised how much the place looks exactly the same.

There's the diner where Mom let me order whatever I wanted ("*Pancakes! Chocolate chip pancakes!*").

There's the local library where I spent my days off, pulling dusty children's books to read by myself.

There's the sheriff's office where I gave my statement. Where my mother waited for me, away from me, the two of us separated from each other while I talked to the social services representative. After I was done, I was told to wait in the hall while the sheriff discussed matters with my mother. Wherever she was. She had suddenly slipped away.

I asked if I could use the bathroom. The deputy shrugged and pointed down the hall.

I sat myself in the stall. I didn't really have any business to do. I just wanted to be alone. Away from everyone. So when the door burst open, I quickly lifted my legs up onto the seat.

Hiding.

I remember hearing Mom's voice rise as she argued with Ketchum over what to say, what they knew, what they thought they knew, what they believed had happened. "I don't give a shit about your goddamn movie," she whispered in a way that was nowhere near a whisper. "They're threatening to take Amber away from me!"

"You're the one who's supposed to be watching her," Ketchum hissed back. "As far as I'm concerned, you're the one responsible. Not the production."

"What about that batshit actress? What about her? Where was she during all this?"

"She's got nothing to do with any of—"

"Amber said Nora dragged her into the woods," Mom insisted, even though that wasn't true. That wasn't what I had told her at all. "She dragged her! *Dragged her!* In costume and makeup and everything! Scared her right out of her mind! It's no wonder she shut down."

"Bullshit."

"It's what Amber says happened and I believe her . . . and I think the police will, too."

I had told Mom it had been Ella Louise. She had drawn the conclusion that I meant Nora. Why wouldn't she?

"I know what's going on with you two." When I heard my mother say this, I sensed her words sharpening. The threat was there. In her voice. "I know you two are sleeping with—"

"That's none of your—"

"I could shut this production down in a heartbeat. I could go to the producers and tell them all about how the director is fucking his leading lady. How that same leading lady is off her goddamn rocker. How she dragged my daughter—*my baby girl*—into the woods, in the middle of the night, in the cold, and scared her half out of her mind, until she had no choice but to hide."

There was silence. Nothing from Ketchum. I remember how heavy that silence felt. The weight of her accusation. I kept my knees pressed against my chest, curled up into a ball on the toilet, suddenly feeling just as afraid of my mother as everyone else in this world was.

"You need us," Mom said. Her final word. "You need my daughter to finish this movie, which means you need me. Try recasting her. See if I don't spill everything. To the producers. To the press. Whoever'll listen. We better be on the same page here. Get our story straight."

How had I forgotten that Ketchum had been in a relationship with Nora Lambert? It had always been an open secret. The cast and crew all knew and chose not to speak of it. Certainly not around me. Did I even know? I had to have . . . But what would it have mattered to a child?

I was only a kid back then.

Just a girl.

It dawns on me, in Sergio's rental car, as the pines sweep by outside, as we plunge deeper into the woods, nearing the Pilot's Creek Cemetery, that I'm doing the exact same thing over twenty years later.

History is somehow repeating itself and I didn't even realize it.

No wonder Nora never spoke to me again. She hated me.

Despised me.

All because my mother had sold her out. Threw her under the bus. When it had nothing to do with Nora at all. Not out here. In the woods. It had been—

It was—

State maintenance on the highway must have ceased decades ago, the cracked pavement veining both lanes. Our tires find every last pothole the asphalt had to offer, tossing our car about like we're rolling through a war zone.

The trees sway all around us. I have to close my eyes to keep the vertigo at bay. They're all spinning. The trees are spinning . . .

Spinning . . .

Spinning . . .

I'm not ready for this, I think. *I'm not ready. I thought I was, I thought I could do this. But I can't. I shouldn't be here. Please take me away. Please take me home.*

Home—

Home—

The word had slipped unevenly out of her mouth, as if Ella Louise had to force it up her throat and all the way over her tongue. Churning the word out, as if her mouth were full of dirt and her tongue were a shovel to dig up the word itself. Disinter it.

Home—

Home—

She kept saying it, no matter how much it sounded like it pained her to do it, repeating it over and over again.

When my mother—it had to've been my mother—found me, she first touched my hand. She thought I was dead. Who could've survived out there, in the freezing cold, all night? Of course I looked dead. I was still in my burn makeup, in my costume, Jessica's cindered clothes, not to mention all the mud and the blood—my blood—seeping out from my fresh cuts.

What a sight I must have been.

What a fright.

My chest rose. Still breathing. Barely.

She picked me up and took me into her arms, carrying me through the woods. *Don't worry*, she said. *I've got you. I'm going to take you back home.*

Home.

Home.

home

"Here we are," Sergio says, snapping me back to the present.

To the cemetery.

Its cast-iron gates loom just outside my window. They're a Serliana design, along with an arch bearing the name *PILOT'S CREEK*, held up by square columns at either side. Rusted angels perch upon the lintels spanning the entryway, the gates always open.

"Welcome back," he says. He can't hide the excitement, the downright giddiness in his voice, even if he tries. Nothing but a little boy about to run into a toy store.

I can't do this. I can't be here. I can't, I can't.

"Ready?"

Please don't make me go please don't make me look please don't make me see—

He must know this is hard for me because he's holding my hand as we walk together. Side by side. He's guiding me along in front of the producers and the cinematographer. Do they know about us? Does everyone know now? Is the secret out?

Everything within the cemetery is right where I'd left it. Practically untouched. The rows of graves don't seem as even as they did when I was younger.

I glance at a few of the headstones. I remember these names. They ring familiar to me.

Here lies Harold Smith.

Here lies Jeremy Hawthorne.

Here lies Tom Watkins.

Here lies Bill Pendleton.

And here lies Wayne Reynolds. I can't help but wonder what he thinks of all this. Probably rolling over in his grave. Yet another production has come to Pilot's Creek, trudging over his final resting place, to honor Ella Louise and Jessica Ford. Let their story be told.

You brought this upon yourself, I say to myself in a voice that feels a little unlike my own. *If you'd shown compassion, none of this would've happened. None of us would be here.*

This is all your fault.

All your fault.

You.

That doesn't sound like me. I have to take a moment to collect myself as we pass the church. It looks smaller now. Much smaller than I remember it. It wasn't in the best condition back then and it definitely doesn't look as if anyone has done any repairs on it since.

Here's the church, here's the steeple, open the doors and see all the—

"What do you think?" Sergio asks. "Looks great, doesn't it?"

"The church? Not particularly . . ."

He laughs at first, then stops himself. "You don't know?"

"What?"

"It's a facade. Had it shipped down in pieces. They just put it up yesterday . . . The original burned down ten years ago."

"Burned." I wanted it to be a question but I end up just repeating the word flatly, echoing Sergio. He nods back, unaware that I still don't quite understand what he's talking about. I can't process this information as quickly as I should. The Ambien is impeding my ability to absorb news.

"We tried to replicate the old one as closely as possible. Wasn't easy. There wasn't much on public record about the original. Not even down in city hall, so . . . we ended up just watching *Don't Tread on Jessica's Grave* and freeze-framing all the shots with the church in the background. Blew them up and printed them out, just to draft this bad boy up. Looks pretty sweet if you ask me."

Sweet. Jesus, he's just a kid. A giddy kid playing make-believe games. Building forts in the backyard.

Sure enough, I open the front door to waltz into emptiness. Nothing but a hollow shell. The outer walls of the church are held up by a diagonal web of two-by-fours.

Burned down keeps echoing in my head. *Burned down.*

Burned down.

Burned—

I walk through the front doors. I wonder if I can retrace my steps from that night. If I can waltz through my memories and see if I can map out everything that happened.

I've blocked out so many recollections from that night. I don't know if I can even if I wanted to.

Do I even want to?

Why would I?

Sergio is talking to the DP about some shot he wants to get. Some angle we had achieved in the original that he wants to replicate. A long dolly down a row of graves. He's talking, his words slipping into the air, but I'm losing the shape of them. Losing their sound.

I can't hear him anymore.

All I hear is breathing.

Someone breathing.

I want to think it's me. *Please, please, let that be my breath.* But it's far too wet. Far too labored. Every inhale rips through tissue, sopping burlap tearing in two, and I know, oh God, I know that sound, I know I've heard those inhales before.

"And there she is," Sergio says, proudly presenting Jessica Ford's grave to the rest of the crew. "The belle of the ball."

No one has repainted the crucifix fence in quite some time. The last layer has chipped away. Flakes of white scatter along the ground, as if it were snowing over her grave.

Weeds choke its trellis. Crabgrass and thistles and wild morning glory weaving and twining over the crosses. Some of the arms are bent now, all crooked.

Her headstone has faded. Decades of weather have worn down her name. The date of her birth. Her death. They want to erase her name. Her very existence. Like she never existed.

But she's still here. Under the ground.

Below my feet.

Sergio feels compelled to say some words, paying his respects to Jessica. Promising to honor her memory.

I'm not listening. I've turned away from her grave. Toward the woods. The pines at our back. They are listening to us. Observing us. Always watching.

I'm looking for Ella Louise. Wherever she may be. She must be watching from a distance, hidden in the pines, at the edge of the cemetery, getting as close as she can without stepping onto hallowed ground. She must be close, I know. I can still hear her breathing.

Or maybe that's just me.

I'm already getting into character, I think, *and I don't even realize it.*

NINE

This feels familiar to me. Have I been buried here before?

There's no air down here. In the dark.

In the ground.

The weight of the cement bears down on me. The burden of it gets heavier as it hardens. I can feel it. Whatever oxygen is left in my chest burns. My throat constricts. All my lungs want to do is usher another breath in, just one more, but there's nothing left. I'm trapped down here.

In the ground.

I'll never see the light of day again. Never feel the warmth of the sun against my skin. I'll be cold forever now. Down here forever. Buried below all this concrete.

In the ground.

I want to scream. Need to scream. But the cement presses against my chest, gripping me. Pinning me in place. Holding me down.

In the ground.

My eyes. I can't open my eyes. They're sealed shut. I feel my eyeballs skimming back and forth behind their lids, but there's nothing to see. Not in the dark. Not in the ground.

I know I'm going to die down here.

I'm going to die.

How many times will they do this to me? How many times will these men bury me?

In the ground?

The worms won't have me. The soil will grow septic. My body will slowly break down and my blood will seep into the earth. If a root ever reaches me, they'll wither. Choke from the inside out. Every last blade of grass. Every nearby tree. I will taint this earth.

This will be my curse, here in the dirt. This is my curse on the people of Pilot's Creek.

On you all—

Someone grips my hand and starts to pull. I am being lifted up. Lifted out of the ground. I can feel a tug at my chest. The earth is peeling back, breaking open around my torso.

Light floods my eyes. I have to squint before the glare of fluorescents above me fades.

I'm in a warehouse. Surrounded by corpses. There are bodies suspended from the walls. All of them in different stages of decomposition. There's a row of decapitated heads lined along a workbench. Five all together. All little girls. Something about them looks familiar to me.

They are me.

Of me.

That's my head.

I mean, *those* are my heads. All five of them. Each and every last one of them is . . . *me.*

As a girl.

Each has its own frozen expression. I'm looking at myself screaming.

Then glaring.

Grinning.

It's a sickening sight, seeing all these different versions of my child-hood self. There's even one of me after the fire. Burned to a crisp. My lips have peeled back, chewed through by the blaze, in a permanent sneer, this halted snarl spread across my charred face.

They're all looking at me, staring back with glossy-embossed eyes. Me looking at me.

"Welcome back," a man's voice beckons. I snap out of it and turn to see him kneeling next to me, holding a rubber mold in his hands.

It's my head. The adult me. My skin. My flesh flops limply through the air, as if I have just shed my snakeskin, the flaps of my exposed chest quivering in the air.

"How you feeling? Okay?"

Howard Kurtz. Now I remember. This is his special effects studio. I'm surrounded by props and prosthetics from all his different movies. Werewolves, zombies, and bears, oh my.

"How long was I under?" I ask.

"Ten, fifteen minutes. The alginate dries quicker than plaster." He hands the mold of my head to one of his underlings, the rubber flapping loosely through the air before disappearing.

My skin. They're taking away my skin. I'm a freshly mottled snake, my flesh tender in the cool air.

It's been a while since I've done a lifecast. Twenty-four years, now? A lifetime ago. But who's counting, right? I have an entirely different body now. I'm no longer a girl.

Somehow, I don't know how, Kurtz and his team were able to reproduce these lifelike replicas of my younger self. My head, at least. His technicians busied themselves painting the various textures to my cindered flesh. A whole army of dead Jessicas, waiting for my command.

Kurtz noticed I was staring at myself. "Pretty uncanny, right?"

I nod. My scalp itches under the swimming cap. There is a remnant of alginate along my temple. My skin is smeared with so much Vaseline that I glisten.

"We had Danielle come in last week. Talk about a trooper. That girl sat here for hours."

I didn't understand. "Danielle?"

"You two haven't met yet?"

I had met her, but I didn't feel like getting into it with him. I played it off as best I could, giving him a dizzy expression: *Yes, yes, of course it's her, how silly of me, that's not me of course.*

"That's her." Kurtz nodded to my heads.

That wasn't me. Those weren't my heads. They were somebody else. Another actress.

Another *girl*.

I felt hollow in my chest. Mournful, almost, as if I'd just lost someone.

I'd lost Jessica.

Kurtz coughed. "We need to do a few more casts . . . Different expressions, you know? You down for one more, or do you want to take a break?"

"I can do another." I could hear my mother's voice in my head, insisting that I smile.

Smile, Amber. Smile. Let them see that you're game. That you're up for anything. That you'll put in a hundred and ten percent. Don't let them down, Amber. Show them you can do it.

Show them you're a star.

The Klonopin certainly helped. I'd taken half a pill before coming in, so the room lost its harder edges. Jesus, where had this stuff been the first time I'd been forced to do a lifecast? If I had popped a K-pin before they poured the plaster on me as a kid, I probably wouldn't be so claustrophobic now. I stared at all the zombie mannequins positioned around the studio, as if they were waxworks in a spook house and I was some silly teenager, stoned and stumbling about.

"This time," Kurtz said, mixing the alginate, "we're gonna need you to scream. I want you to hold your mouth open . . . like this." He dropped his jaw for me in a silent shriek.

"Will any of that gloop get into my mouth?"

"Nah, this stuff sets so fast, we can actually mold it. What you're gonna want to do is slowly widen your mouth, a little bit at a time.

You'll actually feel the alginate tug, like taffy."

A scream. I could do that. *I can be your scream queen*, I thought.

A frozen scream. How hard could it be?

Kurtz started at my ears, squirting a syringe full of alginate within the lobe. After that, he plopped a handful of the cold gel on top of my head and rubbed it down my face.

"Close your eyes," he said as he used his thumb to nudge the alginate into the corners. The crevices of my flesh. Working it in and sealing me up.

The head cast grew heavier, but I was already gone. Lost in the dark again.

Under the ground.

I've spent so much time down here. Lost in my thoughts. In my head. Nothing to do in here, down here in the dark, but dwell. Dwell on the past. The trash fire of my life.

My only friends have been my therapists. Dr. Greenberg. Dr. Miles. Dr. Nolan. None of them ever last. Not after they refuse to fill out my prescription, which is always the inevitable.

Parting is such sweet sorrow . . .

For a while there, back in my teens—the *Exorcist II* Years, as Mom called them—I used to pal around with all the other scream queens on the scene. We formed a support group. Our own little Brat Pack . . . Not that Rob or Emilio or Ally returned any of our calls.

No—we were the Hack Pack.

Hack, of course, because the members of our group were all the dead girls. The kids who'd been eviscerated in our movies. Juliette and Tina and Tiffany and Melanie or Linnea. Who else understood what it was like to see yourself mutilated on-screen, then forced to relive that moment with all the fans? We'd all been there, dismembered that. And God, did we ever tear through L.A., just like we were torn up in whichever sequel our bodies had been butchered in.

The Hack Pack prescribed its own sedatives. I did my first line of cocaine off Linnea's headshot.

I'll admit, I don't remember much from this time. Blackouts were quickly becoming par for the course, particularly after a night at the Whisky a Go-Go. I do remember trying to delineate the differences between myself and the other members of our elite little club, hoping to clarify that I was in fact the creepy ghost girl of the group. Not a victim. Not just another body.

The final girls didn't like that. Didn't like me. They thought I was acting like I was better than them. All holier-than-thou, just because I was a witch. But it's true. I wasn't the cheerleader who got axed in the shower or the bubbly best friend who got electrocuted in the hot tub.

I was the one who killed the kids in my film. I was the monster in my movie.

I was the Little Witch Girl of Pilot's Creek.

I'd shout it out at the top of my lungs along Sunset Boulevard at three in morning, shout it out at the rest of the Hack Pack, at anyone wandering by or willing to listen—"Do you know who I am? I'm the Little Witch Girl of fucking Pilot's Creek!"

It wasn't long before I was excommunicated from the crew. Christ, even among the dead girls of Hollywood I was still a fucking pariah . . .

If those dead girls could only see me now.

Look who's getting remade.

All done up.

How much time has gone by? Has it been ten minutes yet? Why is this taking forever?

Nothing ends anymore.

Movies never die.

A property is never put to rest. It's never at peace. These movies can be resuscitated whenever a studio feels like bringing it back to life. There can be sequels. Sequels to sequels.

Now they do remakes.

Wipe the slate clean.

Start over.

Burn away the old residue to start fresh.

What does it even mean to remake a movie? I wondered under the oppressive shell, my cocoon beginning to congeal around my skull. *What does it mean to retell the same story?*

You're supposed to update the characters.

Update their clothes.

Their lingo.

Think of the cultural differences. Who were we then, when the original movie was first made? Who are we now? How much have we changed?

Have we changed at all?

The studio has always been crass about the original films. Execs believe kids these days won't go see an old movie. It doesn't matter if it's a classic. Or if it's been only a few years since the original came out—if there's even the slightest whiff of antiquity to it, kids won't care.

A movie needs to be new.

It has to be reborn.

What was it about Jessica's story that kept resurfacing? Why did she demand that it keep getting told, over and over again?

These stories will find you.

Your sin will find you, someone whispered from the other side of the alginate.

Jessica had become a cinematic ouroboros. A serpent devouring its own tail, coiling round and round for an eternity. The longer I imagined that snake infinitely spinning, the more its scales slowly took on the shape of celluloid frames. The sprocket holes along either side of the film strip formed scales. When this snake shed its skin, the translucent husk would be fed through the projector. The images trapped within each scale caught the projector's light and made their way to the big screen. Jessica filled that vast canvas, reaching her hand out to me.

This film would never end. It continued to play on its own endless loop. Jessica's story would be told over and over, forever now. She found a new audience.

Fresh blood.

That was exactly what Jessica wanted.

To find new blood.

"You can open your eyes now," Ella Louise's voice beckoned from the other side of my eyelids. At first, I didn't believe I'd actually heard it. It was just another whisper in my head.

It was her, wasn't it?

It had to be her.

My eyelids flutter open. The light is different now. The room is different. I'm not in Kurtz's studio anymore. There is no alginate. There's no lifecast.

No heads.

I'm staring into the eyes of a woman I've never seen before. She looks as if she's straight out of the 1920s. Her beauty feels timeless. Nothing like the dolled-up trollops of today. Her hair is done up in a bob. Clara Bow curls. Her skin is so pale, so phantasmal. A ghost.

I blink, blink again, watching this stunning starlet blink with me. She's mimicking me. Mirroring me.

I'm staring at myself. There's a wall mirror that takes up the entire length of space.

I'm in a trailer. A makeup trailer.

I don't even recognize myself.

It's happening again.

God, I've lost time. How much? This blackout feels big. They're expanding. Opening wider. Swallowing hours. Days. These pitch-dark patches in my memory like sunspots searing through me.

How long have I been out?

How did I get here?

Where am I? In the special effects trailer, yes.

I'm on set, yes.

I'm making a movie, yes.

But *when* am I?

I've seen this face before. Seen it in the woods. Here in Pilot's Creek. The only difference now is the face belongs to me. It's mine. I'm looking at myself.

Oh God, I think. *Oh God, it can't be* . . . can't be *me*.

But it is.

It's Ella. Ella Louise Ford.

There's another mirror along the wall behind me, just over my shoulders, reflecting my reflection back at me, until there's an endless corridor of Ella Louises. The duplicates of her ghost replicate themselves on and on and on into oblivion, infinitely stretching into the horizon.

The mirrors start to spin. The trailer is spinning.

Spinning.

Spinning . . .

I keep staring at myself in the mirror, locking onto the eyes of my own reflection for as long as it takes the rest of the room to settle to keep the vertigo at bay.

I'm Ella Louise, yes.

Always Ella.

Aren't I? Haven't I become a pariah, too? Aren't I living in a pharmacy just like her? What if this whole time I've been on a path that leads from Jessica to Ella Louise?

The makeup tech orbiting me leans over and smiles, glancing back and forth between me and my reflection. There are different fine-tipped paintbrushes poking out from her hair.

"Looking pretty good, huh?"

I look just like her. Just like the woman from the woods. Not Nora Lambert. Not the pretend rendition of Ella Louise.

The *real* Ella Louise.

"You okay?" the makeup tech asks. She's starting to worry.

"Yeah." I laugh at myself. "Think I . . . think I must've dozed off for a spell." I had taken that half of an Ambien before sitting down with Kurtz. But that was weeks ago . . . Wasn't it? How had I gotten here? How many pills had I taken since then? I can't remember if I popped the other half of the same pill or if I'm already on to the next. The days, the nights, are blurring together.

"Night shoots are the worst," the woman says, smiling at my reflection. Not at me. The reflection of me lingering in the mirror. "Throws my sleep schedule off. I just head back to the hotel and crash for the rest of the day. I haven't seen sunlight in like, a week. Feels that way, at least."

I manage to smile. "Terrible segue here, but . . . Well. Because our schedules are so upside down, I . . . I haven't been sleeping so well, either."

She nods. The brushes sticking out from her hair make her head look like a pincushion. She's sympathizing with me. Good. That's good. I have a fighting chance here.

"I must look awful," I say. "They're gonna need to pay you overtime to get rid of my alligator bags."

"I hadn't even noticed," she replies. "You look great."

"Amber," I insist. "Call me Amber."

"Amber."

"I don't think I've slept in . . . *Ooof.* Jesus, two days. I don't know if you know if anyone on the crew might . . . you know, have anything that might help? Take the edge off tonight?"

She doesn't respond, but it's clear she understands what I'm getting at.

"To help," I strain. "Just for tonight?"

She looks back at the door. It's only the two of us. These trailers can start to feel pretty suffocating very quickly. They can become lead-lined coffins in no time at all.

"I'm not asking for you to do anything. Not at all. I'm just asking if, you know . . . If you know of anybody. Who might be able to help. Help me out here." It was getting so hard to maintain that smile, but I had to. I had to let her know I was in control of myself.

"Talk to the gaffer," she says. Quietly. She says it to my reflection. The beautiful image of Ella Louise. "Noah. He might have something, I don't know. But I didn't tell you, okay?"

My spirits lift. My lips lift, suddenly unburdened. Oh, my savior. My guardian angel. "Thanks. Thanks so much . . .?" I stretch the question mark out, searching for her name.

"Blythe."

"*Blythe*. Thank you so so sooo much, Blythe. I owe you one. Really. You're a lifesaver."

"They want you on set in fifteen, Miss Pendleton." The warmth in her voice has gone cold.

TEN

I'm losing too much time. Losing my grip.

Losing hold.

This is not me bouncing back after some bender. Believe me, I know what that feels like. I've had my fair share. This is worse. Much worse. Entire pockets of consciousness have vanished from my memory. Time is gone. I'll admit that I've been meddling with my meds regimen a bit too much. Mixing prescriptions. It took me years to strike the right balance. What pills to take and when. How many.

Nobody can blame me for taking a full Klonopin when half would've sufficed, right?

I've just been under a lot of stress lately. What with the film.

Being back here.

Working through these memories.

Processing the past.

Every inch of this place brings back another memory. Memories I thought I had buried.

How long have I been back in Pilot's Creek? Wasn't I just getting my lifecast?

How did I even make my way to the set?

The production has overtaken the whole cemetery. Towering light kits suspend themselves over the graves, casting their powerful beams across the tombs. One Fresnel fixture flashes on directly in front of my face, blinding me for a spell. I can't see where I'm stepping anymore and I bump into a headstone that wasn't there a few footsteps ago.

It's like I never left this place. Like the last twenty-four years never happened.

Nothing but one big blur.

A black hole.

This is where I live. Where I've always lived. In the dark.

In the ground.

"There she is," Sergio calls out from across the graves so that everyone, cast and crew and the dead included, can hear. "Welcome back, Amber!"

The crew applauds me.

Just for showing up.

Tonight is my first scene. It is my first, right? It has to be. This time around, at least.

"Ready to bring Jessica back from the dead?" Sergio asks. Then, to the rest of the crew, he shouts, "Let's make history!"

He's wrong. So, so wrong. This isn't about making history.

It's about rewriting it.

This story has already been told a hundred times before.

We're here to revise it.

I'm here to edit myself out.

The Legend of the Little Witch Girl of Pilot's Creek retold. Reborn. The force of this story—Jessica's story, my story—has taken on a life of its own. It has evolved through the decades. Undying. Look at how craven pop culture has become. Look how it eats its own films and regurgitates them back onto the screen, again and again. Think of the mother spider whose body feeds its young. The first thing those newborn spiders do after they've hatched is devour their mother. These remakes are the same. They give birth to a swarm of sequels, feasting on the films that spawned them in the first place, only to repeat the process over and over again.

The story, the new story, was somehow even more threadbare than the original. I didn't think that was possible. I imagined the plot, thin as it was, printed on the back of its VHS cover:

Sometimes the dead don't stay dead . . . Cass (The Mouseketeers' Jenna Handley) and her friends are assigned to work together on a group research project for history class. The assignment? Dig through their hometown's past and see what local color they uncover. It's not long before Cass and her pals uncover the Legend of the Little Witch Girl of Pilot's Creek . . . and she wants to play!

Cass learns up on the legend. She'd never heard of it before, but now she immerses herself in the folklore. She becomes obsessed. *Haven't you ever heard of the legend of the Little Witch Girl?* she asks her friends. *They say if you stand on her grave at four minutes after midnight, you can see her, wandering about . . . looking for her mother. But don't take her hand, whatever you do. She'll grab you and drag you down, back into the ground, deep into her grave.*

By the end of the film, when all of Cass's friends are dead and only she remains, the authorities will suspect that she killed them all. The doctors will hypothesize she lost her mind the more she became obsessed with the urban legend. She had been the killer all along . . .

. . . Or was she?

Only Cass knows the truth, along with the audience. You don't mess with the Fords. This is their story. The rest of us are merely storytellers.

Ella Louise and Jessica are the only remnant of the original movie. Everything else has been completely revised. Written away. New characters, new clichés.

Same ghosts.

No matter whose name receives top billing, the real star of this film is Jessica.

Wherever she is.

Her mother is waiting for her. The ghost of Ella Louise Ford is wandering along the perimeter of the cemetery, searching for her daughter.

Yearning.

See her spirit now, her skin translucent in the moonlight. Her scorched evening gown billows in the breeze behind her, bits of ash and cindered lace breaking away and drifting through the air. Her arms are held up in front of her, reaching out for someone off-camera.

She halts among the graves, standing before the headstone of her daughter, Jessica.

I was told to hold the pose the moment I hit my mark. Look longingly into the distance.

Yearn for my daughter's return.

And I'm yearning . . .

Yearning . . .

"Aaaaaand *cut*," Sergio calls out from behind the monitor. He's not looking at me—not the flesh-and-blood me, at least—but the version of me on the monitor's screen. "Great job!"

The crew applauds.

All of them.

I feel like I'm a classically trained thespian gracing the stage, not some has-been in a horror movie. It's the strangest feeling, having the crew cheer the actors after finishing a scene. They clap even louder if the shot is a particularly demanding one. The more you suffer, the more they cheer.

Nobody has ever rooted for me before. There is such a warmth to this set, even if it's thirty degrees tonight. The crew can see how cold it is for me out here. They're all bundled up in winter parkas while the costume I'm wearing might as well be made of tissue paper.

I'm shivering between takes. Half of the acting for this role is simply holding a pose without looking like I'm freezing my ass off.

Blythe, my lovely makeup tech, my guardian angel, flanks me with an extra jacket, just for me, draping it over my shoulders as she circles around to touch up my face. "How're you holding up?" She pulls out one of the fine-tipped brushes from her bun and dabs at my lips.

"I'm dying for a cigarette." The cold has seeped into my bones, I'm shaking so much.

"Wish I could give you one," she whispers. "But then your costume might catch on fire and where would we be then?"

"Too Method for me," I joke. "I don't need to get into my character that much."

Blythe laughs at this. "Let's not have history repeat itself, okay?"

We had started the evening with a quick shot. Nothing too strenuous. Just a simple angle of me traipsing through the cemetery. A monkey could do it. An undead, refried monkey.

But everyone on set is treating me like I'm goddamn Elizabeth Taylor. From the way they're taking care of me, embracing me, you'd think we were on the set of *Cleopatra*.

"Can I get you some coffee?" Blythe asks as she dabs her paintbrush along my lips.

"Please," I say between my chattering teeth. "Feel free to put something strong in it."

"I'll see what I can do." She winks before slipping off.

This crew feels like family. One big, happy family. Had I finally found a family?

Had they met my daughter yet?

I met Jessica. The actress, I mean. A week before production got under way. Sergio had introduced me to Danielle Strode back in Los Angeles. Danielle and her mother.

Her mother.

Her mother was so—so *sweet*. Kind. We all gathered in Sergio's production office to do a quick table read of our scenes. He wanted

Danielle and me to "warm up" to each other.

The warmth at our feet—

The heat of the flames—

Danielle seemed so well-adjusted. So poised. She was just happy simply to be there, on the studio backlot, as if every minute working on this piece-of-shit horror film were a gift. A goddamn blessing.

There was a wideness to her eyes as she took everything in. Absorbing the world around her. When this girl smiled, it was easy enough to believe she was genuinely affected.

That she was truly happy.

"It is an honor to meet you, Miss Pendleton . . ." Talk about a firm handshake. This girl had a grip. Professional. What kind of kid talks like that?

We didn't look anything like each other. How Sergio was going to convince the audience that this was my daughter was anybody's guess. Nobody would mistake her for Jessica.

She didn't look the part. She wasn't Jessica.

"Hi," Danielle's mother interjected. "I'm Danielle's mom. Janet." She held out her hand to me.

"Amber."

Her mother—Janet—didn't hover. Didn't impose. She kept her distance, not wanting to intervene. She carried Danielle's backpack, pressed against her chest. Hugging it.

She looked proud. Proud of her daughter.

Her little girl.

"Well," I said back to Danielle. "Ready to scare some teens with me?"

Danielle giggled at this. This was such an adventure for her. The world was still innocent. Fun. She'd never been frightened—not really frightened—by anything her whole life. Nothing terrifying, truly terrifying, had ever come into her mind's orbit and shaken her world to its core. She didn't know what it was like to be alone, alone in the woods, freezing, so totally numb, the feeling receding from your fingers, your hands, your arms, never knowing if you'll ever see sunlight again, ever see your mother again, retreating into the innermost chambers of your mind, for warmth, for survival, compartmentalizing your own sanity like a squirrel prepping for a long, cold winter, storing those last scraps of reason, of rational thought, into the deepest corners of your skull, where no ghost, no monster could ever find them and steal them away.

"I'm you now," Danielle said, dragging me back to the production office.

"What did you say?"

Danielle looked worried. Like she'd said the wrong thing. Had she said the wrong thing? "In the movie," she clarified, hoping to make amends for whatever mistake she'd committed. "I get to be you in the movie."

She smiled when she said it, uncertain if that was the right thing to do. Smile.

"Well, I bet you'll be an even *better* Jessica than I was." I beamed right back.

"I've got to confess," Janet piped in from behind Danielle. "We haven't watched the original film yet. I mean, *I* watched it. Of course. With Danielle's daddy. We rented it together, right before Danielle auditioned, and we . . . well, we felt it might be a little too spooky for her."

I glanced down at Danielle. Her head was bowed. She nervously rotated her waist as if she were playing with an invisible hula hoop. I could tell she was embarrassed by this. Ashamed. I kneeled down so that we were face to face. Danielle's hips stopped spinning. She looked me right in the eye, both of us lost for a moment. "You know it's make-believe, yeah?"

Danielle nodded. "Of course."

I didn't believe her. "When I played Jessica, you know what I did?

I imagined what it would've been like if we were friends. That me and Jessica were the bestest pals. We would do everything together. We'd play and chat all the time, even if she wasn't really there. The more I imagined us playing, the more I could see her. I watched her, studied her. That way, when it was time to be her, I knew exactly who she was. All her movements. Her laughter. The sound of her voice. I knew everything there was to know about her, because we had spent so much time together . . . even if it was all in my head."

Janet stepped up behind Danielle and took hold of her shoulders. "Well, we can't wait to get started. We've been working on Danielle's lines and we think we'll make you proud."

It was a subtle gesture, but I could see Janet pull Danielle closer to her. Away from me.

She was protecting her daughter.

From me.

Danielle hadn't made her way to the set yet. She must have been still getting into her makeup. Her burns. Maybe she was with her mother. With Janet. Maybe the two of them were working on her lines together or doing whatever the hell they do together as a loving family.

On the call sheet, it said the next scene would be our fated reunion. Jessica would rise up from her grave and waltz into her mother's open arms. The two of us would wander into the woods, together forever. I'm not sure how Sergio wanted to shoot it, but the scene called for Danielle to claw her way out from the ground, to escape her fenced-in prison of crucifixes. We would wrap our scorched arms around each other for the first time in decades. All those unruly teens have been dispatched by this point in the script, save for Cassandra—sorry, Cass—the lone survivor. Our final girl. She must witness this family reunion. Someone needed to live to tell the tale. To keep our story alive. A story needs a storyteller, and fate had deemed her to be the carrier of that torch. Cass would wake up in a sanitarium in the next scene, screaming her pretty head off, insisting that it was real, all of it was real, that she saw the spirits of Jessica and Ella Louise Ford. The nurse injects her with a sedative, sending Cass back off to sleep, to her nightmares, while out in the woods, mother and daughter wander hand in hand.

Finis.

Sergio rushes up to me, looking like a little boy bundled in a winter coat two sizes too big for him, ready to play in the snow outside. "Hey," he says. "That was great. You were great."

"Thanks," I say. "I've been preparing my whole life for this role."

He laughs. "Think you're up for doing another take?"

"Sure. Yeah. Of course."

"Great. It looks great. You look great. Really. I can't wait for you to see it."

"Stop it." This is the most we've talked since our little tiff about the script. Days ago, mind you. At least I think it was. He gave me the cold shoulder at the catering tent yesterday, like some high schooler shrugging me off in the cafeteria. But now, on set, he's glowing. He's in his element.

"I'm serious," he says. "You'll love what we've done. The lighting reaches right through you. It's like you're not even there. So cool." I can't help but notice the look he gives me, how it changes itself. He's not even really looking at me anymore. His eyes trail off by the slightest fraction. He isn't seeing me now, not in the moment, the present tense, not right here in front of him. He's focused on some other version of me. A future version. A postproduction version. Color-corrected. It's a bit discombobulating, feeling this way. That I am somehow unfinished.

"Oh." He suddenly realizes I'm trembling. "You cold? We'll do this really quickly. Then we'll get you back to your trailer to warm up while we set up for the next shot."

He turns to everyone else. The crew has been watching. Waiting for us. They know, they know all about us. It's obvious. Everyone knows. Just look at the way that they're staring. Their eyes. Oh God, their eyes. All those hollow eyes . . . Looking right at me. *Staring.* Not even blinking. Any of them. Gray eyes. So wide. Glassed over. Gummed up in something phlegmy, like oysters. Nothing but pearls of gray snot floating in each socket. I know those eyes. Always staring at—

Janet rushes onto the set.

I hadn't expected to see Danielle's mother. Not during filming. Something about it disrupts the balance of the set. The narrative. I can't focus. Not with her here. Not with her—

Something's wrong. Janet looks as if she's in an absolute panic, trying—and failing—to maintain her composure as a percolating shriek builds into a volcanic swell within her throat.

"Has—has anyone seen Danielle?"

ELEVEN

Danielle wasn't in her trailer. She wasn't wandering around the set. She wasn't spinning in the rotating barber chair in the makeup trailer. She wasn't sneaking stale danishes from the catering tent. She wasn't hiding in any of the production rigs that transported the lighting equipment. She wasn't stranded in any of the porta-potties. She wasn't in the cemetery. She wasn't hiding behind any of the headstones, peeking out when nobody was looking. She wasn't shuffling alongside the gravel road that connected the cemetery to the highway, walking back to town. She wasn't hanging out with any of the other cast members in their spacious heated trailers. She wasn't with Jenna or Freddie or Tara. None of the actors had seen her all night.

That left the woods.

The whole woods.

All those acres of swaying pines at either end of the cemetery.

Shooting halted as everyone, from the producers down to every last production assistant, took to the pines and searched for Danielle. She couldn't have just vanished.

Nobody just vanishes. She had to be out here, somewhere.

In the woods.

I was still in my flimsy costume, freezing to the bone, but I could care less. I grabbed a flashlight like everyone else and dove into the trees. Nobody had said anything, not yet—not to me, anyway, not to my face—about how this was all beginning to feel a little familiar, as if we'd all done this once before. The slightest whiff of déjà vu permeated the set.

"Sure you want to do this?" the electrician asked as he handed me a flashlight. His stare lingered a little longer than I felt comfortable with, insinuating something. Accusing me.

"Of course," I snapped.

History was not about to repeat itself.

Not tonight.

I just prayed nobody else made the connection before we found her.

Before I found her.

The search party branched out. The teamsters had taken the lead, boldly embarking upon their expedition like this was all some kind of gallant quest. *Find the missing princess.* I could see the flashlight beams slicing through the pines. We all called out her name as we traipsed deeper into the woods, a smattering of echoes bubbling up from the dark.

"Danielle . . . ?"

"Danielle . . . ?"

"Danielle . . . ?"

I had a migraine from all the constant chattering. The enamel on my teeth was about to crack. There was a full-on throbbing in my jaw.

I could take a quick detour back to my trailer and rummage through my bag—

Focus, I said to myself. *You need to focus.*

You need to find Danielle.

Before anyone else.

"Danielle?" I called out, my voice cracking just a bit. "Danielle, can you hear me . . . ?"

I knew what it was like.

To be lost out here.

I was the only one who knew exactly what Danielle was going through right now.

To be alone. Out here. Cold and shivering.

To think that everyone else had forgotten you, forsaken you. That nobody cared. Not the director or any of the crew. Not your castmates.

Not even your own mother.

How could Janet have lost track of her like that? What kind of mother lets her own daughter slip through her fingers? She should have been there. She should have protected her daughter. A horror movie set is nowhere for a girl to be left alone. This was all Janet's fault.

I knew what Danielle felt at that very moment. How afraid she must've been.

I wasn't going to give up on her. Not like they'd given up on me.

I was going to be the one to find her, I knew it. Felt it in my very bones.

I knew where to look.

"Danielle?" I called out. "Danielle . . . ? Can you hear me? Danielle?"

The woods hadn't changed. At all. The pines were placed in exactly the same position even after all these years. I knew because I had revisited this forest practically every night for the last two decades, wandering through these swaying pines in my dreams.

It was surprising how easy it was to find my way through the dense brush. The rest of the crew had receded by now, heading in different directions, while I walked along my own path. I could just imagine everyone else struggling to navigate the latticework of low-hanging branches and underbrush.

I knew the way. Knew where to step. Where not to. I knew where I was heading.

The sound of her name from everyone else's voice grew fainter. "Danielle . . . ?"

"Danielle . . . ?"

The echo of it elongated, the consonants stretching out until there was a gaping chasm between each call. "Danielle?"

"Danielle?"

"Danielle?"

Then it was gone altogether. I couldn't hear the rest of the crew calling out for her any longer. Now there was only my voice.

"Danielle? Danielle, are you there? Can you hear me?"

Something didn't feel right. She should be here. I should have found her by now.

Where was I?

I've gone too far into the woods. Too far in this direction.

The wrong direction.

I turned.

Then turned again.

I shined my light into the woods, only for the beam to get blocked by a pine.

"Danielle?"

I turn.

Turn again.

The trees won't let me see. Won't let my light through. Wherever I am, I can't find my way out anymore.

"Danielle!"

I turn. Turn again.

Turn again.

This isn't how it was supposed to happen. I was supposed to find her.

I thought I knew where I was, where she'd be.

Now I'm the one who's lost.

I turn.

Turn.

Turn.

Now I'm spinning. Spinning around and around and around. The flashlight rakes over the pines, creating a continuous ring of light. Of fire.

I'm spinning.

Spinning.

Spinning.

I can't stop myself. Can't stop spinning.

Can't—

Just then, the beam blanches over something white.

Spinning.

Spinning.

A dress.

Spinning.

Spinning.

A girl.

Spinning.

Spinning.

There she is again.

Spinning.

Spinning.

A flash of white embedded among all these shadows. Black and brown and green now white then black and brown and green and white again.

I see her dress for a split second but I still can't stop myself from spinning, losing sight of her for another moment before rotating all the way around again.

My flashlight returns to her, the beam grazing her dress's soft cotton contours.

This time I halt.

My right foot plants itself into the soil, almost stomping the ground like a horse clomping its hooves. My head keeps spinning without the rest of me. A dizzy spell works through my skull. The pines still sway, their branches brushing over my cranium, their needles tickling my skin.

I have to close my eyes. Let the woods settle first. Let this wave of nausea pass over me. Let my brain recalibrate, so, when I finally open my eyes again, I can see her.

See Danielle.

She's on the ground. Huddled into herself. Her back is pressed against a tree. She's brought her knees up to her chest. Her head is buried between her knees, caving into herself.

Hiding. Crying. Silently sobbing.

For a moment, for the briefest, dizzying moment, I feel like I am looking at myself. That's me! That's me on the ground. It's happening all over again.

No—not again. For the first time.

It's twenty-four years ago. Somehow, I've gone back in time. To the first time we made this movie. The night I played Jessica.

The night I disappeared in the woods.

That night.

My night.

But it's not. It can't be. I have to shake the thought away, force it out of my head before it takes root. It's 1995. I'm a woman now. Not some kid.

Not some girl.

"There you are," I say to her. To myself. My younger self. "Everyone's looking for you."

She doesn't say anything.

I don't say anything. I'm too scared. Too cold. I've been alone, out here, in the woods for too long. The dark, the cold itself, has seeped into me. It's in my bones. In my blood. There's nothing else to feel now. Nothing but the numbness of this night. Of this god-awful place.

She looks like me.

She could be.

Be me.

Her hair—my hair—hangs over my face, covering her eyes. The angle of my head is bent down. I'm staring into the dark chasm between my knees. Hiding from everything. Everyone.

I remember that feeling. I remember it so well. It could've happened just yesterday. Just last night. I don't know if that feeling ever truly left me.

I remember being discovered, but somehow not believing it. Not trusting it.

I have to let her know that she's okay. That she's safe now.

That I found her.

I'll protect her.

"It's okay," I say to myself. My younger self. I'm echoing the very same words that had been said to me, that I had said to myself, all those years ago. "I'm here now. I found you."

TWELVE

I bring Danielle into my arms. She's so light. Lighter than I imagined. I feel her fingers slither around my neck, her arms wrapping around me as I carry her through the woods.

Her head presses itself against my chest, just under my chin. She curls in and hides.

"Don't worry," I whisper. "I've got you. I'm going to take you back home."

Home.

Home.

Her grip tightens around my neck. She's squeezing me. It's starting to hurt.

But she's not shivering.

At all.

Her body remains rigid. Such a bundle of skin and bones. She barely weighs a thing. So light in my arms. And yet . . . there's a strength to her that surprises me. The girl has a grip, that's for sure. I try to pull my head away, to free up my neck a bit, but her arms only slither their way around, tighter, coiling over my throat. Her arms don't even feel like arms anymore. They feel like snakes.

"It's okay," I say. "You're safe, I promise. You don't—don't have to hold on so tight."

She's not trembling from the cold. I can't keep myself from shivering—and yet here's this little girl, lost for the last few hours, huddling into herself in the dead of the night, stranded out here in the freezing cold, in a cotton dress with its scorched hem, not quivering a single bit.

Her body is so still. So still.

But she's cold.

Her skin. It's freezing. There's no warmth to her body. I can't feel any heat radiating out from her, even when she's pressed so tightly against my chest.

I feel as if I'm carrying a bundle of kindling. Old wood. Not some child. Not some little

witch

girl

little

witch

girl

My footsteps dwindle. I don't stop walking all at once. It takes a couple strides for me to finally come to a halt. In the woods. Surrounded by so many trees. The pine needles bristling.

I hold perfectly still, like I'm standing on my mark, waiting in place until the director calls

cut

But Sergio never calls out to me. Never stops this madness.

It's happening.

This is really happening to me.

I can see my breath fogging up before my face, these short bursts of steam dissipating into the air. But it's only my breath. Not hers. She's not even inhaling. Her chest is level against mine. She has barely moved all this time. She's so still. Too still. No rise and fall of her chest.

No pulse.

No

no

no

no

I'm standing so still. My legs won't move anymore. They're locked in place. My feet could just as easily take root right here in the earth and my arms would branch out and I'd become just another pine, another swaying tree, lost among all the others, cradling this

this

this

little

no

witch

please no

girl

no

no

no

As calmly as I can, I pull her away from my chest by a few inches. Just enough to get a look at her. To see who I'm holding. I glance down at my arms, trying hard to hold my head upright.

I peer down.

To see.

She's staring up at me. But where her eyes—where her eyes should be—there's nothing. The sockets are hollow. Full of shadows. Black puddles. But they're staring up at me.

With love.

Her lower jaw has unhinged itself. The slack in her seared cheeks lets the jaw hang open wider than it should. The flesh along her face has peeled back. She looks like a gaping, awestruck child.

She's looking at me with wonder.

With such love.

"Mommy . . ."

THIRTEEN

I'm carrying Jessica through the woods.

Slowly.

I've brought her back to my chest, pressing her body to mine. Her arms haven't left my neck. When I tried to separate us, her grip only tightened around my throat. Her arms are now a noose around my neck, choking me if I ever let go.

So I carry her.

Cradle her.

There's a mewling at my chest. Like a congested lamb. It sounds far too wet, the sound she's making, but there's a certain contentment to it. I can feel it hum through her skull and resonate into my chest, the slightest of vibrations. Purring, almost. Such happiness.

Such love.

I don't know where I'm going. Not for certain. But I stop worrying about my way. I've walked these woods so many times, night after night, dream after fetid dream, that I don't need to know for sure.

We found each other, didn't we? We've come this far . . . So I stop worrying. Stop. I let my feet simply lead the way and I let them, I let them. I let them. Let them take me home.

Take me home.

Take us home.

Home.

home

home

This is the role I was meant to play.

Born to play.

I've been preparing for this part my entire life, haven't I? All these years of drug-induced stasis, of emotional paralysis, of lies . . . they have all been leading to this moment in time.

Showtime, folks . . . Time to shine.

Time to be a star.

My life has merely been a dry run. Now it's time to play.

For keeps.

Like the tagline says, *Jessica wants to play . . . with you!*

As a child, I played the part of Jessica Ford long enough to reunite her with her mother.

Just for a moment. Just a breath.

Now I am Ella Louise. For Jessica's sake. It's a phantasmal family reunion come full circle. And it's so easy to slip into this role. I've done my preparation, I've gone over my lines. I know them by heart.

By heart.

I've lived this part.

I'm ready now.

Born ready.

We come upon the clearing before I even realize it. It opens up to us so quickly, the pines pulling back and suddenly I'm stepping out into an open patch of crabgrass and thistle.

I've been to this clearing before. I know who's waiting for us here.

Who's buried below our feet.

Am I humming?

I'm humming a song. A lullaby. It's the opening theme music to *Don't Tread on Jessica's Grave.* I hadn't even realized I knew the score, but there you go. Just a little something to keep Jessica calm. Keep her hands from choking me. She won't let go. Her arms feel like serpents, like snakes wrapping their way around my throat. The charred flecks of her burnt flesh scrape at my own skin, snake scales grating against my flesh. No—not snakes. Film strips. Her skin feels like the tangled reel of a movie, my movie, its brittle celluloid noosed around my neck.

That's all this is. It's only a movie, I keep repeating to myself as I make my way to the center of the clearing. To the patch of scorched earth waiting for us both. *It's only a movie . . .*

Only a movie . . .

Only a movie . . .

Only a movie . . .

Only a . . .

Only . . .

PART FOUR

WHO GOES THERE?
2016

WHEN DID YOU HEAR YOUR FIRST GHOST STORY? WHAT WAS IT LIKE, SITTING *around the campfire as a kid, listening to someone spin a yarn they swore was real? That supposedly happened to someone they knew? The cousin of a friend they grew up with? The sister of a pal they knew in school?*

Where does a ghost story get its power? The imagination of the listener? How does it evolve?

Hello and welcome to another episode of Who Goes There?

I'm your host, Nate Denison. Today, we'll explore one ghost story that has been steeped in infamy ever since it started making the rounds around campfires all across the country . . .

I'm speaking, of course, of Jessica Ford, also known as . . . the Little Witch Girl of Pilot's Creek.

For those unfamiliar with Jessica Ford, perhaps you've seen her movies. Jessica and her mother, Ella Louise, have been the subject of not one but two feature films, beginning with 1971's low-budget fever dream Don't Tread on Jessica's Grave, *directed by Lee Ketchum, and its disastrous remake, 1995's* I Know What You Did on Jessica's Grave, *which was notoriously shut down after the tragic events that occurred on set. Both films tell wildly divergent stories, but each movie roots its central narrative within the urban legend of the Little Witch Girl. What truly puts these films in the echelon of cult film fan infamy, however, isn't so much the movies themselves but the incidents behind the scenes for both . . . particularly when it comes to actress Amber Pendleton. Never heard of her? You're not the only one. Miss Pendleton played not only Jessica Ford in the original film, but her mother, Ella Louise, in its doomed remake . . . and not much else. To this day, it remains unclear what really happened on the set of* I Know What You Did on Jessica's Grave. *Some say the production was cursed, thanks to its haunted source material. Others say Pendleton was driven mad by her role, suffering a psychotic break during production that led to the kidnapping—and death—of her nine-year-old co-star, Danielle Strode.*

Regardless of what you've heard, or what you think you've heard, there's clearly more to this story than what we've been told. For this episode, I'll discuss the historical origins behind the legend of the Little Witch Girl. We'll visit Pilot's Creek and its people, while also examining the impact of these films within the horror genre . . . and beyond. We'll see how movie theaters have become pop culture's new campfires, where audiences gather 'round to hear a good ghost story.

Because what is a movie but a ghost in and of itself? Films are phantoms illuminated upon the big screen for all to see. More on that and the impact of the Little Witch Girl on this episode of . . .

. . . Who Goes There?

ONE

It wasn't that difficult tracking her down. I've uncovered stiffer mysteries. Her name wasn't listed anymore, but nobody's really are. Certainly not tarnished starlets.

But Pilot's Creek? *Jesus* . . . She never left. Moved right where all the action happened.

Nobody chooses to live in that shithole. Not unless they want to drop off the face of the earth. Slip into obscurity and wither away. Nothing but old folks' homes crammed full of desiccated rednecks and mobile homes on cinder blocks with Confederate flags draped in their windows. I'd need to be careful where I poked around *down south*. Last thing I want is to get lynched.

All the long-forgotten trailer parks lining the pine-ridden interstate sound the same.

Sandy Pines Trailer Park.

Three Pines RV Oasis.

Moonstone RV Park.

Amber Pendleton rented a slip in the Whispering Pines Mobile Home and RV Park. Guess what name she's registered under? *Ford.* You believe that? The balls on this woman . . .

Found you, Amber, I remember thinking. *Nice try.*

There's no phone listing. No cell number. Maybe no phone at all.

It's clear she doesn't want to be found. Miss Pendleton's interviewing days are long gone. She hasn't spoken publicly since '97. Not since the trial. But when had that ever stopped me before? A dead end was just a barrier to break on through to the other side . . . Where other journalists gave up, I jumped. I fucking *flew.* Air Jordan journalist right here. Spread those wings!

This is the part of the podcast I love the most, if I'm being honest. Thrill of the hunt. Tracking these people down. Confronting them with their own truths, no matter how hard they tried to hide from them. Their own secrets. Ambush them with my warhorse:

An Olympus LS-12 portable recorder.

This baby comes equipped with two directional microphones that branch off at the top, like antlers, along with an omnidirectional mic nestled in between, a crown capable of recording lower bass ranges.

The sound quality is to die for. My Olympus can pick up everything.

Everything.

I live for that look in my interview subject's eye. The shock. Watching their pupils dilate the moment they realize they've been found. That they can't hide anymore.

Not from me.

I had hopped in my car. Drove all nine hours from Brooklyn to Pilot's Creek, Virginia, for Christ's sake. Slipped through the Mason-Dixon for the first time in not-fucking-long-enough. My family comes from the Carolinas and you damn well better believe I was more than happy to leave it behind in the rearview mirror the second I could. Coming back down to Crackerville was not my idea of a swell time. But you got to follow the story, now, don't you? Follow it to the pits of hell, if you've got to—or, in this case, Pilot's Creek.

Close enough, you ask me.

Now it's time to go knock on Amber Pendleton's door, Olympus in hand. And when she opens up, the aperture of her hidden life expanding to let me inside, I'm going to press record and bring the mic up to her and fire off: *What happened that night, twenty years ago?*

Or something like that. I haven't figured out exactly what I'm going to say just yet. Introductions are the hardest part to script. Still working it out in my head. All the way down I-95. On the drive, I riffed a bit on introductions. The hours in the car offered me a chance to wax on possible preambles. How I wanted to tackle her.

I can respect Miss Pendleton's desire for privacy. But nothing stays private forever. Not these days. Nothing belongs to the past anymore. These stories take on a life of their own, bloating up into urban legends with each retelling. I can't let that happen.

People always forget the source, that kernel of truth buried within every story. The truth was that grain of sand embedded in the oyster, layering up with enough lacquer that it eventually becomes an urban pearl. Beautiful to look at, sure, but its origins are always ugly. Painful. Better left forgotten for those involved. I'm far more fascinated with that first grain of sand, that little bit of grit that everybody else forgets. Tries to hide. Keep secret.

I want the truth. The real story.

It all boils down to perspective.

A point of view.

Somebody to tell the story.

Amber Pendleton had already consigned her life to the big screen. Sold her soul to cinema. If she wants the world to leave her alone, she shouldn't have chosen a career in the movies. What little career there had been. Miss Pendleton's IMDb page is pretty much relegated to one role and one role only:

Jessica Ford. *Don't Tread on Jessica's Grave.* 1971.

Written and directed by Lee Ketchum.

There are a smattering of cameos here and there, leading up to '95. Nothing really to write home about. Forgettable slasher films. Then her CV stops altogether. A dead-end cul-de-sacking with Sergio

Gillespie's unfinished opus *I Know What You Did on Jessica's Grave*.

It all ended that night.

Actors' lives are fair game, as far as I'm concerned. To the fans. To the press.

To me.

I just have to find her first.

Everybody had seen the movie. It enjoyed a bit of a bump on VHS after what happened. Even got a DVD release.

But did anybody know the truth behind *Don't Tread on Jessica's Grave*? The real story behind the making of the film? What did they know about Amber beyond the fact that she was a failed child actress? A diminished starlet eclipsed by her first and most infamous part?

What did people know about the aborted remake? About its director, Sergio Gillespie? Where was he these days? What about the real source of inspiration for these movies? Who knew the history behind the ghost story? Did people even know who Jessica Ford was? Her mother, Ella Louise? How deep did this legend actually go? What had it done to Pilot's Creek?

This is what I do best, if I'm being frank. Let me break it down for you: I seek the true story behind these urban legends and bring them to light, exposing them as the hoaxes they are, discrediting these ham-fisted mysteries and reaping all the downloads my podcast can rack up.

Perhaps you've heard an episode?

Heard of me?

I've spent the last couple years amassing quite a catalog of debunked ghost stories. You've probably listened to Episode 4: "The Haunted Mt. Vista Inn."

Or how about Episode 13: "The Wandering Ghost of the I-95 Rest Area."

Or my personal favorite, Episode 32: "The Pool Witch of Water Country Water Park."

All urban legends I've put to rest, all tales I punctured with proof and lots of legwork. I exposed these hoaxes and a dozen other tall tales for the shams they really are.

I've got no qualms bursting people's bubbles. Hell, I revel in it. There isn't a ghost I can't take down. But this one—Jessica Ford— would be my biggest yet. My white whale.

I'm ready to tackle the Legend of the Little Witch Girl.

Bring her to light.

Expose her.

What makes Jessica Ford's story so tantalizing is the fact that it's two stories, if not three, all wrapped up in one. A nested doll of urban legends. Uncover one and you find another horror story hidden inside.

First, there's the historical account of Jessica and Ella Louise Ford. What happened in real life to those two poor souls in Pilot's Creek. Rooted in this small southern town, its superstitious citizens feared the Fords were witches and ended up burning them both at the stake. Grim stuff, really. Burning a little girl? Brutal. If that weren't bad enough, now the whole town believed—still believes—the ghost of little Jessica wanders along her grave, night after night, just waiting for some dumbass to take her hand and lead her to her mother's resting place. Wherever that was.

Second, there's *Don't Tread on Jessica's Grave* in '71. This is where the myth reaches a larger audience. Where Amber Pendleton first intersects with the Fords. At nine years old, Amber gets cast in the role of Jessica Ford for the movie based on the Legend of the Little Witch Girl. Lee Ketchum only had one movie in him and it nearly drove him insane. The production was a fiasco, all on account of little Amber snapping on set. She claimed her co-star, Nora Lambert, who played her mother in the movie, had attacked her. Dragged her in the woods. Tried molesting her or some weirdo shit like that. I read through enough interviews and even listened to the DVD commentary to pick up on the vibes that Amber Pendleton was one crumbly cookie. This movie must've fucked her up royally.

Truth told, nobody would be talking about Amber or *Don't Tread on Jessica's Grave* today if it hadn't been for what happened on set. Her story took on mythic proportions, gathering up its own momentum until everybody now believes that little girl came upon a real ghost out there in those woods.

The ghost of Ella Louise Ford.

There you have it. An urban legend is born. Now everybody's got to track down a copy of *Jessica*, just to see if they can spot her. See a spook captured on camera.

Bullshit.

Last but certainly not least, the legend's real clincher . . . the remake.

The failed remake.

The debacle on set. The story roots itself in Amber Pendleton once again, somehow. The disappearance of Danielle Strode. The search through the forest. The discovery of her body . . . and Amber, wandering in the woods, practically catatonic.

Three stories for the price of one urban legend.

Can't beat that.

I know Amber is hiding something. I've got a nose for these things—and, well, after *I Know What You Did on Jessica's Grave* capsized, there had to be more to the story than what the press originally reported. There just had to be. Twenty years later, still nobody knows for sure what exactly happened to Danielle Strode. The girl had disappeared and . . .

And then . . .

Well, I'll just have to find out for myself, now, won't I?

I'm more interested in what happened *before* the police came upon her body. The sequence of events leading up to the discovery of Danielle Strode's corpse.

What Amber had done.

That's where the real story is hiding.

Amber's secrets are still out there, hidden within the woods.

Just waiting for me.

These horror fan sites pontificate ad infinitum about what could've happened. The message boards are littered with fan theories. The supernatural conspiracies. It is downright laughable how far some people will go to prove their crackpot ghost scenarios. And yet no one, not a single one of these die-hards, has ever gotten this close.

Nobody has actually tracked Amber down.

Not until yours truly.

She quickly slipped into obscurity after the hearing. Once the lawyers were through with her, pecking at her testimony like vultures stripping the flesh off roadkill, there was nothing left of her. The press hounded Amber for as long as they could squeeze a headline out of her, all through the trial, but once the judge brought down his gavel and the case came to a close, Miss Pendleton vanished.

The tabloids painted a purpled portrait of Amber feeling resentful of Danielle for stepping on her toes. Amber had portrayed the part first, so when this pint-sized actress played her daughter in the reboot and did it better, something must have snapped. Amber just couldn't handle it. So she kills Danielle. Cold blood. That's the going theory, anyway. The defense proposed it, the press loved it, and Amber never denied it. Never said a word. She simply sat in the courtroom, staring off at the wall, not seeing the wall, looking past the wall.

Talk about a witch hunt.

Authorities discovered Danielle's body the morning after she disappeared.

Eight hours later.

Her corpse was found partially buried within a clearing in the woods. Somebody—presumably Amber Pendleton—had begun to inter her body. She was resting in such a way that the police first thought Danielle Strode was simply asleep, a blanket brought up to her chest. She looked like she was resting. Dreaming. Her eyes remained wide open, staring blankly up at the sky. Her skin had a cool blue hue to it, her lips purpled from exposure to the cold. She looked like a doll. A porcelain doll. When I pored over the forensic photos, I couldn't help but think of Danielle as a lost toy. This little girl, so still. So pale.

The police came upon Amber not too far away from the crime scene. She was still in costume, dressed as Ella Louise Ford, wandering aimlessly through the woods. She offered no resistance. The officers guided her through the trees without a single peep from her.

Amber was put on trial for the girl's murder. Who else could it have been? A slam-dunk from the prosecutor's point of view. When Amber was brought onto the witness stand, no matter how much they grilled her, all she ever uttered was, "Jessica was jealous."

That's it. That was her entire defense. When Jessica Ford saw Danielle pretending to be her, dressed just like her, the Little Witch Girl grew very, very resentful.

"No one should step between a daughter and her mother," Amber had said. Said it in such a low tone, the judge had to ask Amber if she would please repeat herself for the record.

That was it for Amber. Not another word out of her for the rest of the trial. I scoured the courtroom testimony and I couldn't find anything.

Amber was acquitted.

Actually *acquitted*.

The evidence never quite added up, even if her defense was absolutely loony tunes. You believe that? Hundreds of innocent black women have been sent to death row for less.

Apparently, when the verdict was read aloud, Danielle's mother, Janet Strode, let out a wail from her seat in the gallery. Just a long, mournful howl. She had to be escorted from the courtroom by Danielle's father, who held her up as she continued to moan the whole way out. Amber never looked back, simply staring at that wall.

The studio couldn't recoup. The remake was deep-sixed before it even got off the ground. No film survives that type of setback. They had to write it off. Whole kit and caboodle.

The footage still remains. They hadn't shot much. Production had just begun when . . . whatever happened happened. The production shut down and the dailies were tossed into storage, never to be seen. The footage took on its own legend. It became just as mythic. Everybody—well, the horror fans, at least—was dying to see. Eventually, it popped up online. I found clips of raw footage on YouTube. Just a bunch of shots of the Pilot's Creek Cemetery at night. The headstones are all backlit. A fog machine pumps a low-hanging veil of mist over the ground. Sergio Gillespie did his best to replicate the feel of the original film. Easier said than done. They were still shooting on celluloid in '95, but there's no grit to the film stock. It looks too smooth. Too sleek. Polished. Nothing like *Don't Tread on Jessica's Grave.*

Then Amber Pendleton enters the frame.

She's stunning. Dressed in this thin dress. Practically translucent. The moonlight seems to pass through her somehow. Like she's not even there.

A ghost.

There are three takes of the same shot on the reel. Amber Pendleton slowly sauntering her way through the cemetery. Staring off into some fixed point behind the camera.

Yearning. That's the only way I can describe it. She's yearning for something.

Someone.

She holds the pose for a beat and, as Porky Pig sputters, *That's all, folks* . . . That's all that exists of her role in the movie. Of *I Know What You Did on Jessica's Grave.*

Amber Pendleton never worked again. Nobody survives that type of scandal. Not in this town. She was a pariah now. The rest of her days had been spent drinking herself into oblivion in some run-down mobile home park, alone, practically in the backyard of the scene of the crime.

Until I found her.

Here we are. Standing at the door of her trailer. Has to be hers. The graffiti spray-painted across its broadside is a dead giveaway . . .

WITCH.

The tendrils of bright pink have faded through the years, but still, there it is.

WITCH.

Rather than paint over it or try scrubbing the letters away, Amber must've resigned herself to the vandalism. Perhaps she washed it away at one point. Perhaps the tag kept growing back, the letters like kudzu over her trailer. Strangling it.

Do people around these parts actually think Amber is a witch? Some superstitions die hard, I guess . . .

I wandered around the RV park a bit, just to get the lay of the land. I spotted a few kids kicking the dust around the parking lot. Local color. *I could get a quote*, I thought.

"Excuse me," I said, clearing my throat. "Is this where Miss Amber Pendleton lives? Is that her trailer?"

There were three white boys. Probably around six or seven years old. Maybe eight. I'm not great at determining age. Their faces were smeared with dirt. They stared blankly back at me as if I'd just spoken in some foreign tongue. Eyes wide. At first, I figure it's because I'm black. That's been my go-to since crossing into Virginia. Hell, just about everywhere I go these days.

I realized one of the boys had a stick in his hand. He'd been prodding a dusty lump on the ground when I first called over to them, quickly hiding the stick behind his back, as if he'd been caught red-handed doing something he shouldn't. Wasn't until I walked over that I realized the lump was actually a hatchling. A baby bird. The wet origami of its crumpled wings was still writhing over the ground. Its thimble-sized beak open and closed, gasping silently. Was it crying? The poor thing hadn't even opened its eyes yet. Never would. The boy jabbed his stick into the bird's purpled eyelid. A jet of jelly spurted over the ground, swallowed up by a whorl of dust.

Nobody said a thing. I only stared, taking in the sight of this hatchling squirming beneath the stick, pinned to the ground, unable to free itself. Its beak open and closed.

Open and closed.

Open and . . .

Froze.

The boys look back to me. Waiting for me to say something. I don't know, scold them or something. Anything.

"Amber Pendleton," I said. My voice very even. Very clear.

The boy pointed his stick toward a trailer, the tip of it dripping in ophthalmic jelly. I turned toward the rusted, dust-covered trailer. *WITCH* was the only address Amber had at this point in her life. The only address she'd ever need from here on out.

"Thanks," I said back to the boy, but the three of them had already run off.

A ring of terra-cotta flowerpots held on to a few withered husks that had been hydrangeas at some point in their life, now nothing more than dried stalks. One pot had shattered, the dirt spilling out from the shards. Nobody had taken the time to clean it up.

I had my Olympus tucked into my pocket, ready to rock. I took in a deep breath. Psyched myself up. Brought up my fist . . . and knocked.

And waited.

And waited.

Glancing over my shoulder, I started to get the sneaking suspicion nobody lived here anymore. Should've slipped those boys a five, asking if Miss Pendleton had flown the—

The door opened.

Turning back around, I'm taken aback by the crescent sliver of Miss Amber Pendleton. Her weatherworn face stares out at me from the small gap in her door. She doesn't say a word. A chain-link lock suspends itself at her forehead. Her eyes have dulled over the decades. She looks nothing like her photographs from the trial. Certainly not from the dailies.

This isn't what—who—I expected to see.

She looks older. Not tired, per se. *Resigned.* Gray streaks run through her hair, nothing but ash now, tresses like spent cigarettes weaving around her head.

". . . Miss Pendleton?"

No response. She's not doing anything but staring impassively back at me.

Waiting.

The words are gone. Faded from my mind. My mouth is so parched. When was the last time I had a sip of water? "My name is Nathaniel Denison and . . . and I . . ."

The chain lock slides along its runners, then falls. Amber disappears into her trailer, into the shadows, leaving the door open behind her. "I was wondering when you'd come."

DEBORAH PENDLETON WANTED TO BE A MOVIE STAR. LIKE MOST YOUNG GIRLS *with stars in their eyes in the sixties, growing up watching Audrey Hepburn and Natalie Wood, Deborah dropped out of high school her junior year and moved to Los Angeles. Coming from Kansas City, however, Deborah wasn't equipped to protect herself from such an unforgiving city as L.A. After a few odd modeling jobs and featured extra work, Deborah became pregnant . . .*

And that was the end. Deborah's dreams of ever becoming a movie star faded to black.

Amber Lee Pendleton was born on September 26, 1962.

Her biological father remains a mystery. His name, his whereabouts, everything. Some have speculated he was the Devil himself, but nobody believes in the Devil anymore. Not in Hollywood. The devils in L.A. are the casting directors. The producers waiting on the casting couch. The men ready to exploit a young, innocent, aspiring actress with no one to protect her.

That devil exists.

Amber possessed a radiance that her mother could only admonish. She looked like her father, as far as Deborah was concerned. She was a constant reminder of the past. Her failure.

Deborah quickly came to resent Amber. For what she stood for. What she could have been but would never be.

Amber's freckled face and button nose were the picture of wholesomeness. People on the street would constantly stop and remark on how adorable little Amber was.

Some went as far as to suggest she could be in the pictures.

Had Amber ever acted on camera before?

Deborah realized she might have a second chance at stardom after all. This time with her daughter. She quickly focused all of her attention on preparing Amber for a life in show business. It wasn't long before Amber was auditioning for television commercials. Local ads. Anything to put Amber's radiant smile out there in the cosmos. A bright, shining star.

But that would all pale to the role of a lifetime, only a few years away . . . That role would be none other than Jessica Ford in Lee Ketchum's seminal Don't Tread on Jessica's Grave.

Amber's life would soon change forever.

Amber would soon meet Jessica.

TWO

The trailer is a mess. The air thickened, congealed, as soon as I walked in. Had to hold my breath. Such a suffocating space. How long had Amber Pendleton been living in this dump?

I attempt a quick tally of all the empties lining the window. The wine bottles clustered along the kitchenette countertop. So many colors. Green glass, brown. Some are half filled with liquid. Others are stuffed with cigarette butts. I spot the crumpled Pall Mall packs. A pyramid of cans on the table. Stray tendrils of sun reach past the slats in the blinds, casting their light through the various colored glass, until the walls are speckled in an alcoholic's constellation.

It reminds me of a tidbit I had read regarding Ella Louise Ford. She was something of an herbalist, back in the day. The walls of her cottage had apparently been filled with mason jars full of primitive remedies. Roots and powders. Eye of newt, probably.

No wonder everybody thought she had been a witch back then.

Maybe Miss Pendleton's working on her own spells out here.

Double, double, drink and trouble . . .

"Have a seat," Amber says over her shoulder as she wanders into the kitchenette. She pours herself a cup of something. I can't see what. All I spot is the coffee mug:

WORLD'S BEST MOM.

I've got to figure out where to sit. Nothing's particularly inviting, if you catch my drift. I settle on a folding chair residing in the dining area. I drag it into the living room space, doing my best not to knock over any of the stalagmites of yellowed movie magazines.

"Thank you for agreeing to talk with me, Miss Pendleton . . ."

"We're not talking yet," she says, sitting herself down on a musty love seat. The slightest puff of dust takes to the air, spiraling through the slits of colored sunlight.

I take her in and imagine her outside, in the woods, the pines, in the snow, the white flakes drifting around her face. At this low level of light, I have an easier time finding the face I remember from all the newspaper articles, the news broadcasts. The *Entertainment Tonight* profile. The hatchet job on *Inside Edition*. Bill O'Reilly downright eviscerated her, making no qualms of expressing his own personal opinions about Miss Pendleton.

The Horror Movie Murderer.

Hollywood's Latest Murderess.

Child Star Killer.

I've got to take a moment to privately acknowledge the fact that I'm now sitting directly across from Miss Amber Lee Pendleton. Former child star. Murder suspect. She's got to be somewhere in her fifties, well beyond the age when Hollywood puts its stars out to pasture. So much ink had been spilled over her, twenty years back—and now, well, now it seems as if nobody cares. Not anymore. Everybody's moved on, leaving Miss Pendleton behind. To marinate in the past. Does anyone want to hear her story now? Her side of the story? Her secrets?

"My name's Nathaniel Denison. I produce a podcast called—"

"Podcast."

Was that a question? I wonder. It's difficult to say. "Digital radio, only you can listen to it whenever you want," I clarify, hoping it might help. I didn't notice a television set or a radio or a laptop or a carrier pigeon. Nothing. No contact with the outside world. "It's called *Who Goes There?* and—"

"Never heard it."

"That's okay. We have around two hundred thousand subscribers, which isn't bad for a—"

"You have a face for radio." She chuckles before slipping into a coughing fit. Something phlegmy loosens itself in her throat after a few hacks, which she promptly swallows.

I hadn't expected Amber to be this . . . *blunt.*

I don't really know what the hell I expected, to be honest.

Definitely not this.

Not her.

"Well, as I'm sure you know, the eighty-fifth anniversary of Ella Louise and Jessica Ford's death is tonight and I was—"

Amber smiles—or her lips do something that almost approximates a smile. There's no pleasure in this, but now that I've said it, said their names, their familiar aural shapes taking to the atmosphere, cutting through the miasma clouding her RV, she seems . . . I don't know.

Relieved.

Now she knows my number. She leans back in her seat, not saying a word. Just staring my way.

So I forge ahead. "The anniversary of their death is tonight and I figured it was time to look back at the history of—"

"Look back?"

Christ, is this woman purposely fucking with me?

She keeps throwing me off. Needling me. I spot the slightest grin playing across her lips just as she brings her mug up, eclipsing her mouth to take a long sip. If I'm not mistaken, I detect the slightest tremor in her wrist. Her hands can barely hold her mug without trembling. Parkinson's?

"Yes," I persist. "Time to reappraise the past. I think it's long overdue that someone reexamine the Fords and all the stories surrounding them. Their lives, their deaths. The town itself. The movies. Both movies. All of it. There's a story to be told here, and I believe people haven't heard the half of it . . . And that means hearing from you, too, Miss Pendleton."

Now I've got her attention. She's listening. Actually *listening.*

I've got her now. She's all ears.

"You want to reappraise my past?"

"I want to hear your side of the story, Miss Pendleton."

"Nothing left to tell."

"I don't think that's true—"

"I've said everything I needed to say—"

"I don't believe—"

"*I've spoken my piece.*" She says it so forcefully, I feel the trailer rock on its haunches. Or maybe I just imagine it. The contents of her mug—dark liquid, coffee, perhaps—fall to the floor, staining the carpet. Joining so many other spills.

Fuck. *Fuck.* I pushed too hard. I backed her into a corner. She's feeling attacked. I've got to coax her back. I soften my tone, almost whispering, "I think something traumatic happened to you as a child that set you on a course that you've never been able to steer yourself away from. I think it has haunted you your entire life. All through childhood. Well on into your adulthood. I think you were forced to revisit that trauma when you returned to Pilot's Creek in 1995. I think it was too much for you, even then. I think you reexperienced something that only made matters worse, not better. But no one ever asked you, really asked you, what happened. They had passed judgment before hearing you out. Am I right? No one understands, Miss Pendleton, because nobody wants to believe. Really believe the true story. Your story . . ."

A cloud must have passed over the trailer park outside. The sunlight recedes. Amber's trailer lapses into darkness. In the silence, within the stillness of the cramped space, I can suddenly hear the slightest tinkle of glass against glass, as if the trailer itself just shifted, the surrounding bottles bristling against one another. The faintest peal of a hundred wind chimes.

Amber keeps still. Her expression is blank, but her eyes have sharpened. She resents me for saying these things out loud, I can tell. Giving her thoughts a voice, like this.

But she hasn't denied it.

Hasn't kicked me out.

Not yet.

I'm no psychologist, but it doesn't take a PhD to diagnose this basket case. She's clearly damaged goods. Probably has been her whole life. She's slowly committing suicide out here, drinking herself to death in her steel-lined coffin of a trailer. But there's one thing I am most certain about when it comes to people, no matter how off their rocker . . .

They always have a story to tell.

Are dying to tell.

All they need is someone to listen.

I want to listen. I have my Olympus ready to record and everything.

"I think people deserve to hear what you have to say. Don't you, Miss Pendleton? Don't you think it's time? I think you've kept this secret for far too long. I think it's taken a toll on you, ma'am. Bottling it up, like this. I'm sorry, but this"—I look around the room, hammily exasperated—"this is no way to live. You can't hide in your trailer for the rest of your life."

"Who says I can't?"

I can picture her on set. Getting her makeup on. Sitting for hours in the special effects trailer, staring at her own reflection in the mirror, watching herself transform into Jessica.

Then Ella Louise.

No wonder she lives in a RV park now. Probably the only moments of peace for this poor woman were when she used to sit in that swivel chair in those suffocating trailers and become someone else.

One of the Fords.

Amber has been a surrogate to the Ford family her entire life.

A changeling.

"Something has kept you here in Pilot's Creek," I say. "Something you can't let go of . . . What is it? I want to hear your side of the story. And I'm not alone. I know you've wanted to talk about it. The true story. Your story. I can tell. But you're afraid nobody will believe you."

"No one," she barely says.

I seize on this. Have to. I'm finally getting somewhere. Gaining some traction. Baby steps. Leaning forward, I implore, "But that's not true. That's not true at all. I believe you, Miss Pendleton. People want to believe. They just need to hear from you. They want the truth."

She isn't looking at me anymore. I may as well have not been in the room. Her attention drifts off to some spot, some far-off place in her mind, losing herself.

"Jessica . . ."

"Yes. That's right. Tell me about Jessica." I need to be careful. If I push too much, the bubble will burst. The moment will be gone. She'll snap out of it and I'll be fucked.

"I . . . I saw . . ."

"What did you see?" Gently, now. Just a little nudge.

Let the question guide her to the answer.

"I . . . I saw Jessica."

Boo-ya.

"Show me, Miss Pendleton," I say. "Please. I want to see her. Will you show—"

Glass shatters not two feet from my face.

The window to my left has burst open.

I recoil as a rock lands on the stained carpet and rolls to a stop just before Amber's feet. She leaps up, immediately electrified, alive again, quickly scooping the rock up with a swift sweep of her hand and grabbing some broken glass along the way. I merely sink deeper into my seat as she pitches the rock back at her invisible assailants.

"You can't scare me," Amber shouts out the gaping window. "You little chickenshits better run! I'll find you! I'll find you in the middle of the night! While you sleep!"

There's laughter outside the window.

Boys' laughter.

Amber turns back. Her hand has tightened into a fist. Blood seeps through her fingers, speckling the floor red. Her leaden breath won't settle, her chest heaving. Her inhales are wet.

"You wanna hear my story?" she asks. "All right. I've got a story for you . . ."

PILOT'S CREEK, VIRGINIA, IS A FORGOTTEN TOWN. JUST WANDERING ALONG *Main Street makes that clear. Most of its storefronts have long since shuttered. Only the diner is still open on the main drag. The shelves of the library are mostly bare, its books borrowed and never returned. A staggering percentage of its people live well below the poverty line. Towns like Pilot's Creek remain frozen in time, trapped within its own past and unable to move forward. To escape itself.*

But there . . . in the window of the library, I see a paper cutout of a woman wearing a pointy hat. She's sitting on a broom. She has a long nose. This blackened silhouette is unmistakable all across town. In storefronts. Tacked to community boards among the other leaflets. They're promoting the only industry left here in town, the only thriving business they have: The Legend of the Little Witch Girl. Cemetery tours. T-shirts (I Saw The Little Witch Girl!). Mugs. Keychains. A small museum run out of someone's living room. Self-published books. Even a doll.

Whether the people of Pilot's Creek are believers or not, one thing is clear . . . They know that the only reason people return to their town is to visit the grave of Jessica Ford. She and her mother have kept their grip on this superstitious town, and they've squeezed the life out of it.

Hmm. Scratch that last part. Doing the segment over. Five, four, three, two . . .

Route 60 remains the main artery between Pilot's Creek and the rest of civilization. When the then-new Interstate 23 was built, forty years ago, most traffic was redirected away from Pilot's Creek. The town suffered a major blow to its remaining commerce. No one drives through Pilot's Creek anymore . . . Not on purpose, at least. Not unless, that is, they have come to see Jessica

And they do. Like believers of a newfound religion, fans of the film Don't Tread on Jessica's Grave *all flock to Pilot's Creek, just to see if they can catch a peek at the Little Witch Girl . . .*

THREE

The diner is the only thing open after five. Whatever storefront businesses are still hanging on for dear financial life here in Pilot's Creek have all closed for the day, save for the greasy spoon. I'm not particularly hungry, but I figure this is an opportunity to fill out the story a bit. I left Miss Pendleton in her trailer, promising to pick her up later that evening.

Time to soak up some more of that local color. Maybe collect a quote or two about Jessica Ford.

Talk about a Formica throwback. This isn't one of those prefab Greek greasy spoons you spot cropping up along the Jersey Turnpike. This is the real soda-jerk deal.

The waitress working the empty tables didn't make eye contact with me when I walked in. The rattle of the brass bell just over my head was enough to announce my grand entrance.

I sat at the counter, alone, taking the place in. The soda fountain. The cake dome perched at the end of the counter, covering a coagulated key lime pie. The place even has tin signs nailed along the back wall, promoting long-forgotten brands of ice cream and cigarettes.

And there they are.

I zero right in on them. I've got a radar for this shit. The Negro faces painted across the bygone advertisements. Their big grins.

Their swollen red lips. Their blindingly white teeth.

Mmm-mmm! Drink this! Hoooo, boy, smoke this!

Aaaand smile!

I spin away from the signs on my stool. Away from Pilot's Creek past, on display for all to see. I bet nobody has ever asked the owners to take that shit down, so they stay up. In front of everybody. In front of me.

Should I? Should I make a stink about—

Hold up.

There, tucked off in the far booth at the corner of the diner, is this wisp of a man. Guess I'm not the only patron in this shit-bucket after all. This fella is hunched over a cup of coffee, hands buried below the table. Has he been there this whole time? He's staring out at the—

"What'll it be?"

The waitress is upon me before I even know it, giving me a start. I play it off as best I can. Not that she minded one way or another. She's a little on the hefty side. Too much of that key lime pie, I bet. She pulls a pencil out from her hair. There are a few other pencils piercing her bun, as a matter of fact, as if she stuck them in her hair and promptly forgot them all. A tired sea urchin.

"What do you recommend?"

"*Recommend?*" It's clear she doesn't like the word one bit, tasting it in her mouth before spitting it back out. "Don't matter much to me. Order what you want."

"How about a coffee for starters?"

Her back is already to me as she mutters, "Suits me just fine."

I turn to the old man again, just to make sure the fogey is still there. That I didn't make him up. Sure enough, he hasn't moved. At all. He still remains in the same position as before, hands still buried below the table, still hovering above that cup of coffee. Nowhere near drinking it. His clothes hang a little too loose for his frame, as if he's shrunk down a size since first purchasing them. Or maybe he raided the Salvation Army for them. They look like hand-me-down attire. Moth-eaten flannel shirt, wrinkled collar, a missing button or two.

A scarecrow.

That's what he reminds me of. This man's spine must be a broomstick. His lopsided head is a pillowcase stuffed with straw, ready to tumble off his own wooden neck.

There's no way that could be a man.

The waitress ambles back with a half-empty pot and pours me a cup. I watch the grit swirl around the bottom of the glass urn. Not the freshest brew. I take a sip and manage to swallow it. Somehow. Tastes burnt. Rancid acid flushes my stomach. This pot has probably been sitting on the burner since this morning when she first opened, scorching the flavor out.

"Anything else?"

Time to slip into action. "I was thinking about going on one of these ghost girl tours . . . Which one do you recommend?"

"All the same, if you're asking me." She leans one hip against the counter, plucking another pencil from her hair. What happened to the last one? "You hungry or is coffee gonna be all?"

I smile, fighting back the black acid rising up from my stomach. "Guess it must get pretty grating, huh? All these tourists swooping in. Snapping pictures of witches and whatnot. I bet you've seen your fill of strange folks flocking around town."

"Way of the world, I reckon."

"Yes, well, if the world has witches in it . . . But you don't believe in witches, do you?"

The waitress doesn't respond. Only stares back with a dull expression that's enough of a retort to my inquiry. She looks tired. Not because of her shift, but the weight of this town. The gravitational pull of the grave has dragged the bags under her eyes down, down, all the way down her cheekbones. Her flesh is slowly falling straight off her face.

"I was wondering if you might tell me a little bit about Amber Pendleton," I say.

"What's to tell?"

"I'd imagine quite a lot."

"Says who?"

"I'm sorry." I regroup, still maintaining that smile. "You must get this all the time. Forgive me." I have a twenty under my palm. I slide my hand across the table, closer to the waitress's apron. She regards my fingers without much of any fluctuation in her expression.

"I'm working on a story," I say. "About Pilot's Creek. About Amber Pendleton."

"You a reporter." Not a question. Just a statement of fact.

"Something like that."

"You is or you ain't, so what are you? You a reporter or not?"

"I'm a journalist. I'd like to ask you some questions about Amber—"

The waitress walks away. Simply plows through the fanning doors leading to the kitchen and doesn't come back.

So much for southern hospitality, I think. *I'd love to see the Yelp reviews for this place.*

"These woods whisper."

Talk about a grizzled timbre. The voice comes from over my shoulder. Just at my back. I would've thought whoever said it was standing right behind me.

I spin back around and find no one there. Nobody else is in the diner, save for the old man in his booth. All the way at the far end of this empty space. He still hasn't moved.

"People think nobody's listening," the scarecrow says to no one. "But that's not true. The trees listen. Always listening. The woods know what the people of Pilot's Creek have done."

"Excuse me?"

"Every last romantic tryst. The suicides. The lynchings. You name it. These trees will testify to them. These woods have witnessed it all . . ."

Secrets. He's talking about secrets.

This town's deepest, darkest truths.

I grab my Olympus and coffee and rush over to the booth. Slide right on into the upholstered seat facing this ancient husk of a human being and place the recorder before him.

The man doesn't seem to mind. Or notice. Or move. His body remains upright, that broomstick of a backbone holding the rest of his weary self, refusing to let him fall.

Now I can finally get a good look at the man.

Up close.

He has more wrinkles than actual features to his face. A constellation of liver spots crowd his forehead and taper up to his scalp, scattering under a shock of white cornsilk hair. His mouth hangs open. There has to be a tooth or two in there, but not much else. Yellow things. Look more like corn kernels.

"What about the woods?" I scramble to catch up to the conversation. Find the thread and follow it. Let it lead me to the right questions. To the story. "What happened in the woods?"

"You wanna hear about Jessica, don't you? Course you do. That's why you're here, isn't it? Tonight of all nights . . ."

Here we go, I think. *Holy shit, this is gold.* The old coot is going to be an absolute treasure trove of sound bites. This is the kind of find NPR goes batshit over.

"What about tonight?" I ask. "What's so special about tonight? Is it Jessica?"

"You brought me a bottle?" The fogey leans forward, bringing his arthritic hands up from below the table and placing them on either side of his coffee cup. His cold coffee. The knot of his knuckles looks painful. It must be impossible for them to pick anything up.

His coffee cup. There's nothing in it.

"Bottle . . .?"

"Don't be stingy on me, now," the scarecrow hisses, licking his lips. "That's my price of admission. You want to hear a story, you better goddamn well have brought me an offering."

"I can—I can get you a bottle. Sure. Absolutely. What are you thirsty for?"

This affirmation sends the old man into a fit of ecstasy. He can already taste the liquor, I can tell. The smile that lifts up from his lips leaves me feeling queasy. "Bless you. Oh, bless you . . ."

How is this man even alive? He has to be a hundred years old. A hundred, easy. There is absolutely no muscle to him. Just shriveled skin and bones and that's about it. The flesh at his gullet is gathered into a grizzled turkey wattle, swaying back and forth with each wet inhale.

"I'll get you something to drink, don't worry. But before I go, I was wondering if you could tell me a little bit about Amber Pendleton. Do you know Amber Pendleton? She lives—"

"Been so long . . ." The man drifts. His eyes are lapsing. Sinking back into his sockets. Jesus, those eyes look disgusting. They've gone all gray. Like oysters. Pearls of phlegm.

Can he even see? Can he see me? Or am I just a voice in the dark?

"Have you met Miss Pendleton?" I keep at him. "Do you know—"

"You hear that, Jessica? I did my part." The old coot's talking gibberish now. He's definitely not talking to me. "Just like I was supposed to. Like I've always done."

"Amber Pendleton," I try again. "She's been living out at the Whispering Pines—"

The waitress slams her hand down on the table, onto my Olympus, as if she were swatting a fly. Spoons rattle. "That's enough of that," she hisses.

"Hold on a sec." I glance up to her stern face and shrink, as if I were some kid caught passing notes in class. "I was just—"

"Pay your bill and move on, you hear? I don't want you coming back."

"I was just asking a few questions."

"I know what you're doing. We don't talk about that in here. We don't talk about that witch in here. Not in this establishment, not anywhere else in this town."

"Are you suggesting you truly believe Amber Pendleton is a witch?"

"Don't say her name! Stop saying her name!"

"I'm within my rights to have a conversation—"

"Haven't you people done enough?"

"Who're you calling *you people*?"

"This is our home. This is our lives you're meddling with. You can't just waltz on in here and peck at our past! Acting like crows on carrion! Now get the hell out before I call the sheriff."

I glance back to the old man. As if he'd be able to help. As if some flame of recognition might reignite in his mind and demand I stay. But the man has already drifted back to that blank spot between this world and wherever his memories refuse to let him go.

"Please," he begs to that emptiness, that black hole before him. "Please forgive us. Forgive us all. Release me."

ACCORDING TO THE MOST RECENT CENSUS, LESS THAN FIFTEEN HUNDRED
people call Pilot's Creek home today. That's a drastic decline for a once-thriving town. While there's no direct explanation for the population drop, it has been whispered among certain townsfolk that a particular citizen may have something to do with it . . . even if she's six feet underground.

Even to this day, Jessica holds sway here.

Pilot's Creek was originally settled in 1803. The wooded community at that point was called "Pin Hook," up until 1823, when Virginia statesman John J. Pilot claimed the surrounding county for his family. Pilot's Creek had been a destination hub for the lumber industry for years. The enormous swaths of conifers surrounding the town were cut and pulped by the local paper mill. Its pines made for perfect masts. But that was the Pilot's Creek of the past. Today, its mills have all shut down. The timber trade has moved on and left Pilot's Creek behind. Only the pines remain.

Eldridge Ford III formed Ford Timberland with his business associates back in 1907. Their first purchase was a modest two thousand acres of timberland in northern Virginia. Ford's logging operation began to stretch along the Blue Ridge until finally finding its way to Pilot's Creek.

It was here that Ford decided to stake his claim in the surrounding conifers and build his base, along with his family home. It wouldn't be long before he and his wife, Prudence, would have their first—and only—child. Ella Louise Ford. After her birth, the Ford family would forever be rooted to the soil of Pilot's Creek in more ways than they could ever have anticipated.

Pilot's Creek would be their grave.

FOUR

The game plan is simple: Record the next episode of *Who Goes There?* on top of Jessica Ford's grave, alongside the infamous actress who played both roles:

Jessica in the original, Ella Louise in the remake.

I'd get her to open up about her experiences there. A blow-by-blow of what happened. This is her chance to set the record straight. Then, once I have everything recorded, with scalpel-like precision, I will dive in and debunk each and every claim Amber makes.

Once I have her story, her version of it, I can do whatever I want with it. I can edit it to fit my own developing narrative. Sculpt it. Already the spine of the piece is formulating itself. Bit by bit, vertebra by vertebra, my own version of this story is growing.

What if I drag the truth out of her? Catch her in her web of deception? There's so much to play with here. Too much. So many details. I keep uncovering little nuggets of gold. I don't think this is all going to fit into one episode anymore.

What if it's three episodes? Jesus, a whole season in itself?

What if this is my Errol Morris moment?

My own reverse *Thin Blue Line*? This could be *The Jinx*! I'll expose her for the fraud she is. History will reevaluate her claims, thanks to my crusade to find the truth.

Who the hell are these people, anyway, turning this town into a theme park? Exploiting the darkest spot of their closed-minded past for money?

The people of Pilot's Creek deserve what's coming to them.

This town deserves to burn.

I booked a room at the Henley Road Motel. One night only. I don't plan on staying in this ass-backward town any longer than I absolutely have to. I'll rest for a spell, do a quick sound check with my recording gear and then head back to the trailer park around ten to pick Miss Pendleton up and chauffeur her out to the cemetery.

That's the plan.

In, out.

When I first checked into the room, I noticed the extra door. One of those inner door thingamajigs. It's two doors, actually, connecting my room to my neighbor's. All these roach motels have them. I hadn't paid it much mind before, dropping my travel case on the bed.

It's not until I start sound-checking my mic—"Testing, testing, one, two, three, testing, testing, one, two, three, microphone check, one two, what is this . . ."—that I hear the soft sweep of the neighboring inner door swiping across the carpet, wood on fabric, in my cans.

I turn. Pull down my headphones and listen. I swear I hear someone open the internal door.

From the other side.

Somebody must have just checked in next door. The room was dark when I walked by. Whoever is in there now must be testing the door to see what's on the other side. Maybe they mistook it for the bathroom. Maybe they want to see if the door works? Where it leads? Assess all possible exit strategies?

I can't hear anything without my headphones on, so I sling them around my shoulders.

I step up to my own inner door. I don't want to alarm my neighbor by opening it, so I lean in. Simply press my ear against the paneling.

And listen.

Someone is standing right there.

On the other side.

Whoever it is doesn't move. Doesn't say a word. But their presence is still palpable. Imposing. *This is silly*, I think as I grab the knob and twist my wrist. *I'll just ask them if everything is—*

The door to my neighbor's room is closed. Locked, as it should be. But it still takes me by surprise. I swear I . . .

Didn't I just hear . . . ?

Then what was . . . ?

Talking. Someone is talking from the other side of the inner door. I can hear it. The words are muffled, shapeless intonations, but the sound is unmistakable.

It's a woman's voice. A woman talking to someone else.

I am one layer closer to the room now. I can't help myself. I have to press my ear against her door. Listen in. Who is she talking to in there? What is she saying?

"—after the day's (*something-something*). Cutting loose. I bet you kids brought along (*something-something-something*) help unwind . . . Right?"

Amber. That's Amber Pendleton's voice.

I can't hear who she's talking to. Whoever she's having a conversation with, they never speak up. Is she on the phone? Is someone else in the room with her?

Did she check into the room next door?

Is she alone?

"That squeaky-clean image isn't so spotless, is it? (*Something-something.*)"

That has to be Amber.

Of course it's Amber. Who else could it be? That's her voice. But I left her at her trailer less than an hour ago. Hour, tops.

It has to be her.

I know what her voice sounds like. That's *her voice*.

Isn't it?

"Amber?" The moment I say it, I instantly regret it. *Idiot.* What the hell am I doing? Of course it's her. Of course it's Amber. I should just mind my own business. Give the poor woman a break. Dragging all this up is clearly taking its toll on her. Better to leave her alone.

Just leave her be.

Things are very silent next door. Whoever it is—*Amber, of course it's Amber, who else*—they're now listening to me. Whoever it is must have their ear pressed against the other side of the same door.

I slowly step back.

Away from the door.

Back into my room.

I push my own internal door shut as quietly as I can, careful not to make a sound. The latch clicks and I remain standing right where I am, staring at the paneling.

I turn on the TV and wrap myself up in a fatty layer of sound. To drown out everything else. To protect myself.

I can't rest. Can't nap. I'm having a hard time taking my eyes off the door, the inner door, almost as if I'm expecting it to open at any moment now.

For Amber to enter my room.

What would I do if she did?

As I leave for the night, I go ahead and peer inside the window next door.

Nothing.

The room is dark. The lights are turned off. My eyes can just barely make out the silhouette of the bed inside, neatly tucked in and made up. No suitcases. No bags. No nothing.

The room is completely empty.

ONE OF THE MORE ASTOUNDING ASPECTS OF I KNOW WHAT YOU DID ON JESSI-
ca's Grave—*for genre die-hards, at least—is that it would have ushered in the pending influx of meta-horror alongside Kevin Williamson and Wes Craven. Sergio Gillespie's failed feature film debut had all the hallmarks of* Scream. *The screenplay has been available online for some time now. You can read it, if you're so inclined. I did. What I find so intriguing about Gillespie's script is that it has the exact same knowing winks, the exact same self-referential banter that became so common in horror for the rest of the '90s. If the film had kept on schedule, Jessica would've just beaten* Scream *to the big screen and would have become the benchmark for all derivative horrors to come.*

It almost—almost—redefined the horror genre for generations. Instead, it became a footnote in a bizarre and lurid urban legend that has continued to evolve over the years. We've all heard of the Weinstein brothers buying a movie and then sitting on it, just to settle a petty self-serving score with the director. But has anyone, living or dead, studio exec or ghost, ever sabotaged a film from the inside out? Has anyone killed a movie before it was finished? Amber did just that.

Maybe a reboot just wasn't enough. To really refashion this ghost story, it needed to expand its narrative scope. This ghost story needed to grow.

An interesting narrative begins to develop, if you look closely . . . Every few decades, beginning with Don't Tread on Jessica's Grave, *the Legend of the Little Witch Girl resurfaces in a major way. Even though* I Know What You Did on Jessica's Grave *never made its way to the big screen, the story of its demise did . . . along with its supernatural source. I'd argue it made a larger cultural impact than any movie could have. More people today know about Jessica and her mom because of the alleged crime committed by Amber Pendleton than if her remake had come out.*

I reached out to Gillespie for this episode to see if he had anything to say to Amber Pendleton. He wasn't the easiest man to find, having moved back to his hometown. He's directed a few commercials for local car dealerships, but beyond that, he remains imprisoned in director's jail, that fabled place where studios consign their auteurs after helming big-budget fiascos. Still living in the basement of his parents' home, Gillespie claims to have moved on with his life. That he's left Jessica and Amber behind . . . but it's clear some ghosts refuse to die.

Gillespie did not want to be recorded for this podcast. He would not let me record our interview, short as it was.

Same with Lee Ketchum. I tracked down the director of the original Don't Tread on Jessica's Grave *in a retirement community in rural New Jersey. Ketchum now spends his days hooked up to an oxygen tank, staring out the window of his bedroom. Watching his movie play out in his mind, I imagine, over and over again. Struggling to breathe. When I visited him one sunny Sunday afternoon, I was met with a similar response as Gillespie . . . He refused to talk.*

Nobody wants to talk about Jessica. Not the men who fashioned their film careers on her story. Whoever has dared to tell Jessica Ford's story has disappeared from the public. They've either run far, far away from her—or they live in total obscurity. Alone. In the dark. As if they're all hiding. But hiding from whom?

FIVE

Their black eyes stare back at me without blinking. There's got to be six of them.

Seven.

No, sorry—eight. The glint of my flashlight reflects off their cold, lifeless eyes.

The litter of rain-drenched teddy bears circle Jessica's headstone. Their fur has faded from all the months out here in the cold. The constant barrage of rain has sapped their color.

The soggy display reminds me of my little sister's bed. It was always covered with a mound of stuffed animals. Even then, at age ten, when I attempted to count all the teddy bears piled up around her pillows, I couldn't help but think of the grainy black-and-white photographs of lynchings from my American history textbook. The dead bodies hanging from the trees.

Their blank eyes. Glaring up at the gray winter sky, unblinking.

Like marbles.

Like the eyes of Danielle Strode.

History is always watching you, I think. *Always at your back. Turn around and you'll find its lifeless eyes staring right at you. Waiting to see if you'll break the cycle.*

Waiting to see if history is gonna repeat itself.

Over and over again.

Not this time.

Not with me.

I'm not afraid of history. Not afraid of the past.

Not some ghost.

There's enough to be afraid of in the present for me, thank you very much. All these people, all these Ambers, the people of Pilot's Creek, living in the past. They're the ones who make the world a messed-up place. Believing this shit. Believing in witches. It's their ignorance, their unwillingness to see the truth, see their own shortcomings, their own bigotry and sexism, that permits these bogeywomen to exist. Makes me sick. Makes me want to shine a big, bright fucking spotlight right into their faces and say, *Don't you see? Don't you get it? The only monsters around here are you. Not some mother and daughter who got burned at the stake. You.*

The molding stuffed animals that lie at Jessica Ford's grave are offerings. Alms for the dead. Even Little Witch Girls need to play with something every now and then.

There are other items. A toy race car. A heart keychain. A soggy Snickers bar, half eaten, a tendril of caramel oozing out from its torn wrapper. Anything to satisfy the witch.

I spot an empty Heineken bottle.

Cigarette butts.

The careless litter of thrill seekers left behind after spending a night out here in the cemetery, waiting to catch a glance of Jessica's ghost as it wanders along her lonesome grave. I had spent an evening back at my apartment sifting through videos uploaded to YouTube. Dozens of personal graveside testimonies. Mini *Blair Witches.* We're talking crappy home movies. Out of focus. Muffled voices. Amateur ghost hunters and dipshit couples wandering out into the cemetery in the middle of the night, filming their vigils with their camera phones.

Waiting for Jessica to arrive. Waiting for her ghost to materialize.

Waiting for her to reach out.

Take their hand.

After several bleary-eyed hours and over umpteen uploaded videos, I had not found one single, actual, real-life, documented sighting of Jessica Ford's ghost.

Now it's my turn.

The headstone barely comes to my knee. I can't make out the inscription. The sandstone has long since worn down. Just the slope of the *J* and the upper flecks of an *s* are left behind.

The graffiti is far more legible. Someone took it upon themselves to spray-paint across the crumbling tomb in bright, neon pink:

HERE LIES JESSICA FORD.
MAY SHE ALWAYS BURN.

It's from *Don't Tread on Jessica's Grave*. Whoever vandalized her headstone decided to paint over Jessica Ford's actual inscription with the one from the film version. They sprayed too close to the surface, though. The pink paint bled before the letters could dry.

It's not lost on me that the paint is the same color as that on the side of Amber's trailer.

I snap off a shot with my camera phone. The image will make a great icon for the website. I'll Photoshop some text across the headstone: *WHO GOES THERE? THE REMAKING OF THE LITTLE WITCH GIRL OF PILOT'S CREEK.*

The crucifixes are sagging. They barely look like crosses anymore, the fence slowly corroding over the years. Each metal pillar leans at its own awkward angle, dragging the neighboring cross with it, until each flailing crucifix droops in one direction or another.

But here it is. I finally found it. I am finally seeing it with my own eyes.

Jessica Ford's grave.

What's left of it.

All this time the story has been so hypothetical. A will-o'-the-wisp in my imagination. Yeah, sure, I knew she was out here, somewhere, but up until I locked eyes on her tombstone, there was still a part of me that couldn't believe any of this was real.

That Jessica Ford wasn't real.

But here she is. Or some version of her, at least. I'm here to cut through the crap. The onion layers of legend. Peel it all back until I reach the core of the story.

Her story.

Her.

I turn to Amber, eager to see her reaction. I've got to admit, I'm feeling pretty charged over our little discovery. My pulse is picking up. There's an electric spark in the air.

But Amber barely registers the grave. Barely looks up from the ground. She has been pretty quiet ever since we arrived at the cemetery, wrapping her arms around her chest to keep warm. Or hide. Who knows what the hell's going through her head right now. She won't say.

I convinced Amber to drive out to the Pilot's Creek Cemetery with me to commemorate the eighty-fifth anniversary of the actual murders of Ella Louise and Jessica Ford. I had to promise a few extra shekels to pave over her current financial rough patch, as long as she kept that part just between the two of us. Look, she's obviously in a bad way. Those royalty checks aren't coming in anymore. Not for a forty-five-year-old film. And Amber hasn't done a convention appearance in over twenty years. No one will take her.

She needs this.

Needs me.

The drive to Pilot's Creek Cemetery with Amber was totally stilted. I figured it might be a good opportunity to start the interview. I had whipped up a laundry list of questions to ask in the rental car. I'd record her answers while documenting our descent into the surrounding pines.

Toward the cemetery.

Everybody loves ambience in their podcasts. The peal of tires over pavement. The hum of a motor. When people listen to these episodes, they want to feel as if they are there.

They want to imagine they're in Pilot's Creek.

In the woods.

I could replicate the aural sensation of the pines swaying in the breeze, the bitter chill in the air, the darkness all around. I've mastered the art of sound design over the course of constructing these episodes, perfecting my podcast with each subsequent chapter. I could go back and embellish the sounds later in post. Tweak them. Enhance them. Even create a few extra clicks and clacks along the way, just to enrich the listening experience.

I want my listeners to believe they're in the car.

With Amber.

I want them to hear the brittle crackle of gravel underneath the tires, getting kicked up and clattering against the underbelly of the car. On our way to the cemetery.

To Jessica's grave.

But Amber, my fading star, is a horrible interview subject. Nothing but one monosyllabic answer after another. Whenever I prod her to elaborate, she only turns away from the Olympus and stares out her window. To the darkness all around.

"So I'm curious," I start for the fifteenth fucking time, straining to mask my questions under the guise of small talk.

"What do you think it is about Jessica Ford's story that sticks in everybody's craw? What gives her urban legend more power than others?"

"I don't know."

"But you've thought about it, haven't you? There are plenty of urban legends out there. Not all of them get movies made about them, let alone two. Why her? What's her deal?"

"I don't know."

"Come on . . ."

Silence from Amber.

Time to change my approach. Attack from another angle. "When's the last time you came out here? To the cemetery?"

"Twenty years."

That's surprising. I had to pick that apart. "For real?"

"For real."

"You've lived here all this time and you haven't come out here since . . . since filming?"

"Yes."

"Not even once?"

"No."

"You're messing with me . . . There's no way that's true."

"No."

"Well . . . Why not?"

Silence.

"There's gotta be a reason. You don't move all the way to Pilot's Creek, after everything that's happened, after everything you've gone through, set up shop down the street from the most decisive moment in your life and not come out here, not even just once, for no reason."

I assumed she wasn't going to answer. I'd get a grunt from her and that would be the end of it. But after a breath of silence, she finally spoke. "Wasn't time."

What was with the cryptic answers all of a sudden? Jesus, I was getting pissed. Why the hell was she shutting down? Why wasn't she talking? Why did she agree to come here, take my money and waste my fucking time if she wasn't even going to answer me?

What was she so afraid of?

"What about your mother?" I asked. A bit more forcefully than I intended, but still. I hoped it hadn't sounded like as much of a dig as it had come out.

Silence from Amber. Her focus was out the passenger-side

window. To the pines surrounding us. So many trees out here. It would be so easy to get lost.

To lose yourself.

I doubled down. "What do you think she'd say about you living here?"

"She's dead."

"Sorry," I had to concede. I already knew she had passed away. Cancer of some kind. The lungs, most likely. "What do you think she would say? If she knew you were here?"

"Don't."

Okay. Okay, now we're talking. I could work with this. "Oh?" My voice lifted an octave. "Why's that?"

"Don't go," she echoed. Her voice was hollow. Distant. I started to fret that the Olympus wouldn't pick any of this up, her voice lost to the ambient sound all around.

The hum of the engine.

The crumbling road.

To the pines.

The radio said it was 10:35. I wanted to make it to the cemetery with plenty of time to get the lay of the land. Record the ambience. Wander the grounds. Perhaps get Amber to give a little tour. I knew the chapel had burned down decades ago. The people of Pilot's Creek still hadn't gotten around to rebuilding it, all these years later. Probably never would.

I parked at the entrance. The gate had collapsed back, no longer held up on its own hinges. I was ready to scale the fence, but it appeared like I could just walk right on in.

The grass was dead. Browned all around. I hadn't checked the weather report, but I didn't remember anything about it being this dry. When was the last time someone tended to these grounds? Had the town completely forgotten their cemetery?

My flashlight found the first row of graves.

"After you," I said.

I should have come during the day first. Bad call on my part. I couldn't get my bearings out here. The cemetery felt super tiny and vast and expanseless at the same time. I couldn't tell if I was three rows in or thirty. Weeds choked most of the headstones, until there was no telling who was buried where. My foot accidentally kicked a toppled tombstone, sending my ass stumbling forward a few steps before I could correct my balance.

Tomorrow, I thought. I'd come back tomorrow. In the day.

When there's sun.

Now all I had was my flashlight and a fucking nutcase who seemed to know exactly where she was going, weaving through the tombs without tripping or—

There it was.

Holy shit, there it was.

The fence! I recognized it as soon as my flashlight brushed over its crucifixes, wilted with rust.

Here was Jessica.

Jessica Fucking Ford.

"Found you," I said.

WHAT IS A GHOST STORY? WHAT POWER DOES IT HOLD OVER ITS LISTENER?

Amber Pendleton believed in ghosts. She had been haunted by them her whole life. Whenever she looked at herself in the mirror or saw her image blown up to enormous proportions on the silver screen, she didn't see herself . . . she saw the phantoms that had been following her ever since she was a girl. She saw Ella Louise Ford. She was Jessica Ford, the Little Witch Girl of Pilot's Creek.

So . . . what happened to Amber Pendleton? The real Amber? She vanished. Disappeared from the public eye. But her films remained. Her ghost lingered, wandering over the screen for all to see.

Amber Pendleton had become her own ghost story.

SIX

It's nearly time.

Amber senses the seconds counting down in her head. She can nearly hear the *tick-tick-tick* all around her, as if each and every last pine needle is the second hand, *tick-tick-tick*ing away. She doesn't need a watch to tell her the clock is closing in on four minutes after midnight.

So much of her life has been spent returning to these woods.

In reality, this is only her third time setting foot in the cemetery. And yet, night after night, for fifty years now, Amber walks down this exact path at nearly the exact same hour. Her dreams have charted out the terrain of the graveyard and the surrounding woods until she knew its layout by heart.

By heart.

From the moment she stepped into the cemetery, every fiber in her body screamed for her to run. Run far away. Run away from this god-awful place and never return.

But there is another voice, a little girl's voice, whispering to Amber. It is clearer to hear in Amber's mind. More forthright. Even with the tender lilt of its intonations, it is simple to sense the strength in Jessica's voice. The absolute power buried within her benign request . . .

Come to me . . .

Come to me . . .

Come . . .

The Fords—their story—still hasn't let Amber go.

Not yet.

Amber has tried to be strong, tried so hard to resist, but the gravitational pull of Jessica's grave dragged her back to Pilot's Creek all those years ago. She has orbited this patch of land for two decades. Waiting. Waiting for her cue to enter.

Amber understands what Jessica is asking of her. What she needs Amber to do. Amber understands that she will help finish telling this story when the time is right.

Tonight.

Now.

Tonight Amber has brought a witness.

But first, she needs to set Jessica free. She needs to find her mother's grave. Take her to the clearing where Ella Louise is buried and reunite her with her daughter at long last.

Bury them together.

Then, perhaps, they will finally release Amber.

Free her of their story.

Let her go.

Nathaniel is off recording ambient sound. They have some time to kill before four minutes after midnight, so he has ventured off, chasing crickets or something silly like that. Lord only knows what. She almost feels sorry for him. *Almost.* But Amber understands now that there always needs to be a storyteller. Someone to tell the tale. Keep it spinning. Spinning.

Spinning.

Spinning.

Spinning.

Amber hesitates. She pauses long enough to take in the sight before her. Nathaniel is busy with his little recorder, not paying attention to what is happening along Jessica's grave.

The soil. It's . . .

Spinning.

Swelling. Something under the ground budges its way up until the dirt itself corkscrews outward.

Whatever it is, it's certainly small. Too small to be a finger. More like a worm wriggling up from the earth. Amber wouldn't have noticed it at all if she hadn't been so focused on her grave in the first place, if she hadn't been staring, waiting, for the page to turn and begin the next chapter of this story.

The soil puckers and cracks, peeling back to release a white filament.

A pale, slender sapling. The ghostly kudzu fans back and forth, unfurling itself even further.

Growing.

Then it bifurcates. The tendril branches out into two segments.

Amber squints. Strains to see what it can be. It certainly isn't a worm. It's too long to be that.

These look like roots. They have the slightest sheen. Almost like porcelain. Some kind of enamel.

Like a tooth.

A tooth.

Amber's tooth. She had planted it right here, right in the ground, over forty years ago. That exact spot. She lost her tooth during the shoot in '71 and she buried it in the soil directly above Jessica Ford's grave. She promptly forgot all about it but now—

Now—

Now it's growing. The roots of her upside-down tooth reach into the air, growing as fast as Jack's beanstalk, branching and segmenting and branching out again, each division uncurling itself, a phantasmal fern fanning through the air. She's looking at a picture of a circulatory system, like one of those images from science class, where you break down the body into its various systems. The nervous, the circulatory, the muscular, the digestive, and on and on . . .

Here—here is the phantasmal. The spectral system.

The palest veins.

The stalk of the tooth swells to a thicker girth, into a trunk. The first pair of fernlike tendrils to branch at the top now sway at their own pace, flexing and tensing through the air.

Arms. The thing that was once her tooth is now sprouting arms.

Sprouting legs.

Fingers.

Toes.

Before long, before reason kicks in and takes over and submits Amber to such notions as calling out for Nathaniel, for help, or running, or screaming bloody murder—she finds herself staring into the hollow cavities of Jessica's eye sockets. The fanning enamel forms into thicker sections, webbing themselves into a human form. Amber is looking at a skull.

Jessica is coming together.

Becoming whole.

How can Nathaniel not see this? Where has he gone? Does Jessica do this every night? Is this a part of her haunting? Or is this all for Amber's sake? It's so hard to tell, to know any of these answers. To know what's real anymore . . . But Amber doesn't mind. She could care less. What she finds most surprising is that she isn't afraid. Not a bit. She knew this moment would come. One day. And now that it's here, finally here, the clock closing in on four past midnight, *tick-tick-tick* the pine needles all whisper, where the ghost of Jessica will wander along the confines of her grave, Amber feels at peace.

The truth shall set you free . . .

And there she is.

All of her.

Jessica drifts along the circumference of her fence. She paces around the inside of her grave, stepping over the teddy bears staring blankly back at her with their marble eyes. The stuffed animals at her feet all turn their heads as she sashays by. She holds her hands behind her back, chin dipped to her chest. She walks like a child. Holds her body like a child. Playful. Dainty. Floating on a cloud. She seems unaware of what time it is or how cold it is, even where she is, blissfully ignorant to the notion that this is her own grave.

Does she even know she's dead?

Jessica glances up to Amber. It happens so quickly, it catches Amber off guard. She gasps as the air sticks in her throat. Jessica must have sensed the presence of people nearby.

Jessica stares at Amber.

And smiles.

She holds out her hand. Her palm faces up, her porcelain fingers fanning out. Amber suspects that this is what must have happened to Danielle, all those years ago. She must have seen Jessica wandering along her grave, just waiting for someone to come play with her. Danielle must have walked right up, and when nobody was looking, she must have taken Jessica's hand.

She's waiting.

Jessica is waiting for Amber to take her hand.

Waiting.

Waiting.

Yearning.

Amber takes a deep breath and does just what all the ghost stories warn people not to do.

Whatever you do . . .

She reaches her hand out to Jessica's.

Don't you ever . . .

She takes the ghost girl's hand into her own. She holds on. Holds on to the cold.

Never ever . . .

And just like that . . .

Don't!

Jessica is gone. Amber's hand remains held up in the air.

Holding nothing now.

SEVEN

"Woods ambience. October 16, 2016. 12:10 a.m."

The battery life on my Olympus is thirty-six hours, so I've got plenty of digital space to record every last footstep, every crackling branch, during our little sojourn through the woods.

These endless woods.

How long have we been walking? I check my watch again. Only five minutes have passed since the last time I looked.

That's odd. I thought it would've been longer.

These woods are throwing off my sense of direction. My sense of timing. I'm losing track of everything out here. Chalk it up to nervous energy. The excitement is really seeping in.

We're close to Ella Louise. So close. I can feel it.

I sling my headphones around my neck, pulling them up to my ear every so often to double-check the sound quality. The recorder's audio isolation is absolutely flawless. I could aim my Olympus at a bird from yards away and practically capture its heartbeat.

When I slip these headphones on, I feel as if I've suddenly removed myself from the moment. The actual walking in the woods. Like I'm now outside listening in.

Listening to myself.

This version of myself. Whatever my body is doing, it feels separate from my sense of hearing.

I'm all ears out here. Nothing else matters.

I might as well be at home, listening in. Listening to myself. My footsteps. The crackle of dried leaves under my feet. The snapping of a fallen branch.

It's all so crisp in here.

The sound in my head.

Much clearer than out there, in real life, the real world. I prefer the sound of it all. Far more than my other sensations. I wish I could mute my sense of sight, of smell, of everything else—and just lose myself to the sound of the buckling pines bending in the breeze, the bristle of their needles, faint but persistent, like the smallest waves rolling over sand.

I can hear Amber's footsteps.

That has to be her feet. For a moment, it almost sounds as if there is a third person walking alongside us—but no, that's just an auditory trick.

Rather than turn to look at her, I simply listen to her strides from within my noise-canceling over-the-ear headphones. Her gentle strides. *Swish-swish.* She never hesitates with her steps, not one misstep, forging ahead of me with an unnerving determination. Like she knows exactly where she's going.

Just who's leading who here?

"When did you become such a power walker?" I joke. "Can we—can we slow down?"

No response from Amber.

I had researched the Pilot's Creek woodlands. The vast expanse of conifers stretches on for miles in either direction. Google Maps wasn't much help. When I clicked around online, all I found was a digital carpet of pines. If Amber wasn't careful, she could end up getting both of us lost. She doesn't seem to be gauging her surroundings at all, simply plowing through the pines without looking where she's even going.

Ella Louise's unmarked grave has to be within walking distance of their cottage. Where it had once stood. For Wayne Reynolds and his co-conspirators to have dragged both her and Jessica out into the woods, they probably wouldn't have gone too far. They had their fair share of pines to pick and choose from. Cut its branches. Tie Ella Louise up and strike a match.

Let them both burn.

It's been debated online where the exact spot of their cabin had been. Considering there's nothing left of it, no foundation, I feel like it's pretty pointless to try tracking it down.

No, I want Ella Louise's grave.

That's the sweet spot. Those superstitious idiots were so frightened of the Fords, even after they murdered them, disposing of Ella's body in the middle of the woods while dropping Jessica in the Fort Knox of all coffins.

I have a few potential hotspots for their burning. But even that's speculation. For an event that happened eighty-five years ago, there's hardly any physical evidence left behind. No scorched earth. No seared stake still rooted to the ground. No singed tree limbs. Nothing.

Ella Louise has to be buried out here.

Somewhere.

I'm going to find it. Find her. Before anyone else. I can just imagine it. Taste it.

A cold case. Solved. By me.

Justice.

Corporate sponsorship.

Advertisers.

A television series. Move over, *Serial*. Buh-bye, Ira Glass . . . There's a new show in town. Here comes *Who Goes There?*, an original Showtime exposé series. A ten-episode show that delves into the unknown and shines a big fat fucking light on folklore's biggest fallacies.

Amber won't slow down.

I've got to pick up my stride just to keep up with the biddy. I can hear myself breathing heavily through the cans. My wheezing is picked up by the Olympus and filters through my headphones. The air has grown much colder now. My throat feels like it's coated in ice. My lung tissue crystalizes with every bitter breath.

Not Amber. She's been acting strange ever since we left the cemetery. Which is saying something. I had softballed a few questions her way and she hadn't answered a single goddamn one. Wouldn't dignify me with so much as a grunt. I might as well have been talking to myself.

Enough time has elapsed since my last stab. Time to try again.

"Tell me . . ." I cough. Clear my throat. The phlegm's building in my chest. The cold air is really going to aggravate my asthma if I stay out here all night. Not that Amber notices.

"Tell me," I try again. "Back in '95. The night when Danielle Strode went missing . . ."

I pause, just for a moment, just to see how she reacts. If she'll buck at the question. Resist. Turn around. Shut me down. But nothing. Nothing at all. She doesn't flinch or huff or puff.

Amber just keeps on walking. Striding. Cutting through these trees with such a sense of purpose. With such a sense of . . . *direction*.

"The news reports all mentioned that the police found you after they discovered Danielle's body. They said you were in some sort of fugue state. *Like sleepwalking*, one officer said. It took several hours before you even acknowledged anyone. You just woke up all of a sudden."

Nothing from Amber. No response. Jesus, is she even listening?

"When the police questioned you, you said you had no recollection of going out into the woods in the first place. That the last thing you remembered was being on set, filming your scene for *I Know What You Did on Jessica's Grave*. You said you remembered Danielle's mother, Janet Strode, running on set, beside herself, asking if anyone had seen her daughter."

Nothing from Amber.

Nothing at all.

"You said you remembered joining the search party. You took a flashlight along with everybody else on set and started walking through the woods . . ."

I point the Olympus at Amber's back, as if aiming a pistol.

Say something, I think. *Come on, come on, come on . . .*

"But then you separated yourself from the rest of the crew. Several witnesses went on record to say they saw you waltz off on your own. Like you knew where you were going."

I strain to hear any fluctuation in Amber's breathing through my headphones. If my directional mics pick up the slightest shift in her demeanor.

Anything.

"For somebody who said they didn't know where they were going or what had happened, it sure seemed to a lot of people like you knew *exactly* what you were doing."

Is her breathing deepening? Is she crying? Is she panicking at all?

What the hell's going on with her?

"You want to tell me where we're going, Miss Pendleton? Is this the way you took Danielle Strode? Did you lead her through these woods? Did you take her by the hand? What did you do with her? Were you two pretending to be Jessica and Ella Louise Ford together? Only Danielle didn't want to play? Did you leave her body out here, then head back to the set, film your scene like nothing happened? Only, when Mrs. Strode rushed in and started shrieking about her lost daughter . . . you panicked. You knew you'd gotten caught. You knew you had to do something."

My voice is escalating now. Growing louder. I can hear the echo of it in the surrounding woods. Reverberating off the pines and bouncing back through my headphones.

"You rushed back into the woods. Where you had hidden her.

You thought you could bury her. Simply dig a grave for her and hide her body out here where no one could find her."

What is Amber doing? Is she hyperventilating?

Is she breathing at all?

Where's the air?

"But when you realized that wasn't going to work, you did the next best thing. You made up a story about it. A ghost story. Lucky for you, there was one right here. Just waiting for you. *The Little Witch Girl did it*, right? *Not me.* No, not innocent Amber Lee Pendleton. Not—"

There's an intake of air.

Amber gasps.

Finally.

I would've been relieved, would have thought I had finally gotten to her, if it hadn't been for the fact that the breath had come from my side.

Amber is directly in front of me.

Not at my left

I halt midstride and turn, aiming the Olympus at the enveloping pines.

Nothing. Nothing at all.

Just the wind, as they say.

Amber hasn't stopped walking. I have to run to catch up. As soon as my feet clomp over the dead leaves, that slight brittle crackle right under my heels, I swear I hear someone whisper just over my shoulder. I don't hear it in my headphones this time, though.

I feel their breath.

On my neck.

Whoever it is stands close enough to whisper their sweet nothings right at my back, the exhale of their words sprawling across my shoulder. My neck.

I didn't hear the words at all. I just *felt* them.

Whispers.

Exhales.

Breath.

The woods. The woods are whispering.

These woods whisper, the old man at the diner had said.

I can hear them all around.

Their voices.

I don't stop this time. No, this time, I pick up my pace. Walking fast. Real fast. Then running. Running, running, running to catch up with Amber.

But Amber has stopped. Stopped walking altogether.

She's now standing before a ring of pines. Their trunks are so close to one another, it almost appears as if they're a wall. A protective barrier. Hiding something.

Amber glances over her shoulder at me, like she wants to make sure I'm still there. Still following her. It's too dark to tell for certain, but I swear she's smiling.

And just like that, Amber turns back, facing the ring of trees, and steps through.

EIGHT

The clearing has a cerulean tinge to it. The moon casts a cool indigo glow over the brush, as if this hidden glade is filtered through a blue lens. It's too blue, if such a thing is even possible. *If this were a movie,* I think, *you'd think it was shot day-for-night.*

Even my breath takes on a blue tint once I pass through the barrier of pines, entering this stretch of barren soil.

No trees grow here. Only weeds. The earth itself appears to darken, as if something has spilled, some pollutant soaking into the dirt and fouling the ground.

Amber stands in the center of the clearing. Her back is turned to me, her head bent down so that her gray hair—blue out here now—falls into her face.

I can't see her face.

"Miss Pendleton . . .?" I didn't realize I still had my headphones on. When I hear my own voice, I give a start. It doesn't sound like me. My mind lapses back to recording my voice on my father's tape player for the first time, back when I was a kid, replaying it and marveling at how different my voice sounded. *That couldn't be me, could it? Whose voice is this on the tape?*

Here it is, years later, happening all over again.

Whose voice had that been?

Did I just say that?

Who else could it have been, if not me?

It strikes me, out here, in the woods, how removed I am from the present situation. I can distance myself from everything happening because I am so focused on the sound.

I'm not here.

I'm not in the woods.

I'm not in this clearing.

I'm just listening to myself. Out there.

In the woods.

See the difference? It's so simple. The headphones make it so easy. *All this has already happened. I'm just listening to myself in the past. I'm not even here.*

There, I correct myself. *I meant out there. In the woods.*

I'm not even there.

So if I'm listening to myself, listening to the recording of my sojourn into the dark woods with Amber Pendleton, that means I must be somewhere else. Somewhere far, far away from the surrounding pines.

Somewhere safe.

Where could I be? My imagination scrambles for a breath before placing me back in Brooklyn, in my apartment, so warm, on the couch, editing this episode. The sound quality to the coverage is great. So crisp. Listening to it on the playback, it almost feels like I am—

Here. Here in the woods. In this clearing.

With Amber Pendleton.

She's staring at the ground. The darkened earth. There's an oil spill at her feet. It seems to be growing. Expanding. Darkening itself even further. Something's welling up from below.

Oil. Bubbling crude. No—no, that's not oil.

Soot.

The dirt here has been scorched. The moon just makes it look as if it's wet. Somebody must've built a bonfire out here recently. It had to have been a hiker or a family camping or—

Or—

Something is burning.

There is a flame. It's blue. Almost invisible in the dark.

Can fire be imperceptible? It looks like one of those Sterno cans, the coldest flames. I have to squint to see the butane blaze flicker and lick against the shadows. The heat of it swells over the ground, the patch of ground directly below rippling and fluctuating from the temperature.

Amber drops to her knees without a sound. Her legs merely fold into themselves, her body softly collapsing like a marionette's strings have just been cut. She's in a supplicating pose.

Like she's praying. Praying to this blackened patch. To this phantasmal fire.

"Miss Pendleton . . . ?"

That's strange. I didn't even realize I had said anything—and yet I just heard my voice seep through my headphones. Did I just call out her name?

I hadn't.

Didn't.

So whose voice was that?

I try again. My lips move. I say the same thing, calling out her name.

But I don't hear anything.

Not in my headphones.

I'm positive I said it this time. I said her name out loud.

My jaw moved.

My lips moved.

My tongue moved.

All the muscles in my mouth did exactly what they are supposed to do.

But there's no sound.

No voice. I couldn't hear myself say the—

"Where are we, Miss Pendleton?"

The sound of my own disembodied voice pours into my ears. It comes out of nowhere, jolting me right where I stand.

There's some kind of delay. That has to be it. I said those exact same words, less than thirty seconds ago. My voice is suddenly out of sync with the rest of myself.

So I speak again. *Forcefully.* A full-throated declaration.

Nothing. Nothing at all.

I'm positive, absolutely positive I just said—

"Miss Pendleton, I think we should leave now."

Jesus Christ! The sound of my own voice bursts my eardrums. I yank off my headphones. They fall to my neck, the cord tangling around my throat.

Everything falls deathly silent.

There's nothing.

Absolutely nothing.

No sound whatsoever.

No swaying pines, no bristling needles. No heavy breaths. No breeze. No cracking branches. No thrumming pulse. It's as if I had accidentally pressed the mute button on my—

On my—

I slowly, slowly pull the headphones back over my ears. As soon as the padded cups settle over the lobes, the sound of my surroundings suddenly returns.

The wind. The swaying pines. The bristling needles.

My own breathing.

Hyperventilating.

Just to test myself, *better safe than sorry*, I tug the headphones off again and return to an empty world devoid of sound.

It's so quiet out here.

In the woods.

I know I'm panicking. I know my breathing has deepened. My exhales fog up the air before me, these bursts of blue. But there's no sound to them.

No gasp.

Amber is digging. Digging with her bare hands. Her fingertips perforate the soil, grabbing handfuls of dirt. She scoops fistful after fistful, tossing them into the air.

Over her shoulder.

At her waist.

I see it.

I just can't hear it. There's no sound to Amber.

No sound at all.

I slide my headphones back on. I return to the comfort of their padded insulation, like a pair of small hands—a child's hands—cupping each of my ears. Squeezing them tight.

I am all ears now.

There. There it is. The soft tear of soil. Each handful of dirt striking the ground

There, that's much better.

I'm listening. I don't need to see. I can hide inside the safety of my headphones.

Now I hear everything. Oh God, I can hear everything.

Everything.

NINE

There was a time, once, when Amber was younger, that she remembered Nora Lambert getting so wrapped up in her role that she completely forgot who she even was. She lost herself within her character.

Amber now realized that it wasn't her mother who had pulled her out of the ground, all those years ago. It had been Nora.

Nora had saved her. Brought her back to life. It was a bittersweet revelation, but fitting in this moment. To be back here, in the woods, where she had first been found all those years ago.

Now it was Amber's turn to lose herself in her character.

Of Jessica. Always Jessica.

She felt the girl's presence slip into her body as soon as she took her hand. They had walked together through the woods, heading for the clearing where Ella Louise waited.

Waited all these years.

Yearning.

Amber's fingernails began to give, but she wouldn't stop. Couldn't stop digging. The nail on her right index finger tore back a bit with each handful, but that didn't matter. Not anymore.

Not out here. In the woods.

In the ground.

Amber knows better. She's always known better. A mother needs to be reunited with her daughter. It's always been her role in life to keep their story alive.

The role of a lifetime.

Amber will let the people of Pilot's Creek, along with the rest of the world, know that Ella Louise and Jessica have always been witches. Their souls will never be at rest. Not truly. Not after what the men of Pilot's Creek did to them.

The Fords aren't done yet. Their story has always been their revenge—and they demand it be told, no matter what the medium may be. Nathaniel Denison is merely a messenger. He will usher in the next iteration of their tale. Jessica will reach out and enter the fresh ears of listeners everywhere.

There.

There she is.

Once Amber's ravaged hands reach Ella Louise's scapula, she allows herself the briefest respite. Her fingers are wet with her own blood, chilling in the air, but she only takes the quickest of breaths before leaning back into the ground and digging around the bones.

Amber's fingers worm through the cold clay until they come upon Ella Louise's skull. She pushes back the soil, rubbing the mud away with her thumbs until the moon casts the faintest blue glow over the slope of Ella Louise's frontal bone. Her eye sockets are clogged with clay, but to Amber, to Jessica, they are full of such yearning.

Such love.

Jessica cups her hands underneath her mother's jaw. She tugs, tugs until the soil finally gives and releases her mother.

Jessica lifts Ella Louise out from the earth, from the ground, and holds her aloft.

Ella Louise blinks. She takes in her daughter. Her beautiful girl.

And smiles.

LISTEN CLOSELY.

We did not choose this life.

You men had.

We had not asked for this.

You men made it so.

So when you kneel next to your beds tonight and pray, why, why is this happening to me, why, why, He will never answer. He never had the answer.

We do.

So hear this . . .

Hear me.

You brought this upon yourself. Suffer a witch to live? We had done nothing to deserve this. Nothing. And yet you could not suffer a witch to live. Now you must suffer. You must all suffer.

Let your suffering be your legacy, let it be the story you tell your children, your children's children, let your dreams of me be the tale you tell for generations to come.

Let this story be your penance, your punishment, for what you have done to us.

Suffer a witch to live.

Suffer a witch to live.

You men always try to tell our story. You men always get it wrong.

So listen. Listen closely.

Are you all ears?

Listen . . .

This podcast was produced by B-Side Studios, with support from the Winters Foundation. Special thanks to Colin Zimmerman, the Geddes family, and most importantly, listeners like you.

Acknowledgments

Bow down to Eddie Gamarra at the Gotham Group. I don't know what I did to deserve you. You always find ways for me tell stories and for that I'm eternally grateful.

Jhanteigh Kupihea saw something in my muddle of a story idea and let me run with it and told me to never look back. She gave me a campfire, a beautiful campfire, to spin this yarn. To her and the rest of the crew at Quirk, bless your dark hearts.

Thanks to Jeffrey Dinsmore and Kyle Jarrow for giving me a chance to write "The Monstrosity Exhibition: Lost Terrors of VHS Sleeve Cover Art" for Awkward Press.

Thanks to Milly Shapiro, Joshua Erkman, Chris Steib, Noah Greenberg, Craig William Macneill, the fine folks at Kilter Films and the Roosevelt Hotel.

To Indrani, Jasper, and Cormac . . . You are all too young to be reading incendiary filth like this.